PRAISE FOR *BEHIND CLOSED DOORS*

"An intense, suspenseful, character-driven mystery that I couldn't put down. Collins expertly weaves a journey of self-acceptance with a page-turning mystery . . . A gripping story from the chilling opening to the startling conclusion."

—Allison Brennan, author of *The Kill*

"With *Behind Closed Doors*, Natalie R. Collins doesn't just treat readers to a taut, compelling mystery, she gives us a riveting look at the very heart of contemporary Mormonism. This book is not, however, fired by an apostate's anger, but rather by one pilgrim's bittersweet search for true justice, faith, and community in the wake of her own brutal loss of innocence."

—Cornelia Read, author of *A Field of Darkness*

. . . AND NATALIE R. COLLINS'S PREVIOUS NOVEL *WIVES AND SISTERS*

"Written with skill and passion . . . it will resonate with women who have never set foot inside a Mormon church."

—*The Washington Times* on *Wives and Sisters*

"This is not a book that can be put down. It's so compelling, so dramatic, with strong suspense and mystery elements, that I had to find out what would happen . . . It's written with a frightening intensity. I had to check the locks before I could go to sleep after finishing."

—Perri O'Shaughnessy, *New York Times* bestselling author of *Unlucky in Law*

"A white-knuckles ride all the way. An expert depiction of a young woman's struggle with the oppressive 'family values' of one kind of fundamentalism. Newcomer Collins is a talent to watch."

—*Kirkus Reviews*

"By anyone' _____ is hard to put down, and _____ dianapolis Star

MORE . . .

BEHIND CLOSED DOORS

NATALIE R. COLLINS

St. Martin's Paperbacks

This is a work of fiction. All of the characters, organizations and events portrayed in this novel are either products of the author's imagination or are used fictitiously.

BEHIND CLOSED DOORS

Copyright © 2007 by Natalie R. Collins.
Excerpt from *The Wife's Secret* copyright © 2007 by Natalie R. Collins.

ISBN: 0-312-93486-6
EAN: 978-0-312-93486-6

Printed in the United States of America

St. Martin's Paperbacks edition / January 2007

St. Martin's Paperbacks are published by St. Martin's Press, 175 Fifth Avenue, New York, NY 10010.

10 9 8 7 6 5 4 3 2 1

This one's for Cele, who manages to be my cheerleader, den mother, reviewer, critic, and kind and gracious friend, all rolled up into one.

ACKNOWLEDGMENTS

I have been fortunate enough, in this crazy writing world, to find myself surrounded by talented and, um, critical friends who willingly read my manuscripts and point out the silly little mistakes I make. In particular, I must thank Jennifer Apodaca, Calista Cates-Stanturf, Karin Tabke, and Rob Holden, all of whom saw this manuscript in one form or another and read and critiqued it, giving of their time and advice freely. I also must thank each of them for talking me off at least one ledge during the writing of this book. A special thank you to Elizabeth Burton who also spent time on this manuscript, helping me fine-tune it.

Thanks also go to my fabulous agent, Karen Solem, who never fails to give me the advice I need, whether I want to hear it or not, and to my wonderful editor Jennifer Weis, who can find the weakness in a manuscript and hand you the answer effortlessly. She is magic. Particularly helpful, as always, is her assistant, Stefanie Lindskog, who patiently answers all my questions and never fails to find an answer to anything I might ask. I suspect she could tell me the location of Jimmy Hoffa, if I gave her enough time to find the answer.

And, as always, to my family, Chad, Carissa, and Cambre, who go into every bookstore they see and check to see if my books are stocked. Thanks for the faith, guys!

BEHIND
CLOSED
DOORS

PROLOGUE

I am Sarah.

At least, that is the new—and secret—name I was given by the temple worker during my endowments several months ago, shortly before I bailed on my wedding. I would not answer to this name if you hailed me with it on the street. In fact, I would probably not even realize you were talking to me.

I need this name so my husband can use it to recognize and acknowledge me and pull me through the veil—which separates this life from the Celestial Kingdom—into heaven. Since I have no husband, and the only man who knows it is complete anathema to me, it seems a moot point. I don't consider myself Sarah. I am—as I have always been—Janica Emily Fox.

My best friend, Melissa, has been wild-eyed and slightly freaked out for the past few minutes, ever since the elderly female temple worker reached under the white vestment and blessed her various parts, washing and anointing her and providing her with the garment of the Holy Priesthood. After that, she put on all the temple garb—worn over her beautiful dress—before she was paraded through the various rooms and movies that make up the endowment ceremony. That's around the time she got her new secret name, too, and I wonder how that makes her feel. Was it as strange and unsettling to her as it had been to me?

I'm sure that the new name, along with trying to learn the secret handshakes and passwords that guarantee one's entry into heaven, have really thrown her off on this day that is supposed to be the most special in a young Mormon girl's life. They don't call them handshakes, of course, or even handclasps, which is more representative of what they encompass. They are called tokens, and along with the signs, they come with an ominous overtone—penalties for revealing the sacred description of the rite. You don't tell people what goes on in the temple. Not without horrible consequences. The powers that be are vague about what those are, but they include the wrath of God, a threat that has left me terrified all of my life.

Knowing Melissa the way I do, having been her best friend for the past twenty years, I knew she wouldn't much like that part of the temple ceremony. The endowment was one of the most bizarre rituals I have ever endured, and my former fiancé swears it led me to bolt before our actual wedding ceremony took place.

He is only partly right. But today is not about me, or Brian Williams, who watches me now from the other side of the room, glowering slightly, as if to say, "This should be us. We should be kneeling before the altar."

This is Melissa's wedding day. The pallor from her slight state of shock has worn off, and she is radiant, beaming with her happiness, almost as though she has completely forgotten what came before. Only I know that's not true. Her arms by her sides, her fingers play a piano scale up and down her legs, always the telltale sign she is nervous. She doesn't show much outwardly. She never has. Melissa has confidence by the gallon jug, and doesn't allow many people to see through to the vulnerable person who exists inside all young women, brought on by the terrors and uncertainty of adolescence and the expectations of adulthood. But I know it's there, because I know her. No one knows her like I do.

And no one really knows what to expect on their wedding day inside the temple of the Church of Jesus Christ of Latter-day Saints. These things are sacred, and only the most worthy enter here. You don't get much preparation. She begged me to tell her, but I wouldn't—I couldn't. Now, the worst part is over, and she is waiting for her husband to pull her through the veil that symbolizes the entrance to the Celestial Kingdom, so they can be sealed for time and all eternity.

She looks lovely. Even though I cannot see her modest white gown, which I helped her pick out, I know it features intricate beading, a tight bodice, and cap sleeves that will cover her garments—the Mormon underwear she will wear from this day forward. The reason I can't see her wedding finery is because she is wearing the Mormon temple garb over them—a green fig leaf apron over a bulky robe, one that fits over one shoulder and then is tied with a sash that must fit over the top part of the green apron, with the bow of the sash on the right hip. It's all part of the ritual.

All the dramas, including the expulsion of Adam and Eve from the Garden of Eden, have been acted out, played before us on a movie screen. All that is left is the sealing, and it is simple, and sweet, and nothing like the dramatic and terrifying endowments. At least, I found them terrifying; my mother always claims to have found them soothing. I spent the majority of the time worrying about how I was going to remember all those signs so my Father in Heaven would know to let me into His kingdom, and suffering an extreme form of claustrophobia that reached boiling point right as Brian called my new name to guide me through the veil.

I could not answer to the name Sarah.

Melissa's parents watch, smiling and nodding, happy and complete in their daughter's achievement—an eternal temple marriage. Michael's parents, standing next to them, beam. My parents also watch Melissa, although my mother's face is easy to read. Why Pete and Angela's daughter? Why not hers? Why did *her* daughter turn tail and run, thrash her way out of the temple, and require paramedics to be called to calm her hysteria? The little old lady serving as a temple matron I had knocked down in my desperation to find an exit had also required medical attention. Three days later, I called my wedding off. Melissa begged me to tell her what had me so freaked out, but I couldn't. I had taken an oath.

So she bravely withstood her own endowment nightmare (she'd whispered to me afterward, "That was very weird"), but the slightly wild look in her eyes when we first entered this sealing room is gone; she now seems quite calm and serene.

The room itself is unremarkable, unlike other parts of the temple, which are elegantly and elaborately decorated. The walls are mirrored, and in the middle is an altar where Melissa kneels on one side and Michael on the other. They take each other's right hand in the "Patriarchal Grip," the

Second Token of the Melchizedek Priesthood, also known as the Sure Sign of the Nail, thumbs and little fingers interlocked, and index fingers placed on the wrist just above the hand. Melissa fumbles around with it a bit, and blushes, as all around them stand the signs of achievement in Mormondom—worthy, temple-recommend-holding adults watching in benign love and grace as yet another young couple commits their lives to God and the church. It is quiet and peaceful. There is no music. No flowers. No young children dressed in their Sunday fineries, playing tag around the feet of the adults. No celebration. It's . . . a little bland.

Michael looks proud, slightly arrogant (as he always has), but also a little humble (which he rarely is). His vanity and calm take-charge manner has always attracted Melissa. Her mother is a little flighty and given to nervous spells where she takes to bed, when she isn't ordering her family around; and her father is quiet, and meek, and unable to hold down a job for longer than a year at a time. I am sure Michael will always be strong and the leader of his family, because that is what she has always wanted—a priesthood holder, a man to lead and support his family. I know Michael will always do that. He is— well, a take-charge kind of guy.

My Brian—my ex-Brian, I should say—has always tried to be the same way, but he pales in comparison to Michael. He is a "second-in-command" type, always waiting for Michael to lead the way. All through school, there was Michael and, following behind, albeit closely, there was Brian. They looked enough alike they could be brothers, both tall with dark brown hair, broad shoulders, and strong, handsome, sturdy features. But whatever Brian did,

Michael usually did it better. Brian got used to letting someone else lead, and so he looked to me to make all the decisions in our relationship, our upcoming nuptials, our marriage.

Poor Brian was always slightly outside, all throughout our childhood and growing up, because his *parents* were outsiders. They were Gentile—non-Mormons—who had allowed their only child to be baptized Mormon so he would fit into our predominantly Mormon community. Because he didn't have the parental backing we did, the family heraldry of Mormonism, he never pushed ahead to lead our group. There were only a few times when he had taken the lead, when he had pushed to be my patriarch, my priesthood holder, and the results had been disastrous. So he backed off and let me lead—and I did. I made the decision that I would never again set foot inside this temple and endure something as creepy as the endowment ceremony.

Luckily for me, I had only bolted my marriage and sealing and had already endured the endowment, so I was able to see Melissa be married—I still had a valid temple recommend. Others were not so lucky, like our school friends who weren't yet married or hadn't gone on missions, or her younger brothers and sisters. It had taken all the strength I had—and some Xanax we stole from Melissa's mother—to get me back through these doors.

When the brief ceremony is over, everyone congratulates the couple as they stand together and smile. It is quiet and we all hug them quickly then shuffle out and down to the dressing rooms to change into our street clothes—or in my case, my sea-foam green bridesmaid's dress and dyed-to-match shoes—so we can stand in front of the temple and on the grounds and have our pictures taken. There are no photos allowed inside the sacred temples of my birth religion.

Melissa holds Michael's hand tightly for one more minute, and then they separate, but not before sharing bright smiles. She follows me to the ladies' dressing room, although, as the bride, she has her own special room where only she and her mother can go. In that room, she will remove her temple garb and put on the beautiful veil that came with her gown in place of the simple veil worn for the ceremony.

"Well, Mrs. Melissa Holt, how do you feel?" I ask her.

"I'm so happy. I've been waiting for this all my life."

CHAPTER ONE

Five years later

I got the call that changed my life forever around two P.M. on Tuesday, June 28.

The coffee I had poured thirty minutes before had gone cold as I stared into my computer screen and talked on the phone, arranging for a restraining order against the husband of one of my repeat clients. Debbie Talon floated in and out of our shelter every several months, convinced her husband, Brandon, was going to kill her. I was convinced, too, but it made no difference. Debbie always returned to him, and they always paid a reunion visit to their bishop, who praised their decision to keep the family unit together. In another couple of months Debbie knocked on our door again, dragging with her a four-year-old son, eight-year-old daughter, and, once, a fetus that didn't live through the night, having been punched and kicked to death while still inside his mother's body.

The Salt Lake City Police Department had finally gotten involved after the last one, even though Debbie begged everyone, including me, not to tell them. She loved Brandon. He was her eternal companion.

Somehow, her eternal companion convinced them she was clumsy and fell down the stairs. No charges were filed, but they were watching him. Without Debbie's testimony, they could do little because there was no proof that anything except a terrible fall had happened. She backed up the "clumsy" story. They knew what I knew, even though they couldn't—and some wouldn't—move against a fellow priesthood holder without black-and-white proof. Apparently, black-and-blue was not enough.

Yesterday, she had shown up with a new complaint—a multicolored patch on her daughter's back. This time, she swore she wouldn't return, wouldn't put up with this, wouldn't even call her bishop. I knew better, but maybe Brandon didn't. So for now, I would try to get her the restraining order, even while knowing it was probably pointless.

I arranged the order and wrote down instructions for Debbie—which she would undoubtedly ignore. After I was done, I picked up the mug and took a sip of tepid coffee and almost spit it back out. Blah. Coffee was evil. I knew that. If anyone from my past life—the one I led before I first attended a session in the Mormon LDS Temple—could have seen me, they would have been shocked.

I was not honest with those who knew me from before. It pained me, but it was necessary. I could not handle their pressure. It was just easier to pretend I still believed, that I attended church on a regular basis, that I never drank coffee or alcohol, or even thought about sex. Of course, the last was not true at all. I thought about it all the time. I just wasn't doing it.

I stood up to refresh my coffee, the phone rang, and I sighed. Some other disaster, some other abuser, some other horrible omen or event to attend to—maybe even Sunday dinner at my parents' house, where I would be grilled endlessly about the singles ward I told them I attended, and about any possible prospects for marriage, and—worst of all—whether or not I had considered going on a mission. Since I wasn't married, and showed no signs of ever being so, that was expected of me. It was the fate of all old maids. Next month I would be twenty-six years old.

"Oh, Jannie," came my mother's voice over the line.

I'd been right. Somebody give me a quarter and call me Madame Zelda.

But I didn't correctly predict what she would say next.

"Jannie, something terrible has happened. Lissa is missing. She's been gone half the day. She never showed up for work, and Jannie? Jannie, are you listening?"

My mother needed constant reinforcement that everyone within miles was attuned to the sound of her voice. The scary part was they usually were.

"I'm listening, Mom. I'm just in shock."

Melissa, my longtime friend, had been missing for six hours and everyone was getting frantic. Steady, dependable Melissa, who always reined her emotions in, would not just up and disappear. She would never just *not* show up for work, or fail to call in, so we all knew that something was wrong.

"Please come," my mother said, her words compact and tight, her unusual brevity a sign that things were horribly out of kilter.

I left my desk at the YWCA Women's Shelter, hurried down the long hallway to my boss's office, and popped my head in the door, quickly explaining that I needed to leave, to join the search party combing the canyons behind

Michael and Melissa's apartment. Millicent Stone, a fifty-year-old former Catholic nun who had saved more women from monsters than any knight in shining armor could ever claim to have done, understood completely. Millie was small of frame and stature, with short, close-cropped gray hair, a heavily lined face, and eyes that expressed more than she could ever say in words. There was usually a touch of sorrow in those eyes. In our line of work, disaster is always little more than a phone call away. We've learned to adapt.

As I drove my Honda Civic toward the Canyon View Stake Center, where the command post for Melissa's search had been set up, fear raced through my mind. Surely Melissa had just lost track of time, or thought she had arranged for sick leave because she had a prior engagement.

But what if that wasn't the case? What if she had been kidnapped, taken by an unknown assailant for nefarious purposes? Although I knew the odds of that were slim, the case of Elizabeth Smart still loomed in my mind. *The obvious suspects are those closest to the victim. Stranger abduction is rare. Look first at the family.* These were my mantras, as a domestic abuse counselor.

But Michael and Melissa had a strong relationship. She laughed sometimes, and I frowned and fought to keep from speaking my mind, because he always wanted to know where she was, who she was with, what she was doing. He bought her a cell phone and then had to up the minutes because he called her so often they were hit with huge overage charges. Sometimes, when we were together, she'd sigh when the phone rang. No one else called her. It was always Michael.

But she loved him. And he adored her. I remembered him serenading her, back when we were in high school, singing silly, sappy romantic tunes and then sulking when she laughed at him, even though she did it kindly.

They had problems, but who didn't? I couldn't even stay in a relationship for twenty minutes. Michael would never lay a hand on her. So who would hurt Melissa? Was she dead? *No, no, don't think that way. No! She's fine. She just got busy and forgot to go to work, and to call in and tell them, and to . . .*

Everyone loved her. She was the type of person who really listened, who met new people and immediately knew everything about them, all their secrets spilling out. They walked away, saying, "What a nice person," without even realizing they knew absolutely nothing about her.

Melissa even knew *my* secret, one I had shared with no one else.

My cell phone rang, and I answered with a quick and breathless hello, praying it was someone calling to tell me that Melissa was fine.

"Jannie, it's Brian. Melissa is missing. Have you seen her?"

His voice sent a cold chill down my spine, and I felt the fear, the anger, and the claustrophobia return. God help me, I really hated him. It wasn't healthy. I kept my voice calm and modulated.

"No, Brian, but my mom called me. I'm on my way."

"Good. Michael needs support. Lissa's car has been found in the parking lot of the 7-Eleven close to their house. It doesn't look good."

I felt as though someone had punched me in the stomach. I didn't want to hear this.

"Why would she have gone there?" I asked, after a moment's silence.

"She went to buy milk. Mike says they were out of it, and she told him she was going to go get some, even woke him up, since he was sleeping. She left, he went back to sleep, and when he woke up again it was ten A.M. He just figured she had let him sleep and gone to work. And you can find out more when you come here. You're great at supporting your friends. You've always been good at supporting everyone but me." He disconnected. I guess he hated me, too. I'd broken his heart. His lack of spirit and chivalry had broken mine. If only my relationship had been more like the one Mike and Melissa shared.

Melissa . . .

Flashes of the last time I saw her played through my mind. It had been an odd encounter. She'd shown up at my doorstep around seven-thirty one evening the week before. We hadn't seen each other in months and had only talked on the phone once or twice. So, to open the door and see her standing there was a bit of a shock.

Her long brown hair was swept back into a harsh ponytail, and her dark brown eyes seemed deeper set than normal, surrounded by hollows that spoke of sleepless nights and stresses I, in my single and unencumbered state, could not begin to imagine. I knew Michael and Lissa struggled for money—her job working as a secretary for an insurance company was not terribly high-paying, but she'd never gone to college, opting instead to marry young and support Michael while he attended first college and then medical school.

"Can you keep this for me?" she asked, without even a hello. She thrust a medium-sized shoe box toward me, and I reached out and grabbed it, stumbling a bit from the force of her movement. I put my hand on the doorway to steady myself.

"Geez, Liss, what's up? You don't look great. Why don't you come in and I'll—"

"I can't stay. I need to get home. Mike will be home soon for dinner. Just keep it for me, okay? Someplace safe?"

"What is it?"

She tightened her lips and shook her head twice, standard Melissa posturing for things she did not wish to discuss. I was used to this type of behavior with her. When we were growing up, it had usually signaled one of her mother's bad spells. What that could possibly have to do with the box I held I didn't know, but I knew I wasn't going to get it out of her until she was ready. Eventually, she would tell me. She always did.

"Okay, it's not anything live, is it?" I asked jokingly, trying to coax a smile out of her. "Something that will smell my place up if I ignore it for too long?"

She finally smiled—not the full, open, wide-mouthed smile she usually displayed and for which she had received one of those silly Senior Spectacular awards at graduation—but a smile, nonetheless.

"Are you sure you don't want to talk?"

"Not today," she answered. "I have to go. Thanks, Jannie. I really appreciate it."

And she turned and left.

"Oh, my God. The box," I said with a gasp, as fear gripped me. Could the box she left with me be connected to this? Her behavior had been strange, her conversation terse, her smile forced. Now she was missing. What, if anything, did the box have to do with it?

Instead of heading straight up 400 South in downtown Salt Lake City, I flipped on my blinker and moved over to the right-turn lane and headed south on 700 East. I had a small apartment in Sugar House, and although it seemed a long shot, perhaps I would find the answers to Melissa's disappearance there.

I had to open that box and find out what was inside it.

CHAPTER TWO

My life as an inactive Mormon was nothing but a balancing act, one that I knew I could not maintain for an extended amount of time. How I had pulled it off this many years was nothing short of a miracle, for which I thanked God daily—my only religious ritual.

I loved my family, yet I had chosen to move out of their home, even though my mother continually assured me I could live in their basement rent-free until I married. There was too much emotional baggage occupying the house where I had been raised, not the least of which was the fact I hadn't even come close to living up to my parents' hopes for me. They gladly told the bishop of my old ward my new address, and my church records followed me there. When the home and visiting teachers came, I told them I was attending a singles ward up at the University of Utah, and promised to call the bishop to have him transfer my records. I never did. They were starting to get suspicious. My big fear was that they would return my records to my parents' ward, and the jig would be up.

For now, I had my freedom, and their ignorance accorded me some bliss as I lived in my own apartment.

I parked in the side driveway of the old red brick house, located on the east side of Salt Lake City, where I rented a back apartment connected to the main home. The sides of 1700 South were lined with trees, all in full leaf on the hot July day, and when I jogged or walked, they afforded shade and relief. The neighborhood was quiet and peaceful, filled with old homes occupied either by elderly people who had lived there for years, or younger, hip, upper-class denizens who could afford the skyrocketing property costs on the east side of the valley. It was close to 2:30 P.M. on a Tuesday, so I knew that my landlady, an elderly woman named Ida Miller, would not be home. Early every Tuesday and Thursday morning, without fail, Ida packed up her old-fashioned flowered canvas suitcase with her temple clothes and caught a ride with me down to 700 East, where I would drop her off to meet her friend Elsie. Together, they would stand there, holding their flowered suitcases and chattering loudly, while they waited for the third member of their trio, LaDonna Ford, to pick them up and drive down to the Salt Lake Temple. It was a rare Tuesday or Thursday when Ida didn't follow this schedule. Despite her age, nearing ninety, she was healthy and active, and since her husband's death, her schedule had revolved around her friends and her temple work.

This morning had been no different. After their temple work, Ida and her friends would go to the Gateway Mall and eat, and then shop a bit, then she returned home around 4 P.M., when she would promptly retire for her afternoon nap. Life was simple for Ida. I envied her sometimes.

I raced around the side of the house, where my apartment

was located, skirting, as always, the wide and tall hedge that protected my door from being seen by the street. Ida kept offering to have the hedge cut, but I declined. The extra measure of safety gave me a small amount of peace of mind, and since that was already in short supply, I needed all I could get. I reached for the doorknob, the keys in my right hand, and saw that the door was already slightly ajar. Startled by the gap, I stood for a moment and considered my morning. My already racing heart picked up a notch as I tried to remember what I had done before I knocked briskly on Ida's door and told her I was ready to go. Had I forgotten to lock the door and pull it closed when I left that morning? I couldn't remember pulling it shut, but it was rote. I had never before left my door unlocked and open. There were too many burglaries in this affluent east side neighborhood.

I listened closely for sounds, but there was no noise. Just the week before, the neighbor across the street had returned home in the middle of the day to find her house trashed by thieves who had stolen whatever they could tote quickly away. The police said it was young gang members looking for money to buy drugs. Were dangerous criminals inside my apartment right now?

My next thought was even more frightening than young addicts. What if it was one of the violent men whose wives and girlfriends it was my job to protect? I had a concealed weapon permit because of the nature of my job, but I had left my purse—complete with the gun I always carried—on the front seat of my car. I had raced to my apartment door, sure that I would only be a moment, that the box would contain nothing of importance, and that I would quickly be back on my way to the command post where they were setting up searches for my missing friend.

Now I backtracked, threw open the car door and grabbed my purse, pulled out the small-caliber weapon, and headed back to my door. It was probably nothing, but I wasn't taking chances.

I pushed firmly on the door, and it swung wide open. I aimed the weapon, took a proactive stance, as my instructor had taught me, and looked around. Nothing seemed amiss in my sunny apartment—I hated the dark, and always left the blinds wide open. My mother claimed this heated my place up, and scolded me for not closing the draperies and keeping my apartment cool and more cost-efficient, but I ignored her chastisements. I liked to see where I was going, and what I was walking into, at all times.

It only took me a few minutes to determine that no one was inside, and I breathed a sigh of relief and returned to my bedroom, setting the gun on the dresser as I moved to my closet. I had to have forgotten to lock the door and pull it closed. Stupid. I'd be more careful in the future.

I'd placed Lissa's box at the top of my closet, in between four other shoe boxes that held mementos of dates and events, which I liked to save. I'd picked up the habit of keeping ticket stubs, fortune cookie slips, greeting cards, and other things from my days of keeping a Treasures of Truth book. While I no longer took the time to place them in the scrapbook my mother had given me years before, during my time attending Young Women's Church events, I had never stopped collecting them.

I threw open the closet door, and my heart jumped as I saw the mess. All the shoe boxes were upended and on the floor, my mementos jumbled and strewn about among my shoes.

A sound behind me caused me to turn, and I caught a glimpse of blue as heavy footsteps bolted from my room and across my wood floor, the creak of the door reinforcing that someone had been inside my apartment all along, most likely hiding behind the bedroom door.

I fought the panic and quickly crossed to my bedside table where a cordless phone rested in its base. I dialed 911 and reported the intruder, then hurried to my front door and locked and bolted it. I turned abruptly and the room began to spin, my chest tightening, and I shut my eyes tightly and leaned against the door for support, willing myself to calm down, to breathe. *Focus, Jannie. Focus. Don't lose it.* I could smell a hint of something musky, cologne, distinctly male.

I could not tolerate any invasion of my space, my privacy. No man had ever set foot inside my apartment. Not even my father, who accepted my endless excuses with odd looks and shakes of his head. I knew that was no longer true. I had been violated. But why? Why now, and why my closet, with the boxes . . . with Melissa's box.

Could it be related to that?

I forced myself to calm down and cross to the bedroom, and jumped about ten feet when my doorbell rang. I returned to the front door and looked out the peephole to see a young uniformed officer. The police had arrived much quicker than I expected.

I opened the door, and for the second time that day, a man violated my space, although this one came inside with my permission.

I was going to have to find a new place to live.

CHAPTER THREE

After the police officer took my report and determined that nothing of importance had been taken, he gave me a funny look, asked a few more probing questions, then encouraged me to get better locks on my doors. He didn't seem terribly interested in the fact that the intruder appeared to have been looking for a shoe box, which had been left behind. I guess it did sound a little silly.

"Whoever did this didn't break in. There aren't any signs of forced entry. Are you sure you didn't have a fight with your boyfriend, or—"

"Officer, I do not have a boyfriend," I said, my voice shaky with the dread and fear that filled me like fire. "No one else has a key to my apartment except my landlady and my friend Melissa—and she's missing."

My landlady was undoubtedly still shopping, but I told the policeman her name and phone number. And Melissa was missing. He gave a start when I explained exactly who Melissa was.

"It's probably not related, but I'll look into it," he said, before he left.

Whoever had come into my personal space, my living quarters, had entered with a key. Melissa was missing. She had a key. She had given me a box. Did I need a billboard with a flashing neon sign? Surely, this *was* related.

I scurried back into my bedroom and knelt before the open closet door, sorting through the odds and ends that had landed on the floor when my intruder had searched for something he wanted. But what?

Among my playbills, torn movie tickets, and fortunes from cookies, I found two items that had to have come from Melissa's box, because I did not recognize them. One was a sparkly blue composition notebook, the inexpensive kind you could buy in every drug and dollar store. The other was a pregnancy test, obviously used, in a plastic bag. The pink plus sign told me that whoever had used it—Melissa, obviously—was expecting a baby. I was stunned by the sight of the pregnancy test. It had been the last thing I expected. Of course, Melissa had always wanted children, but she was waiting, as they couldn't really afford them until Mike was out of college and had a decent-paying job. And there had been no joy on her face when she dropped the box off.

I set the bag aside, and grabbed the notebook, sitting down heavily on the floor as I opened it. Inside I found a journal, of sorts. The kind Melissa and I had tried to write in faithfully as we were growing up, journaling having always been taught as a part of our heritage.

With our church's emphasis on genealogy and passing on our stories, journals were a big part of Mormon culture. Mine were boring. I tried, I really did, to infuse something different and exciting into my journal, but I was just a boring Mormon girl from a boring Mormon town. Nothing

ever happened to me, at least nothing exciting. At least until my fiancé raped me, and no one would listen.

"Don't go there. Stop it right now." I had to concen-
trate on my breathing and the journal in front of me.

I decided to start from the back, the logical choice. It
might tell me what had caused Melissa's odd behavior
right before she dropped the box off at my house. But when
I opened the notebook, I saw there was only one notation,
on the front page. There was no date, and no name, but I
knew Lissa's handwriting. We had passed too many notes
during high school, and shared too many exams and papers
for me not to immediately recognize her careful script.

"I cannot handle this," the journal page began. "It's all a
pack of lies. I don't understand why all of this has happened
to me. Where did it come from? And why? All of my life I
have striven to be a good person, to read my Scriptures, to
follow God's plan for me. I had a temple wedding, and I go
to church every Sunday. So why has God handed me this
travesty? What did I do to deserve it?"

And that was it. The rest of the pages were blank. I rose
from the floor and grabbed my purse from the bedside
table, then stuffed the journal and pregnancy test inside it.

What the hell was going on? Was she talking about
Michael? Was he angry she had found herself pregnant?
Takes two to tango, Mike. It was time to confront Michael.
And to find Melissa.

I carefully locked my door as I left. Maybe in my new
place, I would have a landlord who would allow pets. I
was thinking rottweiler.

CHAPTER FOUR

As I drove north toward the Canyon View Stake Center, my car stereo blared the latest information on the search for my missing friend. Melissa was a good Mormon girl, from a good Mormon family. Waiting would serve no good purpose. The entire state had been on high alert ever since the Elizabeth Smart case. But would the same effort be put forth for some of my clients—the drug-addicted, or those from minority or poverty-stricken backgrounds? I chose not to consider that right now. I was glad that they were looking for Melissa. I was also glad for the outpouring of support from the Mormon community in which we lived. I would save my umbrage for the day when one of my clients was missing, and it was needed. The radio announcer broadcast the plea for volunteers to search for Melissa.

"Mr. Holt realized something was terribly amiss when he discovered there was no milk in the fridge," he said.

Milk? The lack of milk told him something was "terribly amiss"?

"He called his wife at work, and was told she had never come in for the day. Now, we will hear from Michael Holt at the command center where the search for his wife, Melissa, is being coordinated."

There was a small hesitation, a bit of static, and then I heard the voice I knew well.

"Please, if you have any idea . . . if you have seen her, or seen someone who looks like her . . . We need your help to search for this person who is hurt, or missing . . . Please help."

This person? What a weird thing for Michael to say. Hurt or missing? We all knew Melissa was missing. Where did the "hurt" come from?

Michael's voice was followed by a plea from her father, Pete Holtzbrick, whose voice was filled with the raw emotion of a father dealing with unimaginable loss.

"Please help us find Melissa. She is the center of our universe, and we can't imagine life without her. Please help us." He choked up, and the radio announcer's voice came back on just as I pulled into the parking lot of the Stake Center.

As always happened, at least for the past few years, the minute I saw the spires of the church I began to sweat profusely and my stomach started to churn. I forced myself to focus and breathe deeply. When I saw the setup, I let out the deep breath and sighed. I didn't have to go inside. Relief soared through my body like hot cocoa on a cold day.

A canvas canopy had been staked down on the dark green side lawn of the church and beneath it were folding chairs with hundreds of people milling about and others sitting behind tables, giving directions and orange vests to volunteer searchers. One plus about the tight-knit Mormon community was they could field an army in less time than it took to say a prayer.

The grounds of the chapel were extremely well cared for, with planted flowers, freshly mowed lawns, and no weeds in the beds. *All is well here,* the entire scene seemed to say. *See these immaculate grounds? It's the same inside.* I was walking proof this was not always true. And, of course, Melissa. There were several police cars parked in the lot, and I saw a few uniforms among the crowd, perhaps giving advice or perhaps casing the scene, looking for someone acting hinky. Sometimes this worked. But all my perspectives were colored by my line of work. I knew that with victims of domestic violence there were often no signs someone was seriously twisted—until they killed the family pet, or boarded a wife up inside the house, locking the doors from the outside when they left. Although this wasn't the case with Melissa. It couldn't be.

I stepped out of my car into the hot, dry blast furnace of the day, and as I approached the canopy I tried to avoid looking at the building all this was set up around—not an easy thing, considering its size.

"You're here for Melissa. Be strong," I told myself under my breath.

I saw my mother sitting behind one table, and Angela Holtzbrick sitting toward the back of the canopy and sobbing into her hands as several of the Relief Society sisters tried to comfort her. Among those women was Marlene Holt, Michael's mother. There was no love lost between the histrionic Angela and no-nonsense earth mother Marlene, but Mike's parents had loved their daughter-in-law, and all grievances would be put aside while we searched for Lissa.

I saw no sign of Michael, and assumed he was out looking. He was proactive, a doer. Never one to sit back and wait, he always stepped up to the plate.

My mother saw me and motioned to the woman sitting next to her to take over. She rose and came over and pulled me away from the crowd. Even on a hot summer's day, my mother was immaculately dressed in a smart, light pink, short-sleeved pantsuit, probably from Nordstrom. She looked fresh and her gray hair was beautifully coiffed, cut short in an attractive bob.

"Oh, Jannie, this is so awful. I can't believe Melissa's missing. It's just like Elizabeth Smart. I hope she's okay. I hope she's not . . . Oh, Jannie."

I hugged my mother quickly, then moved away, before her familiar scent—apple pie, cinnamon, and Joy perfume combined—could overwhelm me. I heard my name and turned to see Angela motioning to me wildly as the sisters surrounding her tried to slow her down.

"Jannie . . . Jannie . . ." she wailed. I wasn't sure how she had noticed me. When I'd last looked her way, her face had been buried in her hands.

"Oh, Angela," my mother whispered under her breath. We'd been dealing with her histrionics and "spells" for years. Melissa had taken refuge at our home during some of those times, and my mother had been there for Melissa a lot more than her own parents had. Life had been a lot better for the family after Prozac was discovered, but eventually that wore off, or Angela stopped taking it, or she just got tired of being happy—because no one paid her much attention that way—and she had reverted to the woman we'd known growing up.

I reluctantly walked toward the wailing woman, whose

brown hair was messy and wild, mascara smeared under her large blue eyes, hollow rings surrounding them. Her face was gaunt, almost skeletal, and if I hadn't known her so well, I would have thought the entire incident had destroyed her. But I knew better. She had looked this way for years. *Finally, she has something to really be upset about,* I thought unkindly, and winced at my nastiness.

I turned away from her, not wanting to be such a vicious person, and noticed I had caught the eye of a tall, dark-haired man wearing a suit, even in the sweltering heat. The bulk under his jacket screamed "cop." I knew them well, many of them personally, from my work with victims of domestic violence, but this was one I had not met.

He followed me as I made my way to Angela. She hugged me tightly and cried.

"Where is she, Jannie? Where is my baby? Please tell me why this happened. I don't understand. I don't get it. Why would someone take her, my life, my light, my love? Why?"

Frustration boiled in me. I had no answer, of course, and if she had taken even two minutes during her life to actually talk *to* her daughter instead of complaining *at* her, maybe *she* would know . . .

These thoughts and my negativity were getting me nowhere.

"You need to lie down, Angela." The voice belonged to my mother, who was carrying a double-edged sword I knew would be used to fillet me later. I'd been saved by the mother rather than the bell. She had followed me, and she nodded toward the other sisters, who scurried Angela off to a car so they could drive her home. Mike's mother was angry, tight-lipped, disdainful. She didn't offer to go

with those taking Angela home. This was a good thing.
She was a go-getter, who could find any needle in any
haystack. If Melissa could be found, somehow Mike's
mother would engineer it. She had raised six boys. Not
much fazed her.

She was a strong woman, different from my mother in
many ways, but so similar in others. Growing up across the
street from her, I knew her well. I'd spent countless hours
in her kitchen, eating homemade cookies and brownies,
and drinking cold milk or lemonade on hot summer days,
while my own mother was tending to the other members of
our ward. Marlene Holt used her kitchen for power. She
was content to stay at home, raise her children, and cook
for everyone who was hungry. It made people gravitate toward her. My mother also had a commanding presence, although in a different way. I did not miss how easily my
mother had made things happen. Mom had been Relief Society president for years; and even though she had been released from that calling and given a position in the Young
Women's organization, the women of the ward still looked
to her for guidance. She was a queen bee, a position firmly
established last year when my father had been called to
serve as stake president.

Unfortunately, I knew well enough that my mother's
intervention would require payback. I sensed a blind date
with someone's brother's uncle's son whose wife had
died while giving birth to their ninth child.

Seeking refuge, I turned to the man in the suit, who
had been observing the scene with interest, and offered
my hand.

"Hello, Detective. I'm Jannie Fox. I'm Melissa's best
friend."

He nodded at my acknowledgment he was a cop, a slight smile crossing his strong, masculine face, and shook my hand quickly, his grasp hard and strong.

"Detective Colt Singer. Salt Lake City Police Department. Do you have time to answer a few questions?"

"Of course, I'll do anything at all to help find Melissa."

"Why don't we go inside the church? They've been nice enough to let us set up shop in there . . ."

Panic speared through me like a knife, and I began to sweat, my heart accelerating, my stomach lurching. I couldn't do it. I loved Melissa, would die for Melissa, really, but I could not set one foot in that church. I would search for her barefoot instead, walking on glass, on a freezing day . . .

"No, no, I'd rather stay out here, if you don't mind. I want to stay close to where things are . . . are . . . happening."

I clenched my fists to try and fight back the terror that threatened me at the thought of stepping inside the familiar church. No matter the design or color, all Mormon churches were instantly recognizable, as long as you had seen one before. I had actually found a route to drive to work—and to do the errands that life required—that allowed me to avoid passing any LDS chapels at all, and therefore warding off the instant panic I felt whenever I saw the familiar building. But my reaction to this church was the worst one of all. I had attended here all my life. I knew this place like the back of my hand. Melissa and I knew every cubbyhole, every tiny hiding place, every shortcut in there. This church was guilty. All the others were innocent, included in my phobia strictly because of their affiliation with my birth religion.

But this particular church turned me into a quivering mass of useless human being, one totally unable to explain the terror I felt right now.

Detective Singer could see that terror, and he took a closer look at me, his eyes narrowing, his face turning slightly, his head cocked as he considered what I knew had to be written on my face.

"Why don't you want to go inside?" he asked quietly.

"It has nothing to do with Melissa." I spat the words out like knives, clenching my teeth to stay in control. *Breathe, Jannie, breathe.* "I would just rather stay out here."

"It's nearly a hundred degrees."

"I like heat." It didn't matter to me that my behavior was odd, that he might now be watching me closely, wondering if I—imagine, me!—could have had anything to do with Melissa's disappearance. I knew that my legs would freeze, that I would never be able to take those steps to the door, that my heart would beat so rapidly, sooner or later I would have to pass out, just to slow my body down.

"I don't," he countered.

I knew there must be a million eyes on us, and most inquisitive of all would be those of my mother. I couldn't embarrass her in front of all the members of her ward, not to mention all the strangers who had shown up to help in the search. I had already disappointed her profoundly, in ways she was totally unaware of.

"I can't," I said to him in the quietest voice I could manage, one that I knew my mother, standing ten feet away, could not hear. I hoped her lipreading skills, so deeply honed when my brother and I were teenagers, had faded with lack of practice. "It's a . . . a phobia. One I'm working on. But I can't go into that church. You can take me to the station and talk to me there. I'll go to any restaurant. I'll sit in your car. But I can't go in that church. And I can't explain why. Not right now."

CHAPTER FIVE

Colt Singer was a gentleman, but he was also a police officer, and I knew I would have to explain, and it had better be good.

"All right, let's talk in my car," he said, grabbing me by the elbow and steering me toward his vehicle, which I guessed was parked somewhere near my own. I could feel the prying eyes of my mother and all her cronies scoring into my back as we walked. I imagined my mother searching his shoulders for the telltale garment line—even though it would be impossible to spot through his suit jacket—that would tell her if this man was a returned missionary or active Mormon, and thereby good enough for her daughter. She had undoubtedly used her radar to see that he had no ring on his left hand, a fact I had also noted, although not for the same reason.

It was habit with me. Every man was under suspicion. I trusted none of them. I had learned to look for signs and then quiz them to see if I could catch them in a lie. Sad, what I had become.

We reached the unmarked brown car Detective Singer

opened with a keypad; and he pulled the passenger door open for me, then shut it tightly when I was seated inside. He walked around the front and entered on the driver's side, inserted the key in the lock, and started the car up, adjusting the air-conditioning to full blast. Then he turned to me.

"Tell me what's going on, please, Ms. Fox. Or is it Mrs.?"

"Jannie. And I'm not sure you'll understand."

I was dealing with the enemy here, no matter how good the enemy looked, or how often my mother had told me to trust the nice police officers and run to them if I was ever in trouble. I worked with the wives of police officers. They could be among the worst of abusers.

"Try me," Colt Singer said.

"Fine. I can't go inside a Mormon church. I haven't been able to for about six years. It's a phobia, and I'm seeing a therapist to try to get it under control, but no luck so far. I'd appreciate it if you didn't share this with anyone, please."

Fat chance of that.

He didn't respond, just stared at me, waiting for me to go on.

Finally, I couldn't stand the silence.

"What? That's it. It's stupid, I know, so just write me off as a whackjob or whatever, but it has nothing to do with Melissa, or her disappearance, and I'll take a lie detector test or whatever you want to prove it."

"Is it all churches, or just Mormon ones?" His question, when he finally spoke, surprised me.

"I don't know. I haven't tried to go inside any other churches. There really hasn't been a reason. But I'm sure it's Mormon churches, because . . . just because."

I'd almost said too much.

"Guilt?"

"What?"

"Is it guilt that does it? You did something wrong, and now the guilt is driving you away?"

Color infused my face—color I could feel, although not see—as I remembered the night my world had changed. It was the same night I vowed never to let another man touch me. It was the same night the beginnings of an unforgivable sin took seed, and I would never get past it.

"I had nothing to do with Melissa's disappearance, she's my friend. Something bad happened to me in a church, and that's why I have this phobia. But it's not related to this, and I don't intend to say anything else about it." Unless he kept probing, and I had no choice. My heart was already racing, I was sweating, and I felt light-headed. I couldn't talk about it. I couldn't.

"Okay. Tell me about Melissa."

He changed direction so quickly I sat stunned, then turned and looked out the window to regain my composure. I wouldn't have to explain what had happened, and how I had become the shell of a person I was now. I had another reprieve. My whole life was full of reprieves.

I began to talk about Melissa, about how close we had been growing up. I told him about her mother, and their strained relationship, and how relieved Liss was to move out of her parents' home after she married Michael. I told him about Melissa's odd behavior in the last week before she disappeared, about how she had shown up on my doorstep with the box. I told him about my intruder, and Colt Singer's face tightened as he wrote in a small notebook, asking me the name of the officer who had come to the door.

"What was in the box?"

"I'm not exactly sure. She told me not to open it."

"And you didn't?"

"Of course not."

"So, after the intruder came, you said the box was turned over upside down in your closet?"

"Yes."

"So the intruder didn't take the box. What was in it?"

"There was a journal with a weird entry, but there wasn't a note telling me, specifically, that something was wrong, but that wasn't Melissa's way. She was always closemouthed. She never really opened up until she was ready, and on her terms."

Melissa was a stone wall when she didn't want to talk. But she shared more with me than anyone else, and I remembered a strange meeting we'd had the year before, one of the many times I was forced to endure Brian's company, and be hit in the face with the success that was Mike and Melissa. But this night had been different. Something was wrong.

Despite the fact I'd grown up with the three people sitting at the restaurant table with me, we stared at each other like strangers meeting for the first time across the hood of a dented automobile, lives crashing into each other with reckless abandon and no control.

Melissa held her arms close to her body, hugging herself, scooting as far away from Mike as the booth would allow. They hadn't said much at all to each other ever since we sat down, and the tension was spreading to Brian and me. We didn't need any help in that department. Something was wrong, and I didn't know what it was, because I'd made myself so distant from this group of people, friends I used to be so close to.

Brian had set up the meeting and I'd agreed to it because he said that Mike and Melissa were anxious to talk to us both about something. I was caught in a moment of loneliness, and a desire to recapture the relationships of the past, so I gave in. It was obvious that all was not well in the Holt household, but I started to doubt that Mike and Melissa wanted to talk to anyone, including each other, and this had just been one of Brian's desperate manipulations. "I think I'll go use the ladies' room," I said, anxious to get up and leave the scene of whatever wreck this was.

"I'll go with you," Melissa said, jumping up and almost sprinting away from the table and ahead of me. As we walked, I turned and saw Mike put his hand to his forehead and Brian reach out and place one hand on his shoulder.

"All right, what's up, Melissa? What's going on?"

She just shook her head as she entered one of the stalls and slammed the granite door shut. When Melissa didn't want to talk, not much would get her to open up. But I sensed this was something serious, and I knew that I truly was the only one she could vent to. So I kept quiet, and waited for her to come out of the stall. When she exited, she gave me a funny look and then proceeded to the sink to wash her hands, not saying anything about the fact I had not used the facilities.

She dried her hands slowly on the paper towel she pulled from the wall container, and then turned and met my eyes for the first time that night.

"Liss, what's wrong?"

"Mike did something." It was almost painful to hear the words from her mouth, they were so sharp and edged with tension.

"Did what?" I felt myself tighten up with fear. Surely Mike and Melissa would be okay. Surely Mike would not do something so horrible that their relationship would be destroyed.

She sighed deeply, and then opened her mouth and leaned forward, as though to force the words to spill out. Her curly brown hair fell forward and moved in waves as she spoke. "He ran up a credit card again. One I didn't know he had. I finally had them all consolidated, and then this bill came and I saw we were right back where we started."

"He's done this before?"

She sighed again. "Yes. He gets in a jam, and he's afraid to tell me, so he figures he can cover it, borrowing from Peter to pay Paul. I grew up with that kind of stuff from my mom, and he knows I can't tolerate it. So he doesn't tell me about it, because he knows it will make me mad. The worst part is, I don't know what he spends the money on, and he won't tell me, or can't tell me. Jannie, I'm just tired of it. I'm working myself to death to put him through college, and if he could just control himself we would get there! But he can't, or won't. And I don't know how much more I can take."

"How bad is it?"

"This time? You ready for this? Twenty-five thousand dollars."

I gasped as the impact of the number hit me. That was just a little less than I knew Melissa made in one year. How overwhelming it must be for her to be faced with this.

"Why didn't you tell me? I never knew any of this was going on."

"I didn't tell anyone. The first time I just got a loan and paid them all off. He promised it would never happen again. But here we are again. And this time it's even worse."

"Oh, Liss, I'm so sorry. What are you going to do?"

"I don't know. Bail him out again, I guess. What else can I do? We're married for time and all eternity."

"Those bonds can be broken, Liss, if it's that bad for you."

"I love him, Jannie. But I want him to grow up. I want him to be the man I thought I married. I want the life I thought I was going to have."

I couldn't fault her for that. I'd had my own dreams, too, once upon a fairy tale. But the more I lived, and the more I learned, the more I knew that the fairy tale was never true. Melissa and Mike were the closest thing I'd ever seen to someone actually living the dream. And, selfishly, I didn't want to hear about the human faults that were marring the relationship I'd idealized for so long.

"We'd better get back, or they'll think we scooted out the window and took off." No sooner had I said those words than a knock came on the door and Mike's voice echoed through it.

"Melissa? Are you still in there? God, baby, tell me you're still in there. I'm so sorry. Please don't leave me. Please don't leave."

At Mike's voice and words Melissa burst into tears and tore the bathroom door open, and they flew into each other's arms. Brian stood behind Mike, surveying the twosome with a look I couldn't identify, but which made me uneasy, and then his eyes swung up and met mine.

I squirmed under the scrutiny of his hazel eyes, and guilt flooded through me, as it always did whenever I was around him.

Brian's eyes were pools of unanswered questions, and need, and hurt, but I also saw something else there. I saw desire. That, I could not handle.

"What are you thinking about?" Detective Singer's voice interrupted my reverie and I started as I pulled myself out of the time warp with Melissa, Mike, and Brian.

"Michael and Melissa. I grew up with Michael. He's like a brother to me. He lived across the street. In fact, our parents still live in the same houses."

"So they had a normal relationship? A normal marriage?"

"They had their problems, just like everyone does. But nothing that would bring this about. Nothing . . ." Except a huge amount of credit card debt and money unaccounted for. I hesitated, then spoke up. "Maybe things have changed between them, even though I still don't believe he would ever hurt her. Melissa wanted a life very different from the one her parents have had. Her dad has never been good at keeping a job, and her mom's a basket case. You might have noticed."

"But what do you mean that things have changed for Mike and Melissa?"

"You know, disappointments when things don't work out the way you planned. When someone doesn't live up to your expectations, or do what they told you they were going to do or become, that it can be hard. We all dream of a life that is usually pretty damn different from what we get. Melissa is no different." I hesitated for a moment, and then said, "I think she was pregnant, and I'm not sure she was happy about it."

"Pregnant?"

"Yes," I answered. I had already told him about the journal. Now I pulled it and the pregnancy test out of my purse and handed them to him. His face was serious as he took them, and his jaw pulsed with tension.

"You should probably go stay with your mother," he said after a moment. "Your place isn't safe."

"I can't do that. And please don't ask me to explain. I'm looking for a new apartment now, so soon I'll be gone." My heart sank as I thought about explaining to my elderly landlady why I had to move. She would be devastated. I was the ideal tenant—I paid my rent on time every month, I never had parties or male houseguests, and I drove her all over town, since I had nothing else to consume my time except my job.

"All right, Jannie, I'm done with you now. But I need to know how to contact you. I have the number of the domestic shelter, but do you have a cell number?"

He knew where I worked. Probably had the entire time, although he hadn't said a word. I didn't know if that bothered me or not. In a way, it made me feel oddly safe. It appeared that Colt Singer, like me, was not very trusting of humans and human nature.

"What now?" I asked him.

"What do you mean?"

"What happens now? In the search for Melissa?"

"We have searchers combing Memory Grove and the Avenues, and all the areas around the 7-Eleven where her car was found. We also have officers at her apartment building, and they are searching the Dumpsters—"

He stopped as I winced, the thought of Melissa's body hidden inside a big trash bin like yesterday's garbage almost more than I could take.

"They're looking for clues, Jannie. Anything that might tell us what happened to Melissa."

"Mike must be devastated," I said, as I rubbed my temples and closed my eyes.

"His behavior has been a little odd. I'm sure you've seen it before. He's out searching right now, with his friend Brian."

I turned and stared at him, not wanting to hear what he was saying, but the message got through nonetheless. They believed Mike was the prime suspect.

"You think he did it."

"Let's just say I'm not convinced he didn't."

"But he loved her. He wouldn't hurt her." The words seemed hollow, and I realized I had heard them parroted time and time again from the families of victims. Still, I couldn't help myself. "He never has before. It makes no sense."

"Love usually doesn't."

CHAPTER SIX

After Detective Singer took my cell phone number down, he let me go back to the command post; and I spent the evening, signing up volunteers and helping organize the hunt for Melissa. At sundown, as they shut down for the night, I reluctantly left the command post and drove to my apartment, anxiety filling me as I considered my intruder that afternoon. He wouldn't be back, of course. The police had been there. They had promised to watch the place.

But if the intruder had been looking for Lissa's box and the contents, he hadn't found it. Or at least not all of it. I had no way of knowing if anything else had been in that box, and had been taken by . . .

Could it have been Mike? It made no sense to think that it had been anyone else, and I really wanted to believe it had been random, but I was not stupid. Would he be waiting for me there?

I grabbed my purse and tightened my grip on it. I turned off the engine and pulled out the keys, placing one between each of my fingers so they could be used as a weapon, if it became necessary. I also pulled the gun out of my handbag and released the safety. If someone was waiting for me inside my apartment, they were going to get more than they bargained for.

I trod quietly on the walkway past Ida's open window, and I could hear the television set playing in her bedroom. Shadows from the flickering light of the television cast an eerie glow across the walkway. My door was ajar.

Heart pounding, I took several steps back and ducked into an ivy-covered alcove. Not letting go of the gun, I dropped my keys inside my purse and fished out the cell phone, dialing 911 and whispering my address into the receiver. Then I made my way slowly to the front of the house, keeping in the shadows and close to the house. In less than three minutes, the flashing red and blue of police lights bounded back and forth from the front of the house, although there was no siren. Another car followed closely on the first. I ran toward the first vehicle and identified myself to the two officers who stepped out, pointing them in the direction of my back apartment.

Down the street I could see the approaching lights of a third police car, and a flash of embarrassment roiled through me. This might be nothing. I pushed that thought aside—better safe than sorry—and then decided I'd better let Ida know what was going on, so she didn't panic. Since it was nearly ten P.M., I imagined she was sleeping soundly in front of her television, which was her usual routine, but just in case, I decided to warn her.

I told one of the officers who had remained behind to guard me that I was going to check on her, and he followed me to her doorstep. I knocked softly. There was no answer. The screen door was unlocked, and her front door ajar, but Ida had been forgetful lately.

"Ida?" I called as I stepped inside. "Ida, it's Jannie. Are you okay?" There was no answer. "Her bedroom's back here," I told the young officer who had followed me, and I walked toward the closed door. Again, I knocked gently. "Ida?" When there was no answer, I pushed the door open and peeked inside. There was no sign of Ida, although the television on her dresser was blaring. The bed was slightly mussed, as though she had been there relaxing but had risen.

A quick run-through of the house told me she was not there. Alarm ripped through my body. Ida's only daughter lived in Boise, and my landlady never left her house in the evenings, unless it was for a church event. She certainly never left her doors unlocked and lights and television blaring.

"Something's wrong. She should be here," I told him, panic beginning to fill my chest.

The two-way radio attached to his shoulder beeped, and he backed away as he spoke into it, identifying himself by a call sign. "This is Tango Two."

The speaker on the other end used some ten-code that I could not identify, and the officer gave me a hard look as he asked me to step outside with him. The panic deepened, and I turned to walk out the door and ran smack into the broad chest of Detective Colt Singer, who stared down at me with what I imagined was a look of extreme suspicion.

"Jannie, I'm afraid I have bad news. The officers discovered a body in your apartment."

CHAPTER SEVEN

Life was funny, in a very unha-ha way. It was filled with surprises that you could never see coming, and could never anticipate, even if you lived to be a hundred years old, an age that Ida Miller had come awfully close to, but would never see.

I demanded to see the body, despite Singer's insistence I would not want to look. I could identify her, though, something they couldn't do immediately.

He'd been right about my not wanting to see her, of course. There was blood everywhere, spattered on the walls, soaked into the carpets. It would never come out. *Good thing I had already planned to leave.*

Ida Miller's body was clad in her nightgown covered with a lightweight silky robe, both light blue in color—at least what wasn't stained dark red with blood. I knew it was her, even without looking at the face, which was virtually unrecognizable so severely had she been beaten. I recognized her hands, long fingers twisted and gnarled from arthritis, her large diamond wedding ring still on the third left finger.

Even though Ida had been taller than I, she looked so tiny, so frail, lying on the floor of my apartment. How could someone have done this? And how was it related to Melissa's disappearance? *Was* it related, or just some strange random crime? Why was Ida even *in* my apartment?

The amount of blood and the spatter indicated that this was, in fact, where she had been murdered.

"It's Ida," I said through the tears that bubbled up from a place deep inside me. My home life, which I had carefully ordered, everything the same, predictable, steady, had been upended with Melissa's disappearance. Poor Ida had not deserved this horrible death, and the guilt came crashing in. She was in my apartment. It was all related to me. What else could it be? But why?

Now I sat in an interrogation room of the Salt Lake City Police Department and recounted—over and over again— my actions and whereabouts of the past twenty-four hours. Since I had a bevy of witnesses who had seen the time I left the command post, I knew I was pretty much off the hook for Ida's murder, except perhaps as an accomplice, which really was laugh-out-loud funny. I had no one in my life to "accomplice" with. Of course, the police would not be convinced of that.

With Ida's death, Melissa's missing status suddenly seemed even more dire. Mental videos of Melissa's life kept running through my head, accompanied by the horrific still pictures of Ida's brutalized body. Melissa had always been so alive and vibrant, so filled with the promise of youth and exuberance, and with years of living ahead of her. Was her fate going to be the same as Ida's? I was irrevocably tied to these crimes, and yet I had no knowledge of who was doing it, or why.

Detective Abrahams, who was interviewing me, was a tired-looking man of about forty. I knew he must be exhausted or burned out, because he kept asking me the same questions. Maybe this was a new variation of good cop/bad cop. Instead you get tired cop, who drones on and on until you scream your guilt just to get him to stop.

I was relieved when Colt Singer stepped into the room and dismissed Abrahams.

"You don't really think I had anything to do with any of this, do you?" I asked Singer after Abrahams left. "Melissa was my best friend. And I took care of Ida. I would never harm her."

"What I think doesn't matter," Singer said, his voice tense and abrupt. "I have to follow the clues, and the clues so far are these. Melissa gave you a box. A week later she disappears. Someone breaks into your apartment to try to find the box, and fails, or at least fails to retrieve *all* of it. Then an elderly woman who never left her house after seven P.M. turns up dead, brutally murdered in your apartment. You are the key here. You hold the answers."

"I don't have the answers. Unless it's about revenge. I work with domestic abuse victims. I don't make a lot of friends among the bullies and abusers of the world."

"But no one has outright threatened you, at least in the past few days?"

"No. No one. But right now I'm working on the Talon case. You might recognize that name."

His blank look told me he didn't. "Brandon and Debbie Talon. He beats her up pretty regularly, then convinces her it's her fault, they go see the bishop, he gives them advice to keep their family together, and she goes back to Brandon, where they live happily-until-he-loses-his-temper. Last time he beat her up she was pregnant and the baby died. He convinced the world it was an accident, that she was clumsy and fell. She backed him up. But she came to me a few days ago and showed me a nasty bruise he gave her daughter. She swears she's done with him this time. And he threatens me every time it happens."

"You have the address?"

"Ten sixty-five Madison, Sugar House. He's living there, and Debbie's at her mother's. I know their home address by heart, since I've written it on three or four restraining orders a year for the past three years." Sugar House was officially established in 1853, six years after Brigham Young declared the Salt Lake Valley the "place" for the Mormon settlers to make their new home. The district was named for a planned sugar mill, which I heard was never really established, but it was a wonderful place to live, and in the past twenty years had become very upscale and the "it" place for young yuppie couples and the financially well off.

Brandon Talon came from money, his father being one of the founders of a premier real estate firm in Salt Lake, as well as one of the church's general authorities. As far as I could tell, that was the only reason the Talons lived so well, because Debbie was always vague about exactly what Brandon did, even though he put on a suit and went into his father's office every day. I suspected she was vague because she didn't really know, another way for Brandon to keep control over her.

Singer pulled the cell phone off his belt and dialed a number, speaking with rapid-fire urgency to the person on the other end, telling them to pick up one Brandon Talon, immediately. With Ida dead, and Melissa missing, they couldn't afford to take chances. *Ida, oh, poor Ida.* What a horrifying mess this day had turned out to be.

"So there's no clues at all where Melissa might be?" I asked him, my heart pounding, even though I already knew the answer.

"Nothing substantial. You know, for someone who has a dead lady in her apartment and whose best friend is missing, you seem pretty damn calm."

I sighed and looked away for a moment, tears stinging my eyes as he attempted to chip to the core of the real me. I didn't want anyone going there. I wouldn't let him know how, deep inside, I was totally destroyed. But I'd been that way for years. "That doesn't make me guilty, Detective. I work with chaos and destruction for a living, kind of like you. I've learned to cope. So, what do you mean, nothing substantial?"

Singer's lips tightened. They had found something, but he wasn't going to share with me what that something was.

"What the hell is happening here?"

"You tell me."

I shot him the best glare I could muster, given the situation. "I have no idea. And you are barking up the wrong tree if you think I do."

His phone rang before he could respond, and he answered in short bursts of verbiage—yeses and nos, mostly.

"Patrol can't find Talon. Seems he's disappeared. We'll keep looking for him, though. Hopefully, we'll find him skulking around his wife. Violation of the restraining order gets him a go-to-jail card."

"Good. And when you do, just keep him there."

"We'll find him. And when we do, if he had anything to do with Melissa Holt's disappearance and Ida Miller's murder, he'll never see the light of day again."

The sinking feeling in the pit of my stomach told me it wouldn't be that easy. I couldn't see Brandon Talon killing an old woman and kidnapping a young one just because he was angry at me. He usually contained his rage and only directed it at those closest to him, even though he threatened me verbally every chance he got.

Instinct told me Ida's killer was not Brandon, and Melissa was in grave danger, unless she was already dead. Who was responsible? Was it Michael?

"How is Michael holding up?" I asked nonchalantly, not wanting to indicate that my thought processes were leading me to question whether or not he might really be innocent. I knew the police didn't need any help looking at him as a suspect.

"He's not. He collapsed about an hour ago. He's conveniently being treated in the hospital right now."

Detective Colt Singer's eyes told me that, for him at least, there was no question who was guilty of at least one of the crimes committed in the past twenty-four hours, if not both.

Mike Holt was his prime suspect.

CHAPTER EIGHT

Before we left my apartment and headed to the police station, I had packed a small bag and turned my keys over to the police—it was a crime scene that I would not be allowed into for at least a few days. I never intended to return. I would hire a moving crew to pack up my possessions, and would use the next few days to find a new place to live. Maybe I would call my boss and ask for some time off. I could use the time to search for Melissa, as well as arranging to move.

Every time I thought about moving, I thought about Ida, and tears threatened to overcome me. She was dead. Had Melissa met the same fate?

Detective Singer drove me to the first place that came to my mind, which usually would have been the last—my mother's house. He also assured me that he would arrange to have my car delivered—I had ridden to the station in a police car, which had undoubtedly been a good thing for the other drivers on the road. However, it meant that I was now stuck in my mother's care, and dependent upon her until my car was dropped off.

"Can you do it soon?" I asked him as we sat in front of the large, three-story colonial-style house I had grown up in. It was just around the corner from the church where the search command center had been set up and where my father, as stake president, had his offices.

Colt Singer nodded as he surveyed me closely. I blushed under his inspection and turned to stare at the brightly lit house where untold terrors awaited me. *You are being very shallow and selfish, Jannie,* I told myself harshly. Think about Melissa. Think about Ida. What was a night spent with my mother when I considered what had happened? Even if that night would be spent answering my mother's four million questions and listening to her exhortations against my dangerous lifestyle and living alone in the city. Never mind that all of this seemed to stem back to young, happily married Melissa's disappearance. My mother would find a way to attribute all the chaos and destruction to the fact I had not yet settled down with a nice, steady, dependable, successful Mormon boy. A boy like Brian.

For Evelyn and Hugh Fox loved Brian. He was everything they wanted in a son-in-law. My family was everything Brian wanted to belong to. He had little to do with his own smoking, drinking parents. For them he had mostly disgust, so he had adopted my parents instead. They were thrilled. The only disagreeing party was me.

As proof, Brian's car sat in the driveway, and I knew he was inside the house comforting my parents, attempting to show them what a stalwart young man he truly was—trying to weasel his way back into my life, something that would never happen. He knew why, even though he had rationalized it all away. My mother and father remained blissfully ignorant about what had occurred between Brian and me even though I had gone to the bishop of our ward after it happened and sobbed out the whole sordid story. Afterward, I had felt too much shame to ever tell my parents what had occurred. The bishop had called us in together and spoken in that monotone voice all Mormon authorities use. I was at fault, too, it seemed, for I had allowed the necking, light petting, and—

"Uh, are you going to go in?" Detective Singer's voice jolted me back to reality, and I tried to shake off the unsettling memories that visited me at least once a week.

"I think maybe I should just get a hotel room," I answered, staring forlornly at Brian's brand-new Lexus. He had done well for himself, graduating first from Brigham Young University and then from BYU's J. Reuben Clark Law School. Now he worked in downtown Salt Lake City for McConkie, Young, and Smith, one of Utah's most prestigious law firms—and one with direct ties to the LDS Church and the church's leaders. With no family and no real expenses, he spent his money on self-esteem builders, like the car sitting in my parents' driveway.

He was my mother's dream son-in-law. He was my nightmare.

"Want to explain why you are staring so intently at that car? Someone you know that makes you not want to go inside?"

"It belongs to Brian Williams. He's Michael's best friend . . . and my former fiancé."

"Former? Why is he here?"

"He's always here. He's never gotten past the fact that I let us get as far as the temple, even going through our endowments, and then I walked—well, ran, really—out before we were married. It's kind of nuts. Everything he achieves—every milestone—he always comes back here to show me and my parents what we are missing out on."

"You ran out of the temple?"

"It's a long story." I grimaced as I considered the fall-out from the decision I'd made that day.

"And one I'd love to hear."

"Maybe another time." Melissa's disappearance and Ida's murder had me frazzled, and I was saying things I'd probably regret. I looked away from the Lexus and across the street at Michael's childhood home. It was dark, abandoned, with no sign of activity.

"And he's still trying to get you back?"

"God, no. He despises me. Can't even bring himself to be civil when he sees me. He just wants me to know how well he's done, and how much he's achieved."

"He's still trying to get you back."

"That's not true. You don't understand. He knows I want nothing to do with him, and he's just trying to get at me by showing up all the time, but he really doesn't want me back."

"Yes he does. You don't understand men very well, do you?" Singer asked me, a quizzical look on his face, one eyebrow cocked higher than the other.

"Oh, please, I understand this situation fine and I understand him fine. And he knows I would never let him touch me again, not after—"

I stopped short, having said way too much to this man who was a complete stranger.

"Not after what?"

"Not after I broke up with him."

"That's not what you were going to say." Colt shook his head, and I remained steadfastly silent. I couldn't explain.

I wouldn't. Finally, he spoke again. "How long ago were you engaged?"

"It's been six years."

"Six years? And this guy is still coming around? He date anyone else?"

"I think so. My mom moans about it all the time. 'Look what Brian's doing now. Just look.' Looking makes me sick."

Detective Singer was silent, staring straight ahead, drumming absentmindedly on the steering wheel as he thought about the man who wouldn't leave me alone, or at least let me be single in peace.

"Six years. Six years, he's not married, and he still comes around your family. Yet you say he can't stand you. Something is definitely wrong with that. He's behind it, isn't he? He's behind the reason you can't go inside churches."

I suppose it wasn't that hard to reason out, but I would still be damned if his detective skills were going to make me end up spilling secrets about my life that were better left buried, deep, and never uncovered.

Of course, they would never be that deep. Brian's constant uneasy presence in my life made sure of that.

I turned to look at the man sitting next to me, and for the first time, really saw him. He had dark brown hair—almost black—and his eyes were such a dark green they reminded me of mysterious oriental jade. I wondered what else existed behind those eyes. His face was angular and strong, and his lips . . . I couldn't think about that. I couldn't believe I *was* thinking about it.

"Yes, he's behind it. Can we leave it at that? Will you take me to a hotel?"

"You can't keep running from him. Sooner or later you have to stand up to him, tell him to get lost, to stay away from your family. Get out of your life."

"Easy for you to say," I said to the window, not meeting his eye or looking at him.

"What did he do, Jannie? Did he rape you?" His voice was gentle and concerned, and the use of my first name, said so softly, unnerved me greatly.

I should have been surprised that he guessed about the rape, but, really, wasn't it obvious? Wasn't I a walking billboard that screamed "victim"?

"They said it wasn't rape." I spoke suddenly, determined to get this information out and then never speak of it again. "The bishop said I had allowed it to happen, because we were alone together, and I was wearing some revealing clothing, and I . . . It happened after a ward singles dance one night. Brian was in charge of the dance, and had a key to the church, and was responsible for locking it up. We stayed late. I agreed to it. I *wanted* to be there with him. I guess if you look at it that way, it was inevitable, but I said no. I told him to stop. I said no."

I reached up to my face, surprised to find I was crying because I wasn't feeling the pain. I was numb.

"You said no, and the bishop told you it was partially your fault?"

"Yes. He made us repent, and we had to meet with him weekly, and discuss our sins, and we had to wait six months before we could go to the temple and be married. I buried it, decided it was my fault, and I was able to say no to his touching me, because the bishop told us to never get ourselves into that situation again. And we stayed so chaste for about three months, until I discovered . . . I discovered I couldn't go into a church anymore. I started finding excuses not to go to meetings. I was sick. I was visiting a friend's ward. I didn't know how I was going to make it through the temple ceremonies. Actually, I didn't. That's when I walked—actually ran—out of the temple and out on my own wedding. And I've only been inside a temple or church once since. I had to take Xanax to get me through it."

"And you've told him to leave you alone, but he still comes around?"

"I've told him, but he won't let go, for whatever stupid reason he has. We were part of the golden foursome, though, you know? Melissa and Mike. Me and Brian. We were all going to hang out together, live by each other, raise our kids together. Fairy-tale lives. I screwed that up."

"You said no. He didn't listen. That's rape. Date rape is still rape."

"We were practically married." I'm not sure why I was making excuses for him. Perhaps it was to ease my own fear of culpability in the situation, to help me deal with my guilt.

"No means no."

"Well, it's old news. Been a long time. I just wish he would find someone else and stop haunting my life."

"He's still assaulting you, you know? Keeping you under his thumb. That's what this is all about."

"I know," I answered, then sighed wearily. "Will you take me to a hotel? I'm just not up to dealing with this tonight."

"Yes, I will. But I'm not leaving you alone."

"What do you mean?"

"I'll take you to a hotel. I'll check you in. But we'll get adjoining rooms. You aren't safe. Someone killed your neighbor in your apartment. There's a murderer out there, and we don't know who it is. Melissa Holt is still missing. Maybe I'll get lucky, and the killer will show up and I can solve the whole damn case tonight."

"But you think it's Michael, and he's in the hospital, right? Under observation."

"Michael is my main suspect, at least in Melissa's disappearance," Singer admitted, his mouth a grim slash. "Until we determine a time of death for Ida Miller, we don't know that he isn't the one who did it. But it isn't ironclad."

"So it could be someone else?"

"Yes, it could be."

"You can't come inside my room."

"Pardon?"

"We can get adjoining rooms, but you can't come into my side. Not even a foot. I can't . . . I can't . . ."

"The only thing that would get me inside your room, Jannie, is if you are in danger. I'm not that puke in there," he said, with a sharp jab toward Brian's car. "And we're virtual strangers. I've never forced myself on a woman before, and I'm sure as hell not going to start now."

"I didn't mean to offend you. It's just, if you come in the room, I won't be able to sleep."

"Are you trying to say if I step into the room, you won't sleep at all, even after I leave? Even if it's only for a moment?"

"Probably not."

"You getting some help for that?"

"Yes," I answered shortly, not amused by the tone in his voice. I knew my phobias were silly and ridiculous. I knew I needed to get control of them. I also knew I had been unsuccessful so far.

He started up the car just as the front door of my parents'

home opened, and out stepped Brian, followed by my mother and father. The entire tableau was illuminated by the porch light. He hugged my mother, and something in my chest tightened as I watched her hold on to him tightly. My father stood behind her, gazing fondly at the son-in-law they wished they had. I turned to Detective Colt Singer and urged him to quickly leave, but it was too late. My parents and Brian had noticed the car, and all three were staring. Brian took a step, and then another, and before I knew what had happened he was running toward the car and pulling the door open, yanking me from the passenger seat.

He let go of me abruptly when he heard a sharp click and a gun touched his head.

"Brian, meet Detective Colt Singer, Salt Lake City PD," I said.

CHAPTER NINE

As good as it felt to see Brian totally cowed, even though it took a gun and a badge-yielding man, I knew the encounter would have repercussions, the greatest of which would be my mother's reaction.

"My stars, what on earth are you doing? You have a gun? Hugh, why on earth is this man holding a gun to Brian's head?"

My mother, who had run forward followed closely by my father, was fond of asking questions her husband could not possibly answer.

Detective Singer pushed Brian to the ground, and ordered him to put his hands behind his back. Brian complied, a look of sheer anger and arrogance on his face, backed up by some very real terror. Only when he was on the ground did Singer lower the gun.

"What in heaven's name is going on?" my father asked the detective.

"Well, this man just attempted to pull Jannie from my car without her permission, which led me to believe he was attempting a kidnapping."

"Kidnapping? Don't you know who this is?" My mother was flustered, an uncommon state for her. "This is Brian Williams, he is Jannie's fiancé."

"Mother, Brian is not my fiancé. We broke up years ago. Can you please get over it and let me move on?"

Brian sputtered a bit but didn't speak.

"Oh, I know that, Jannie. I'm just, well, for heaven's sake. Would you put that away?" She pointed to Singer's gun. "Brian is an old family friend. We've known him all his life, and he certainly wasn't trying to kidnap Jannie."

Singer obliged by putting the gun away, and a quick upward quirk of his mouth told me he'd never really thought Brian was trying to kidnap me at all but he had certainly enjoyed taking him down.

Brian stood and brushed off the knees of his expensive suit, disdain and anger lighting in his dark blue eyes. His brown hair was fashionably cut, and he smelled like expensive cologne. He gave me a condescending look, and then turned to Singer.

"I'll have you know that I'm an attorney and a false arrest can garner millions from a lawsuit. I saw Jannie in a strange car, and considering what is going on, I assumed she was in danger."

"But I didn't arrest you. You rushed to the car, threw open the door, and yanked Jannie out of it. We are in the middle of a situation where one young woman is missing, and an elderly woman is dead, and no one seems to know who is doing it. As Jannie seems to be the target of someone's wrath and murderous intent, I had to be cautious."

Brian's eyes closed up tighter as he glowered at Singer.

"Surely she told you who I was."

"She didn't get a chance." I ignored his lie, basking in

Brian's moment of degradation. Colt continued to speak. "And did you really think that someone would abduct Jannie and then drive her to her mother's house, and sit out front waiting for someone to spot them?"

It was a standoff, and Brian knew it.

"What did you mean, an elderly woman is dead?" my mother asked, Singer's comment suddenly having penetrated her ever-sharp mind. "Who is dead?"

"It's Ida, Mom," I explained wearily. "Someone killed her in my apartment."

"What in the world have you gotten yourself involved in?" Brian asked, edges of both concern and derision in his voice. I knew he was trying to drive home, as he always did, how much easier my life would have been had I just followed through and married him, as had been preordained by the God he always insisted we pray to before our dates.

"This has nothing to do with me," I spat back, irritated by his beliefs, both spoken and silent.

"Well, that's not exactly true, now is it?" Brian countered. "*Your* landlady was killed in *your* apartment. It has to have something to do with you."

"Of course, we have no knowledge that either crime is connected," Singer said, then motioned me to get back in the car. "I was just going to take Jannie to a hotel to stay. She wanted you to know that she would be safe, and wanted to tell you personally about Ida before you heard it on the news."

He directed all of this to my parents, ignoring Brian as though he weren't standing there.

"You'll do no such thing," my mother said, moving toward me and hooking her arm through mine. "Jannie will stay here. She'll be safe here, with her family."

"Jannie?" Detective Singer said, the question in his voice letting me know that the decision was mine. Either I stayed here with my mother and father, in a house filled with memories of all that I had not become, or I stayed in a hotel room with an adjoining door that led to a man I barely knew.

I picked the man I barely knew.

CHAPTER TEN

We checked into a Quality Inn in downtown Salt Lake City and, as promised, were given adjoining rooms. Detective Singer unlocked and opened his side, and I did the same, although not without some trepidation. He did not step across the threshold, but simply told me to get some sleep, then retired to his room, where I could hear the television set softly burbling what sounded like a canned news program.

In the bathroom, I opened the small duffel bag I had packed and pulled out a T-shirt and shorts, slipping out of my clothes, which I wanted to burn. While not physically ruined, they held the taint of death and disappearance on them, and I never wanted to see them again. After I washed my face and brushed my teeth, I pulled my long blond hair into a ponytail, then made my way to the bed. I could still hear the television going in the room next to mine, but I didn't turn on my set. I had several reasons for this. I didn't want to relive Ida's death again, over and over, on the news; I knew that Melissa was still missing; and I wanted to be aware of every noise, every sound, every possible movement.

The rational side of me knew I trusted Colt Singer not to try anything, but since my rape, my phobias had been anything but rational.

Once in bed, I pulled the covers up to my chin and determinedly closed my eyes, not thinking I would ever sleep.

The next thing I knew, I heard a man's voice calling my name softly. "Jannie? Jannie, it's morning, and I have to leave."

I sat up and turned to the adjoining door. In the early morning light I could see the outline of Colt Singer, and an unfamiliar jolt speared through my stomach. It was odd, because it wasn't fear. Until that moment, I wasn't sure I knew anything *but* fear.

"Jannie?"

"Yes, I'm okay. You can go. Thanks for bringing me here, and staying."

"Uh, can I come in?"

Could he come in? Would I be able to withstand that? Since this was a hotel room, I could leave it at any time and check into another one. I would take the chance, for an opportunity to be normal for the first time in many years. I so desperately wanted to be normal.

"You can come in."

He moved one step into the room and stopped. "You sure?"

"Yes, I'm sure. Come in. Please. Sit down. Take a load off."

He moved forward into the room and stood a few feet from the bed. "Sleep okay?"

"I slept like the proverbial baby. Which is a little hard to explain considering—"

"Considering you had a strange man in the room next to you, with the adjoining door open."

"Yeah, that."

"I have to go to work. You stay here, stay out of sight, and don't make any calls or tell anyone where you are."

"I have to call my work, and I'm not going to stay in here like a prisoner, Detective."

"Call me Colt, please. And you're not a prisoner, but you're not exactly safe, either, are you?"

"I haven't felt safe for years. I'm used to it."

"Maybe it's time you stopped being used to it."

"Psychoanalyzing me, Detective?"

"Colt."

"How on earth did you get that name, anyway?"

He quirked an eyebrow, acknowledging my attempt to change the subject without words.

"Long story. You wouldn't believe it, so I'm not sharing."

"Try me."

"I have to get to work. Another time."

"Okay, well, after you leave I'm going to do some snooping around my apartment, and then go to visit Brian and see what he knows about Michael and his odd behavior, and then—"

"You're trying to bargain with me?"

"I'll stay here if you tell me how you got your name."

He tightened his lips, and then shrugged his shoulders, and pointed a finger at me. "You have to stay here, if I tell you this."

"I keep my word, Detective . . . er, I mean Colt."

"Fine, it's my middle name. Named after Colter Bay, in Wyoming. Near the Tetons."

"And what's your first name?"

"Not telling."

"Then I'm on my way out, as soon as you leave."

"That's bribery. It's illegal."

"Arrest me."

This was getting us nowhere fast, but I found myself enjoying the banter and the "something more" that I felt but didn't want to acknowledge. Fear was not a part of it, a thought that was both freeing and extremely frightening in itself. That was as deep as I wanted to examine on this early morning.

Colt Singer reached for his wallet, safely stored in the back pocket of his rumpled suit (Had he slept in the suit? In his underwear? In nothing? What was *wrong* with me?) and pulled it out, flipping it open with skill and retrieving a small square item that he tossed to me on the bed. I picked up the copy of his Utah driver's license, and almost burst out laughing.

"Moroni Colter Singer. Quite a moniker."

"I have a gun, you know."

"Your parents named you Moroni? You don't seem very Mormon to me. How come you don't go by Moroni?"

"How would you know how Mormon I am? And would you go by Moroni, if your nickname could become Moron just by dropping one letter?"

"Good point." He was right about the Mormon stuff, too. How would I know? I had met him yesterday. The day that Melissa disappeared and Ida Miller was murdered in my apartment.

"I'll stay here."

"Good," was his only reply, and then he left. I had no idea when or if he planned on returning. And I'd lied.

I didn't intend to stay put. Melissa was still missing, and might be alive. I saved women like her for a living. Just because I couldn't function myself didn't mean I couldn't go on being superwoman, saving the world from horrible men, one female at a time.

CHAPTER ELEVEN

When I was a little girl, my mother spent countless hours shopping for the perfect Sunday dresses. We were Mormon royalty, as opposed to Melissa's family, who equated to Mormon trailer trash. We had to look the part.

My mother's father was DelMar Carlson, a famous general authority. She married into the Fox family, relative newcomers to the Mormon hierarchy, my father's father being a convert and all, from Scotland; but nonetheless, Grandpa Fox managed to rise fairly quickly in the ranks and become a member of the First Bishopric. It didn't get much better than that.

I grew up in fluffy, foofy, Sunday-go-to-meeting wear. Nowadays, I wore nothing more than jeans and T-shirts, sweatshirts in the winter, and an occasional power suit when I had to go to court for my clients. I had become a simple person, wearing my blond hair long and straight, my face mostly free of makeup, my clothes simple and nonrevealing. Of course, my mother did not know this, and on every occasion that required a gift I received a nice, fancy—though modest—Sunday dress, usually from

Nordstrom. Unknown to her, I donated them to a closet that had become known at work as Jannie's Closet. From it, I dressed those of my clients, and others who made their way through the doors of our shelter, who came to us with little or nothing. We were trying to help them get jobs, become self-sufficient, stand on their own two feet, and not rely on the abusive partner who had landed them at the shelter. The tradition had grown, and we received donations from local businesses and women's organizations year-round. Part of my job was helping women find something to wear. Today was JC day, and I was going to be at work to help the women who needed me. Then I was going to find Brian and question him about Michael. I wasn't much looking forward to that.

After a quick shower, I changed into the second outfit I had brought from my apartment, gathered up my things, and left the key card to the motel room on the dresser. I wouldn't be back, for I had the perfect place to hide, where no man could reach me, including Detective Moroni Colt Singer, who appeared to be penetrating me in ways I did not care to be touched.

I had the concierge call me a cab, and a short while later I arrived at the shelter. I exited the vehicle, looking around carefully to make sure I had not been followed. I could see no one. I made a quick dash to the shelter entrance and waved at Charlie, the retired cop who was now our daytime security guard. He sat in a chair, one arm resting over his large belly, covered by a light blue shirt, the other holding the coffee cup he was never without.

"Hey, Charlie," I said into the buzzer/intercom, and he hit the open button and waved me through.

"Morning, Jannie," he said cheerily, sipping from the

same mug he used every day—it had stains so engrained it would never come clean. He said it gave the coffee flavor. I was always afraid some mysterious amoeba was going to attack him and slowly finish him off. He had enough girth, it would take a while.

I walked quickly through the hallway and scurried to my office, tucking my purse into the cabinet where I stored it, then walked down the hall to the utility closet that had become the fashion boutique for the abused women of Salt Lake City.

I opened the door and poked my head inside and groaned. The closet was a shambles. I had an hour until the women started lining up for clothes, and I had a lot of work to do.

The sudden light touch on my arm nearly sent me through the roof.

"Good God, Jannie, what on earth is wrong?" Millicent Stone said as she gasped and crossed herself, as though to ward off the heart attack I had nearly given her—and she had nearly given me.

"Sorry, Millie, I'm jumpy this morning. The thing with Melissa . . ."

"Yes, I just came to ask you how that was going. No sign of her, at least from what they said on the news. Probably the husband. It usually is."

"Oh, but not Michael. I just don't get it. I can't see it, Millie. He really loved her."

"Well, it might not be," she said with a quick shake of her head, "even though it usually is. You know this. But you know him. Maybe you're right."

"No, the problem is I *knew* him. Back then. And he's always been controlling. Wanting to know where she was all the time. Maybe things had changed, and something flipped that switch, and then he . . . and I was so out of touch with Lissa and her life, I just didn't see it coming."

Millie patted my shoulder and grasped my arm tightly. "Maybe she'll turn up, and it will all be a misunderstanding."

Day two. Still no Melissa. This was no misunderstanding.

"No, something's terribly wrong. And unfortunately, I seem to be tied up in it. She brought a box to my house last week, and someone broke in yesterday trying to get to it. And then my landlady was murdered in my apartment last night."

"No!" Millicent was aghast. "In your apartment? What was she doing in your apartment?"

"We don't know."

"Janica, why are you even here today? You should be somewhere safe."

"Uh, Mill? Can you think of a safer place than this? We protect women for a living. In fact, I need a favor. I need a place to stay. I can't go back to my apartment, and I really can't afford a hotel room until I find a new place, and God knows I'm not going *home,* so can I stay here? I'll take the smallest room."

"Of course, dear," Millicent said, patting my arm. "We aren't full up right now. Take the one by mine. You can stay as long as you want. If it gets too crowded in the shelter, we'll bunk up together." Millicent lived here full-time caring for the flock of women and children that had become her extended family. Since she had never married, she treated them all like her children. It led to lots of heartache for her, especially when we saw them return time and time again to situations that sometimes ended in a violent death, but she was stronger than she looked. Only five feet tall, and extremely petite, Millicent had an iron will.

"Are you going to be okay?" she asked me.

"Yes, but I need to find out where Melissa is, and what happened to her—and to Ida."

"I'll help however I can," she said, and then gave me a hug and left me to organize the closet before the women arrived. No-nonsense Millie. She cared, but we had work to do. Important work. It would help keep my thoughts off Melissa, Ida, and all the others parading through my mind—at least for a few hours.

I called Brian on a brief break before the women started arriving, and he sounded startled to hear my voice. "Jannie, I'm glad you called—surprised, but glad. Any news on Melissa? I'm just so worried about her, but I'm in the middle of this case, and I don't have a lot of time to take off. And then I have you to worry about now, too, with Ida's murder, and this detective—"

"I'm not *your* problem, Brian. But I do need to see you. Can we meet for lunch?"

His tone was considerably cooler when he answered. "I have a full schedule today, Jannie. Maybe this evening."

"No, this evening won't work. Perhaps tomorrow would . . ."

He gave me a deep sigh, and then said, "Well, I can re-arrange my schedule, I suppose. One o'clock at Market Street?"

"Twelve-thirty." I wasn't ever going to give him the

ground he wanted. I had made a concession to go to his choice of restaurant because I needed to see him, even though inside I wanted to scream and rage at him. It was always that way.

I arrived at Market Street exactly on time, and saw him sitting in a corner booth. He waved me over before the hostess could approach, and I made my way through the close aisles, steering clear of busboys carrying dishes and waiters and waitresses with full trays of food.

"Brian," I said, nodding my head to acknowledge him.

"Jannie. I ordered for us, so that we can make this quick. I'm in the middle of a big case and don't have a lot of time, so for once in your life, don't argue, okay?"

I wanted the mother of all arguments with the man seated across from me, but it would do no good. I needed information from him, and antagonizing him wasn't the way to get it. I wasn't very hungry anyway, so it made no difference what he had ordered.

I ordered a Diet Coke from the hovering waitress, then set the napkin on my lap and reached out to grab one of Market Street's famous sourdough rolls. Buttering it carefully, I posed my first question.

"Brian, do you think Michael had anything to do with Melissa's disappearance?"

I expected immediate denial and vitriol aimed at me for thinking such a thing, but he surprised me.

"No, I don't think Michael had anything to do with it, but he sure isn't helping his case by acting like a nutjob and having to be checked into a hospital where the cops can't question him."

"But could he have been involved? I mean, he's always

been controlling of her, and maybe she rebelled and fought back, or just didn't want to deal with him anymore, and was going to leave."

"Jannie, Melissa is not you. She doesn't just run when things get a little tough."

My eyes got wide, and I could see from his face he knew he had gone too far.

"Just pretend I didn't say that, okay? Let's just talk like civilized human beings, if not for us, then for Melissa's sake. She's missing, and we both want to find her and make sure she's safe. I loved her as much as you, Jannie, and I can't bear to think something has happened to her."

I bit back the acrid words that wanted to spring from my mouth.

"You loved her?" Why was he speaking in the past tense?

"I love her," he corrected himself, and tightened his lips in that little-boy way that told me he was going to pout—really soon.

"Okay, well, by my experience, Brian, it's usually the husband. Stranger abduction is rare."

"It happens," he countered. "Look at Elizabeth Smart."

"Come on, Brian, someone broke into my apartment yesterday, and returned last night and murdered my landlady. Melissa came to my apartment last week and dropped off a box, and asked me to keep it. I think that's what the killer was looking for. Do you really think it's a coincidence?"

His eyes widened with shock at the announcement that I had had something personal of Melissa's, something I believed could be the reason she had been taken. "What was in it? The box."

"I can't tell you that. The police told me not to." This wasn't entirely true, but I knew that Brian would stand by Mike's side, no matter what, and so I was unwilling to share this information if there was the slightest chance that my friend's own husband was responsible for her disappearance.

"Jannie, this is crazy. Someone is after you, maybe because you have something of Melissa's they want, and you still won't let me help you? You must really hate me if you would put yourself in jeopardy and not come to me, or at least to your mom and dad. Was I really that awful?"

Was he? I didn't know. What I did know was that my life had spiraled out of control after he pushed me too far, and forced me to submit to him sexually, when all of our teachings had told us that it was a sin. And then when he expected me to forget it, to just move on, I realized how far his delusions went. He would do it again. I wasn't going to be there when he did.

"I don't hate you, Brian," is what I said, not revealing my inner thoughts. "And I am perfectly safe, trust me."

"Where are you staying?"

I stayed mute, not willing to share with him where I was holed up. How dumb was that? He couldn't get through the security, and then find me, just to force me to become his eternal companion again. It didn't work like that. My fears were never rational regarding Brian. Even the bishop had said so. We had simply gone too far. Too far to go back.

"It doesn't matter. I'm safe. And I'm here to ask about Michael. Could he be behind this?"

He looked as though he were going to argue with me, then changed his mind. "No, Michael couldn't be behind

this. I think Melissa was up to something, and that something caught her. It happens a lot."

"Up to something? What?" I gasped.

"Michael thought she was having an affair. He had
caught her in some lies, and found some phone calls to
numbers he didn't recognize, and he confronted her. She
got really defensive, and said he had no right to pry, and
he lost it. Started screaming, and yelling, and then left the
house. He came to see me. When he got back, Melissa
was gone."

I was stunned. Melissa having an affair? It wasn't possible. I would never believe it. "Melissa would not cheat
on Mike. Besides, that is not what Mike told the police.
He said she went out to get milk yesterday morning."

"He was trying to protect her. In case she came back.
He was embarrassed, and didn't want anyone to know
that she was cheating on him. And people do all kinds of
things you don't think they are capable of, Jannie," Brian
said, a slightly sarcastic tone coloring his voice.

"They certainly do, Brian," I responded, and abruptly
stood. "I think I'll take a pass on lunch. My appetite is
gone. You have a great day, although I don't know how
you can, living with yourself."

Cold chills ran up and down my spine, and I felt the
nausea begin to build. I had this physical reaction to
Brian mostly under control, or thought I had for the past
few years, but apparently not completely. It didn't take
much to set it off. I despised my weakness but knew I had
to go, and had to go *now*. I left the restaurant before he
could stand or say another word. In the pit of my stomach, I felt despair along with the panic. I was not helping

Melissa this way. Why couldn't I be strong? When I got outside I broke into a run.

When a hand grabbed my shoulder from behind, and held on tight, I nearly screamed.

CHAPTER TWELVE

"You aren't very good at keeping your word," Colt Singer said, irony lacing his words.

"How did you find me?"

"I'm a cop. That's what I do."

"Supercop?"

"You didn't have a car. I never had yours delivered, purposely, so I could keep you in one place. So I used my reasoning skills and asked the front desk of the hotel. They told me that they called you a cab. From there, it wasn't hard at all to find the cab driver and he was more than willing to tell me where he dropped you off."

"He dropped me off at the shelter. That still doesn't explain how you found me here."

"Power of deduction. No one at the shelter knew where you had gone, including your boss, Millie. Nice lady, very closemouthed, even when a shield is flashed in her face. Now, if you were somewhere you should be, she would have just spilled it. It told me you were doing something that I might not approve of. Say, trying to track down clues in a case I told you to leave alone. Maybe even going to someone you despise in order to try and help Melissa."

"Still not following, Detective. How did you find me?"

"I don't know you very well, and yet I picture you as the type who will confront anything head-on just to prove you can, no matter the personal discomfort it causes you—anything except going into church buildings, of course."

"I'm waiting." I raised both my eyebrows and met his stern gaze, my arms crossed, one toe tapping in direct imitation of a stance I had seen my mother take time and time again. It always worked on me. It was worth a try.

"I figured you'd go directly to the source. But you didn't go to the hospital, where Mike is, so the next place to look was wherever Brian was. I called his office, pretended to need him for an emergency case, threw my police credentials around, and voilà, I knew where he was."

I just shook my head. "That's a secretary whose job is in jeopardy."

"Why?" he asked. "You going to tell him how I found you?"

I turned to walk away, and he grabbed my arm. My heart, which had stilled slightly since the original confrontation, began to race again, but it wasn't a panic attack this time. I couldn't identify exactly what I was feeling, although fear was definitely a part of it.

"So, why did you leave, when you told me you wouldn't?"

"I need to do this." I didn't really want to tell him I didn't trust any man, and would do whatever I had to do to stay safe. I just didn't know what it was about him that I feared the most.

"You're in danger."

"I carry a gun—registered, so don't freak—and I can take care of myself."

"This is a little bit bigger than anything you've dealt with before."

I knew he was right, but wasn't willing to back down and away. Melissa needed me.

"Why did you come to find me, anyway?"

"Let's go. Since you're so determined to ignore me and my warnings, you are going to have to stick close to me. And I think you might be able to help me." He grabbed my elbow and steered me toward his car, which was parked in a red zone in front of the restaurant.

"Where are we going?"

"To the hospital to see Michael."

On the fourth floor of the LDS Hospital lay the neuropsychiatry ward, a complicated and fancy term for what others called the "loony bin." Michael knew this ward well—he had worked here all through college, as he planned to go to medical school after graduation. He and Melissa were waiting to find out which medical schools had accepted him, and then they would be moving away, something that had given me slight twinges of regret in the past because Melissa and I had grown so far apart.

When we got to the ward, it was locked; and an orderly questioned us as to our intent. When Singer told him what we wanted, he shook his head firmly.

"He isn't talking to anyone right now, I'm sorry. The family has left strict instructions."

Singer shook his head, and I was perplexed.

"But doesn't he have to talk to you? I mean, you are the police."

"He hasn't been charged with anything, so, no, he doesn't have to talk to us. It's in his best interest to do so, but so far, his best interest seems the farthest thing from his mind."

The automatic door that led into the locked ward opened and out came Marlene Holt, Michael's mother. She gasped at first, then ran to me and enveloped me in her arms.

"Oh, Jannie, I'm so glad you're here. This whole thing is so terrible. So, so terrible." She pulled back, still holding both my arms, and perused me, tears streaming down her face. "Did you come to see Michael? He really needs his friends right now."

"She actually came with him," the orderly pointed out helpfully, and Singer gave him a look that could do almost as much damage as a nine-millimeter.

"Who is this? Is this someone special, Jannie?"

"This is my, uh, friend. Moroni. Moroni Singer."

"Oh, what a lovely name. Moroni, I wish I could have met you under better circumstances. Are you and Jannie close?" She leaned in even closer to me, and whispered, "Does Brian know?"

Singer's bullet-loaded gaze was now directed at me. I raised my eyebrows and tilted my head. After all, I'd done it for him. Just the name should set her at ease with a man she didn't yet know suspected her son was guilty of murder. Now she wouldn't be so suspicious of him.

"Moroni is just a friend, Sister Holt. Can I see Michael?"

"Well, maybe for a minute. They have him sedated, because he hasn't slept since Lissa disappeared. He's just so distraught, he collapsed." She glanced toward Colt Singer. "I think you better wait out here, though."

Singer didn't look surprised. "I'll be in there," he said

to me, pointing to a waiting room where a television was blaring *Days of Our Lives*.

I made my way through the automatic door after the orderly pushed a button opening it, and Marlene guided me to Michael's room, located down at the end of a long hall. I could hear shrieks and moans, and a chill ran up my spine as I considered where we were. Why was Mike in the pysch unit, anyway? If he was just being sedated and collapsed from exhaustion and stress, is this where they would put him? A lockdown ward?

"Oh, Jannie, we're just so worried about Melissa. This is terrible. Everything is such a mess." She stopped and shuddered for a moment, then set her shoulders and threw her head back, as though to give herself strength. After Marlene pushed through the door, I had my answer. Lying in the hospital bed, eyes closed, face ashen and wan, was Mike Holt, looking weaker than I had ever seen him. Both of his wrists were taped.

Big, strong, dependable Mike Holt had tried to kill himself.

CHAPTER THIRTEEN

Marlene saw where my eyes had traveled, and she shook her head lightly and put a finger to her lips, then grabbed my arm and pulled me from the room. Michael didn't stir.

"I should have warned you. This has to stay here, Jannie. It can't get out that Michael was so distraught about Melissa that he tried to end his life. It will be taken wrong, and you know that. He was just at the end of his rope, and so tired he didn't know what to do. He can't imagine going on without her, and yet she is nowhere to be found. And there are some other things that, well . . ." The tears started to fall again, and I had a feeling I knew what those other things were. Brian had hinted Melissa had been having an affair, and obviously Michael had shared that with his parents.

I still couldn't believe it. I also couldn't believe Michael would take his own life. Unless he believed Melissa was lost to him forever.

"The police don't know about this?" I knew they didn't but wanted to hear her answer.

"No, Earl found him and brought him straight here. It

wasn't a serious attempt. I think he just, well, cracked under the pressure."

I knew that all suicide attempts had to be reported to the state, but this was a process that took weeks, not days. With Michael not under arrest, the hospital wouldn't be required to report his attempt to the police, and I was sure they had accorded him some protection as a courtesy, as he was a member of their staff.

"Look, Jannie, maybe this wasn't a good idea." My questions were making Marlene uncomfortable, and I cursed myself for putting on my professional hat.

"No, I want to see him. We need to find Melissa, Marlene. And Mike needs to know I'm there for him."

"All right, but just for a minute." She followed me into the room, obviously unnerved enough by my questions to not allow me to see him alone.

"Mike, Jannie is here to see you," she called out softly, her voice a singsong lullaby tone, as though he were a baby again. Michael turned his head first one way and then the other, then slowly opened his eyes and stared at me without much focus.

"Hi, Mike, are you okay?" It was hard not to immediately start questioning him about Melissa. The more time that passed, and the more things happened, the more I began to believe that he had had something to do with her disappearance, although I would never have believed it possible had you asked me just a week before.

"Hi, Jannie. I'm not okay." His words were slow and slurred. "Mom, is there any word? Anything at all about Lissa? I need to get out of here and go find her." He began to turn from side to side and attempted to sit up.

"Shh, shh," she comforted him, scurrying to the side of

his bed to rub her hand over his forehead, pushing him back down. He didn't resist. "They are still searching. No sign of her at all. You need to rest."

Lack of sleep, superficial wounds from a botched (purposely?) suicide attempt, and exhaustion, and his mother was treating him as though he had been hit by a car. I was a little perplexed, but supposed maternal instinct would do that. Marlene was one of the most motherly people I had ever met. At times, it had almost seemed to be too much, as she constantly raced after her children with coats on slightly chilly days; forced chicken noodle soup down their throats after they got wet; and kept them home from school if they seemed even slightly sick. I had none of that maternal instinct for Mike, and I wanted to smack him and pull him from the bed. Lissa was missing and all he could do was create sympathy for himself? Why would he be here unless he knew that the search for Melissa was pretty much fruitless?

At that moment, I knew that Mike either knew what had happened to her or had been responsible for it.

It made me physically ill.

"Mike, what really happened here? Where is Melissa? I know you, and if you thought she was out there somewhere, hurting, or hurt, or needing help, you'd be searching every nook and cranny of this valley until you found her. Instead, you try to kill yourself? What the hell is going on with you?"

"Jannie," Marlene said with a gasp, moving quickly from the other side of the hospital bed to where I stood. She grabbed me by the arm. "Maybe you better leave."

A derisive snort from Mike stopped her from tugging at me, and we both turned to him.

"Oh, she might as well know, Mom. Your beloved Lissa, so honorable, was having an affair. I caught her. I don't know who he is, and she wouldn't say, but she's obviously run off with him. Everyone is looking for her, and she's off somewhere holed up like a two-bit whore who couldn't keep her legs shut."

Marlene's eyes about popped out of her head as Mike let loose with his diatribe, and I felt my blood begin to boil as he denigrated my missing friend.

"Michael Holt, I did not raise you to speak that way," Marlene said.

"Mike, how can you say those things?" Anger tinged my words, emotions I could no longer, and did not want to, control. "Lissa? Having an affair? She wouldn't! I know she would never do such a thing. Why would you say these things, Mike?"

"I don't want to talk anymore," he said, and turned away from us both.

"You better leave, Jannie," Marlene said, her tone firm but not unkind. "I think Michael's father needs to have a chat with him."

I knew I wasn't going to get anything more out of him, so I turned and walked away, hearing Mike heave a huge sigh as Marlene got on the phone and placed a call to Earl.

It occurred to me that Utah was an odd place. With our huge emphasis on family and the patriarch leading the home, even when we were adults we were still treated as children by our parents.

I was a perfect example of this. I'd spent the past five years worried that my mother and father would find out I hadn't been—and couldn't go—inside a Mormon church or place of worship since Melissa married Mike. And yet

I was a grown woman, holding a good job, paying my own rent, driving my own car.

And Michael's father had now been called to come deal with his son's behavior and language.

And Lissa was still missing.

As I walked through the automatic door, I nodded at the orderly. Singer leaped to his feet in the waiting room and looked awfully relieved to see me.

"Those soap operas are pretty stupid," he commented as he followed me down the hall. I wasn't going to say another word until we were outside, and he seemed to know it instinctively.

"So," he said, when we were in his car. "What did he have to say?"

I pursed my lips as I considered what I had found out. "He tried to kill himself, or so they say."

"You're kidding me. And of course, no one told us." His handsome face tightened in anger.

"I was ready to point a finger at him and say, you did it. You've hurt her, haven't you? And I can't believe that I was, but his behavior doesn't fit a worried husband. It doesn't fit what I know of *Michael*. But then he said she was having an affair and had obviously run off with someone. And Brian kind of said the same thing. That Mike caught her in some lies, and she was having an affair. Then he said that they had this huge fight, and Mike left and went to Brian's, and when he came back she was gone. The whole milk story was a lie. Brian said Mike was trying to cover for Melissa, in case they got back together."

"We pretty much knew his story was bogus. We've talked to the neighbor who heard the fight. There's been no sign of her since. He could have killed her, dumped her body, and then gone to his buddy's house in order to shore up an alibi."

I turned to him and said, "She was pregnant. At least I think she was pregnant, because of that test in the box. Obviously, she wasn't happy about it. I guess if the baby wasn't Mike's, that would explain it."

"Do you think that is possibly what happened?"

I considered all I knew of Melissa—and I knew her well—and then shook my head. "No. I don't. I just don't believe she would do that."

Singer's cell phone rang, and he flipped it open and answered tersely, starting up the car and pulling out of the hospital parking lot. When he hung up, he just shook his head, and my heart sank. It wasn't good news. I prayed that they hadn't found Melissa's body.

"They found a bloody mattress in a Dumpster about three blocks from Mike and Melissa's apartment."

CHAPTER FOURTEEN

Singer dropped me off at the YWCA Shelter, and he insisted on seeing me inside. I'd already told him that was where I would be staying until I found another apartment.

"Until the danger is over," he corrected. I agreed.

He let me know he didn't trust me. I couldn't blame him, but I truly did not want to die. I only wanted to find Melissa, and would do whatever was necessary in order to succeed. The discovery of a bloody mattress did not bode well for her, but I refused to give up.

Singer had promised to have my car delivered to the shelter. He extracted yet another promise from *me* that I would not go anywhere unless I told him first.

"You are not my mother," had been my retort.

"I most certainly am not," he'd agreed, but did not back down. I promised, and this time I meant it.

The search for Melissa had resumed early this morning, and nothing had turned up, at least from the volunteer corps. I knew the police were now searching the Dumpster where the mattress was found, and also had moved back into the apartment and were taking it apart, trying to find clues to Melissa's disappearance—this time with a different focus.

They would also be looking for signs of foul play—signs that Melissa had been hurt, or worse, murdered. I blanched at the thought. I wanted to know what was going on. I picked up my phone to call Colt Singer, and realized I had neglected to get his cell phone number, even though he had mine.

I tapped my fingers on the side of my leg as I considered whether or not I should try to track him down. After all, who did I think I was? *You're you, Jannie. You're a domestic violence counselor, and if this was one of your clients, you wouldn't even give it a second thought. This is your best friend. Why are you waiting now?*

I quickly dialed the main number for the Salt Lake City Police Department, ignoring the strange stirrings in my stomach. I was transferred to dispatch and informed that Detective Singer would be called and told I needed to speak with him.

"Is this an emergency?" the dispatcher asked.

"It's extremely important. Please have him call me."

I sat in my office and considered my options. There were plenty of volunteer searchers out combing the canyons and parks around Melissa's apartment, and I didn't think I would be much help there. Instead, I decided to start calling everyone we had gone to school with and all of Melissa's work acquaintances to see if any of them had ideas where she might be. I was sure the police had already done this, but as a friend of Lissa's, I might be able to pick up on something they said because I knew her so well.

My cell phone rang, and I picked it up, expecting to hear Colt Singer's deep, melodious—and always slightly sardonic—voice. Instead, I heard the familiar tones that belonged to Brian, and the always present, unwelcome chill went down my spine.

"Jannie, it's Bri." He hadn't shortened his name like that for a long time, and it set something off in me, an unfamiliar longing for the time when things were easy and simple and I knew what was expected of me and exactly how to do it. That time would never return.

"Brian, what is it?"

"Look, I just wanted to apologize . . . I mean, we should be working together to try to find Melissa, not still fighting over the past. Can't we at least be friends?"

"I don't think so."

He sighed heavily. "Jannie, I've said I was sorry. We just got too close, and I couldn't stop. It's the biggest mistake I ever made, and I'll never forgive myself for it. But are you going to continue to hate me forever? Please, just forgive me. Maybe if you forgive me, I can forgive myself, too, at least a little." The genuine pleading tone of his voice hit me deep inside, along with his plea for forgiveness. He had always seemed so nonchalant, so uncaring as to what I was feeling, but did he truly feel remorse that he had forced himself on me? And who was I to not forgive?

"Brian, I . . ." The beep on my phone told me I had another call, and I asked him to hold on for a minute. "Hello?"

"This is Colt. Are you in trouble?"

"Trouble does not follow me around, Detective."

"I know. You go looking for it," he said wryly. "So what's up?"

"I just wanted to find out what was going on. I know you are searching Mike and Melissa's apartment. Have you found anything?"

"Nothing substantial."

"Don't play games with me, Singer. This is a block I have been around, and around, and around. This is my friend. My *best* friend. Please tell me what is going on."

When he answered, I was not prepared.

"We found blood spatter."

The impact of his words hit me hard, and I felt tears gather in my eyes and begin to run down my face. *Please, God, don't let Melissa be dead. I'll come back to the church. I'll find some way to get inside, and sit through the meetings without screaming. I'll do anything, just please, God, don't let Lissa be dead.*

"Jannie?"

"Oh, God, I don't want her dead." My hard-guy demeanor was completely gone. "I want her alive and well, and if that means she ran off with someone and *is* having an affair, then I think that's wonderful. I know it sounds dumb, but that's how I feel." I hastily swiped at the tears.

"Jannie, I'm so sorry. I should think about what I say and how I say it." I heard regret in his voice. "I guess I've gotten used to talking to the detectives, and even you seem harder, because you've seen so much. But I forget how much she meant to you."

A sudden click on my cell phone reminded me that I'd had Brian on hold. Apparently, he had given up and disconnected.

"No, don't be sorry. It's reality, but I want her alive. I want to renew our friendship, and sit down and talk, and I want to know what was going on in her life. What changed her. She was so different when she stood there on my doorstep. So unhappy."

"I know. You can't totally give up, Jannie, but please be prepared. You know how these things usually end. Call me if you want. I have to go now. But I'm going to come and pick you up to get some dinner. Six o'clock. I'll be out front. Don't argue." He hung up before I could say a word. Interestingly enough, I had no intention of arguing. I was tired of my lonely existence. Colt Singer seemed to have found a way to get inside my protective bubble. I didn't know how far it would go, but I needed someone close, and I would take what I could get.

I spent the next four hours calling every high school friend I could think of. Many had moved away, and I got a lot of disconnected numbers, and spent more than a few precious minutes answering questions from people who had heard of Melissa's disappearance but hadn't seen her in years. I struck out.

I then proceeded to call her work, and asked to speak to Teresa Furneau, who I knew had been close to Melissa, sharing lunch and breaks every day.

"This is Teresa," came the older woman's slightly tinny voice.

"Teresa, this is Janica Fox. I'm a good friend of Melissa's, and I'm trying to find out if there's anything she might have said, or done, or something that indicated she might be going to . . . . Well . . ."

"Janice?"

"No, no, my name is Janica."

"I don't remember ever hearing her talk about a Janica. Is this a reporter?" Her tone was hard and brittle.

I'd never met Teresa personally, but based on her voice

I saw her as a tall, skinny peroxide blonde with too-short skirts and an overbright smile.

"No, Melissa was my best friend. I'm not a reporter. She called me Jannie."

"Jannie? I remember her talking about Jannie . . . But how do I know you aren't a reporter?"

"I work for the YWCA Women's Shelter in downtown SLC. I graduated from Skyline High School with Melissa. I went out with Brian Williams, who was best friends with Mike, Melissa's husband. Mike lived across the street from me. His mother used to make us cookies. Melissa had a birthmark on the back of her right knee that she really hated . . ."

The woman chuckled slightly and her tone loosened a bit. "Okay, okay, enough name, rank, and serial number. You wouldn't believe the number of calls we've gotten from reporters. Gary shut down the office, but I stayed here to field the calls, just in case someone called with a tip about Melissa, or . . . Oh, I know it's useless. No one is going to call here, but I didn't know what else to do." I could hear the despair in her voice. I also suspected this woman had shared a lot with Melissa, especially in the years that we had grown distant, and maybe knew something that I did not. Maybe even knew if Melissa could have had an affair.

"Can I come see you? Have you eaten? I could bring you something to eat."

"Not hungry, hon. But I could take a big old honking Diet Coke with lemon, since you seem determined to come over."

I told her I'd be there in ten minutes, and hung up the phone.

• • •

True to his promise, Colt had arranged to have my car waiting for me when I exited the building. Charlie had waggled the keys at me, and asked me how I managed to get such personal service from the Salt Lake City Police Department. I just smiled.

When I arrived at the insurance office, I found I'd been entirely wrong about Teresa Furneau. She was short and fairly plump and at least ten years older than I'd suspected. She also wore matronly clothes and I could tell she was wearing garments, the telltale lacy lines showing through her thin summer blouse. Even though I had gone through my endowments and had been given the sacred garments to wear, I only donned them when I suspected I might run into my mother, father, or someone who knew them. They were long and awkward and terribly ugly, and reminded me of things about which I did not wish to reminisce.

Thinking of the garments reminded me of my promise to God to go back to church should Melissa be found safe, and I grimaced a bit. But if Melissa walked through that door right now, I would do it.

"Here's your Diet Coke," I said, handing it to Teresa. She motioned to a room where there was a small round break table. The insurance office was in an old Sugar House neighborhood, and it was formerly a home, built around 1940, so the rooms were small and quarters tight.

"Well, I sure am upset about this," she said, after she heaved her large body into a chair. "I cried all night. My husband finally got up and went to sleep on the couch, but I couldn't help it. How could someone do this to Melissa?"

"Teresa, Lissa came to my house about a week ago, and she asked me to store a box for her. She didn't look happy. Now I found out that Mike said she was having an affair, and that he thinks she's just taken off. I hadn't talked to her about this stuff in a long, long time, but Lissa having an affair, well . . ."

Teresa's lips tightened, and she looked away from me, staring at anything but my face. Good God, could it have been true?

"Teresa?"

"Look, she wasn't having an affair. I'm sure she wouldn't do that. Mike's just trying to place the blame elsewhere. Anywhere but solidly on his shoulders, where it belongs."

"What do you mean?"

She finally met my gaze. "He was getting obsessive over her, not letting her go out and monitoring all her phone calls, and she was getting really upset over it. He wouldn't even let her go on a girls' night out with me! What kind of trouble would she get into with me? We were just going to go to the movies and to dinner. But he told her no. I think he was afraid she would find a life without him, because of all the shit he pulled on her, so he just kept tightening the rein."

"By 'shit he pulled,' what do you mean?"

"I probably shouldn't talk about it. She made me promise never to tell another soul."

"Teresa, it's pretty important. She's missing, and no one seems to have a clue where she is . . ." I decided to take a gamble. "With Mike's telling people she was having an affair, I'm afraid they might believe him, since she isn't here to defend herself."

"The creep. I bet he did this. I just bet he did it."

"Why do you think that? Was she ever afraid of him?"

Teresa considered the question, then wrinkled her nose. "No, I can't say she was. Disgusted with him, sometimes. Tired of his controlling behavior. He was running up credit cards, and then wouldn't tell her where he spent the money. He'd go out sometimes, and tell her he was going to study at the library, but leave without books. She just kept forgiving him, and I guess I can understand why. Nobody wants to admit they are being taken for a ride, especially by someone they love. Only the last day she came in to work, the day before she disappeared, she was really upset. Worse than I'd ever seen her. She made a phone call, and then she started crying. I asked her what was wrong, but she wouldn't say, just kept shaking her head. She was so upset she had to go home. I figured I'd call her that night, when she calmed down, and I tried, but there was no answer. The next day she was gone."

"Did you hear the phone call?"

"No, she went into Gary's office to use the phone because he was playing a round of golf with some clients and hadn't come in yet. I only heard her crying, and when she came out, I saw she was distraught."

"So you don't know who she was talking to?"

"No, but she did say one thing that bothered me. She said, 'He's not going to do this to me. Not ever again. It's the last time.'"

I prayed those words would not be prophetic.

CHAPTER FIFTEEN

As I was driving back, I scrolled through the received calls on my cell phone, and found Colt Singer's number. I called and got his voice mail, leaving a message. I drove on autopilot, ignoring my surroundings. Teresa Furneau assured me she had told the police all of this, and I realized that Singer had some information he was not sharing with me. Of course, I was not a member of the police department, but for some reason this bothered me.

My phone rang, and I answered expecting Singer. I had grown to expect hearing from him a lot in the past couple of days. Instead, it was my mother.

"Jannie, where on earth are you? Where have you been? I've been calling you at work all day, and they just keep saying you're busy, or you're out. I was awake all night worrying about you. You didn't even tell us where you were going, and we have no idea who that man was with you . . ."

"Mother, he's a Salt Lake City detective. You *did* know that."

"Well, why on earth were you with him? And why did

you insist on leaving? We're your family. Honestly, I just don't think I even *know* you anymore, Janica Emily Fox."

"I was with him because we came from the police department. In case you missed it, there was a terrible crime committed, and I seem to be in the middle of it. He drove me to your house, but I decided it would be better for me to stay somewhere else . . . to keep you safe." That last part was pure genius, off the top of my head. Perhaps my balancing act would last another day or two.

"Oh, Janica. I was just so worried. With Lissa missing, and, well, we heard some things from the Holts. They called your father up and needed counseling, because Mike—"

"I know, Mom. Mike tried to kill himself, and he's claiming Lissa was having an affair. I don't believe it."

There was no communication network like the Relief Society network. My father told my mother everything, and she dished out whatever she deemed necessary to other interested parties. I groaned inwardly, knowing that these allegations, and the fact that Mike had injured himself, could do considerable damage to the search for Lissa. If they believed Mike's version, interest in the search would wane, and she might never be found.

You're still refusing to believe that Melissa could have had an affair. But you didn't really know her anymore.

"Jannie, please come home. Your brother is coming in from Provo, and we're having a family dinner tonight."

My head began to pound—Mother had called for reinforcements. My brother, Jack, was a professor at BYU, a huge honor at the age of thirty. He was also my parents' pride, especially as he spent much of his time on the Internet as a Mormon apologist who defended the faith. I loved

Jack, but his one-track mind was wearying, especially when my train had derailed long before.

"Mom, I have a million things to do, and I really can't tonight. Tell Jack I'm sorry, but I'm right in the middle of this search for Melissa, and I—"

"Jannie," my mother said. I knew the tone. Warning and patronizing all in one. I was not going to like what she had to say. "It's probably a waste of time to look for Melissa. It looks like she ran off, honey. I feel really bad that such a thing would happen, but, well, look at the stock she comes from."

"Mom, sometimes I'm ashamed to say I even know you, let alone be related to you. How could you say such a thing about Melissa? You make me sick."

I hung up the phone and felt my stomach heave. One did not talk to the Mormon Maven that way. There would be hell to pay.

When the phone rang again, about half an hour later, I jumped. I'd been doing some paperwork that had piled up on my desk and which desperately needed attention. It also gave me some time to *not* dwell on Melissa and all the things I *wasn't* doing to find her.

"How could they do this?" sobbed a familiar voice from the other end. "It's not him, Jannie, it's not him. He wouldn't do this."

"Debbie?" It was my client.

"You have to tell them it's not my husband. He wouldn't do this. Brandon would not take some woman and kill her. Especially a stranger! Why do they think it's him? What could it possibly have to do with him? Did you tell them it was him?"

"Debbie, calm down. First of all, do you know where Brandon is? This can all be cleared up really quickly. He needs to turn himself in, and the police will question him."

The line went quiet. Debbie's sobbing stopped, and when she spoke again, her voice was deadly calm.

"The only person Brandon would ever kill is me."

Debbie swore she didn't know where Brandon was, but continued to proclaim his innocence. She didn't seem to realize she had just told the person sworn to protect her that she knew eventually Brandon would kill her. It went in direct violation of all her claims before, and I knew I shouldn't feel the shock that coursed through my body— not after years of doing this work—but I did.

It must be some kind of addiction, living life with a man you knew would eventually destroy you. Despite our religion's emphasis on staying married, I knew that wasn't the real problem, as other states had an equally big problem with domestic violence. It didn't help, though, especially with someone like Debbie.

She'd married Brandon for time and all eternity. That's something you had to take seriously. Just like Melissa did. The only real way out of a Mormon marriage, at least one that leaves you without recrimination and saving face, is death.

CHAPTER SIXTEEN

Promptly at six o'clock that evening, I walked to the front doors of the YWCA, arriving at almost exactly the same time Colt Singer did. I pushed through, and he raised his eyebrows.

"Weren't going to walk out without me, were you? No intention of making yourself a walking target?"

"No, Detective, I was waiting for you." Irony laced my voice.

"Good."

We walked to his car, and he opened the door for me, guided me in with a firm hand on my elbow, and then shut the door, as if it were a date. Was it a date? The quake in my stomach told me it better not be. Would I ever be normal?

"Normal?" he said as he slid into the driver's side and fastened his seat belt. Apparently, I had said the thought aloud.

"Uh, just wondering if life will ever be normal again."

"Probably never the same," he commented, and I was struck by how true this was. People never really did get back to normal, especially when something like this happened. We were all so good at pretending. I was the queen of pretense, never letting my mother and father know just how far I had fallen since the day I had lost my virginity to the man I was supposed to marry.

"No, never the same," I agreed. "Where are we going to eat?"

"My place."

"Uh, what? Where?" Alarm filled my voice, and irrationally, I wanted to fling the door open and flee.

"My place," he said, this time less nonchalantly, and he kept looking over at me, perhaps reading my mind as I searched frantically for an escape. "I made dinner, Jannie. I didn't plan a seduction scene. But if this is freaking you out, we can just go out."

Sick of my life, sick of being alone, sick of how I got here, I shook my head violently. "No, I want to go. I do. But . . . can you please just understand how hard this is for me?"

"I thought it was just churches."

"No, it's not. I can't be alone with a man, either. The few times I tried, it didn't go well." Somehow, talking was calming the huge panic storm that had begun to build in my stomach and chest. So I would keep talking. "The first date I went on was a double date, so that was okay, until he tried to kiss me good night. I screamed, he screamed back, jumped, and took off like a bat out of hell. Oddly enough, he didn't ask me out again."

Singer chuckled, and the warm sound further quelled the army of ants that seemed to have invaded my body.

"The next few times I tried, it went just as bad. One time I couldn't get in the car. Just stood there, frozen. He kept asking me why, and all I could do was shake my head. Finally, he drove off. After a few incidents like that, I gave up, and accepted I was damaged goods and would never be normal. I stopped trying."

"But you didn't stop trying to save other women."

"Yes, look at me. The protector of all the abused, who can save everyone but her own damn self." I was surprised to hear the anger in my voice. I was equally surprised to realize I was fairly calm.

"We don't have to do this," he said as he pulled into a driveway in the Avenues and stopped the car. "This is my house, but we do not have to do this."

"I think we do."

He shook his head. "Okay, but if you scream, I have a next-door neighbor who is extremely jumpy. You can fully expect the entire police department to show up."

I giggled at the thought. He got out of the car and walked around to my side. My stomach started to churn. He pulled open the door, and I stepped out, trying to pretend my heart was not racing and my eyes were not swimming.

His house was a nice, two-story brown brick dwelling built in typical Avenues style. It had obviously been re-stored, although the yard was a bit unkempt, and there were no flowers or bushes adorning the front of the house. I wanted to see inside, I told myself. I wanted to see more.

"Jannie," he said, eyeing me carefully, seeing the distress on my face.

"Can it, Singer. I am doing this." I took a small step forward, and was totally unprepared when I felt a rush of wind and then my body flew to the ground, someone on top of me. I screamed, fleeting thoughts of the nosy neighbor rushing through my head.

"Get up, you motherfucker."

Colt Singer's voice echoed through the screams, and suddenly I was not covered anymore. I slowly sat up and looked over to see Brandon Talon sprawled on the ground with a gun pointed at his head. It didn't stop him from hurling a string of invectives in my direction. Singer put the gun directly on his forehead, and he shut up.

While the detective expertly whipped out his cell phone with one hand and called for backup, I stared with a lack of understanding at Brandon.

Somehow I had misjudged this situation. If he wasn't responsible for Melissa's disappearance and Ida's death, why had he just—quite stupidly—tracked me down, apparently following me, and tried to kill me. Had he tried to kill me?

The sound of sirens filled the air, and I shook my head trying to clear it. Was this it? Was it over?

"Are you okay?" Singer called over to me.

"I am." I was. Surprisingly, I was filled with anger, and the panic and fear was quelled. Who the hell did Brandon Talon think he was? *I* knew *what* he was—a spineless coward. Stupid, too, not realizing he was following a cop.

Four police cars pulled up, and Detective Singer handed Brandon over to a uniform who would transport him to the Salt Lake City jail; he walked over to me and put his hand on my shoulder.

"How are you, really?"

"I'm okay. No, I'm mad. He's such a spineless creep, such a lowlife scum, tormenting his wife and children, and then moving on to me . . . I want to get his balls in a vise and squeeze."

"Ouch."

"Yeah, well, he deserves more than ouch."

"Yeah, he does. Especially since I spent three hours cooking homemade lasagna and now it's going to get cold."

"Homemade lasagna?"

"Yup. But I have to go down to the station and interrogate Talon. You, however, do not. So, I want you to stay here. I'll introduce you to Beavis. He'll keep you safe. Anyone comes close, he'll lick 'em to death."

"Beavis being your dog?"

"Yes, and you will have time to get used to my house without me in it. I'm leaving a patrol car out front."

"Detective—"

"Colt."

"Colt, you don't have to do this. Just have someone take me back to the shelter . . ."

"Not a chance. I intend to show you that not all men are abusive creeps."

"Why?"

He gave me a funny look and then took my hand. "Jannie, you're a smart girl. You figure it out."

He led me into his house and introduced me to Beavis, a tail-wagging seventy-pound yellow Lab with a propensity for crotch-sniffing, as I quickly discovered.

"That is rather annoying," I said as I pushed him away for the millionth time.

"He's a guy. Can't help himself," Singer said. "Beavis, down." He pointed a finger in the direction of what I assumed was the kitchen, based on the smells issuing from it, and the dog slunk away, throwing furtive sad glances over his shoulder as he walked off to crotch-sniffingless exile.

"He'll be up again as soon as I walk out, so if he's bugging you, put him in the backyard. I'll be back in a couple of hours. Television's in there," he said, pointing to a small living room off the main entryway. "Sorry, I don't have any chick flicks."

"So am I to assume that I am free to wander around your house and explore at my leisure?" I asked, the realization that I was standing inside a man's home, alone with him save for a horny dog, hitting me with a clarity that was both paralyzing and freeing. I had done it without screaming. And he was leaving, which upped the odds I wouldn't scream in the next hour or so.

"If you want. You might scare yourself. I am *not* a good Mormon boy."

"With a name like Moroni?"

"I didn't say my mother wasn't a good Mormon mother. We just don't always embrace what our parents embrace, much to their chagrin."

Yes, chagrin. My mother felt that on a regular basis. Moroni Colt Singer leaned forward, pecked my forehead with a quick kiss, told me to dish up some lasagna—which was being kept warm in the oven—and help myself to anything in the fridge. Then he was gone.

I felt a strange warmth and comfort flood through me, immediately followed by this thought: If Melissa had not disappeared, none of this would ever have happened. God works in mysterious ways.

CHAPTER SEVENTEEN

Melissa needed me. She reached out for me from behind the church pulpit, where she stood with my mother behind her. Mom had her hand on Melissa's shoulder, so she couldn't move, couldn't leave the pulpit, but still she reached out to me.

"Tell them," Mother urged. "Tell them all the truth. It's the only way."

"No, I can't," Melissa protested. "Jannie, help me. She thinks I did it. She thinks I'm nothing more than trash."

The sound of a door opening interrupted Melissa's impassioned plea for help, and I sat upright in a panic as she faded away, unfamiliarity in my surroundings flooding me with a well-known fear. The events of the evening came back to me, and I took a deep breath, willing the panic away. It miraculously quelled, and I wondered just what it was about Colt Singer that could bring this about. A flash of anger speared through me. A man should not be able to "fix" me. I should be able to fix myself.

I'd fallen asleep on his couch, waiting for him to show up, Beavis curled up below me at the base of the sofa. The dog was not as dumb as I had first thought, quickly realizing that if he continued to sniff my crotch he would stay in exile.

The dream of Melissa was still fresh, and with a horrible ache I realized how much I missed her. I wanted her to come back. Tears poured down my face, a river of sorrow I couldn't control, even though I desperately wanted to.

Colt Singer, his face weary, his eyes tired, came over to me swiftly from the place where he was standing, next to the front door, and pulled me into his arms, holding me, comforting me. He didn't ask why I was crying, just let me weep until I could cry no more. If anyone should be missing, life in peril, it was me. I had strayed from my teachings, letting paranoia and panic keep me from attending church. I was not faithful. Melissa had gone to church every Sunday. Why was this happening?

When I calmed down, I asked him what had happened with Brandon Talon, without offering an explanation for my tears. Again he did not question me.

"He's proclaiming innocence. Says he just wanted to talk to you, to convince Debbie not to leave him and give him another chance. However, he cannot account for his whereabouts the night that Ida was killed, or the night Melissa disappeared. Jannie, I have a huge favor to ask of you. Can you just stay here? I'll give you my bed, and I can sleep on the couch. We need to talk to Debbie in the morning and try to find out just how deep his hatred for you went, and I have a feeling she'll open up if you're there. I need your help trying to get information from her. It would just be easier. I won't try anything. And I'm beat."

I knew he was telling the truth.

"I'm comfortable here," I said, motioning to the couch.

He gave me a questioning look, and I nodded. I could do this. It was a big step.

"Okay, good night, Jannie."

"Good night, Detective Singer."

He had turned to leave but did an about-face and stared at me.

"Good night, Colt," I said.

"Good night."

Despite—or perhaps because of—this being a milestone, I was uneasy and couldn't sleep. I turned from side to side, trying to get comfortable. My brain was on overdrive, though, and I alternated thinking about Melissa with thinking of the man asleep not far from me—and again, wondering what, if anything, he was wearing.

Jannie, you are in so much trouble.

How would I react if I were in his room, lying next to him in the bed? How would I react if he reached out to me, touched me, held me, kissed me . . . ? Warmth flooded my body and I forced myself to think about Melissa.

How long had things been bad between her and Mike? Had this all started years before, and I had somehow just missed it? Ever since she'd disappeared, I'd spent a lot of time reliving the past, when before I refused to even let myself go there. But now, I was looking for clues, hints, something that would help me to understand this situation.

Mike and Melissa never really fought. Not much, anyway. Once in a while I would sense something in Melissa, but she never said much. I remembered the time we went to the drive-in theater shortly after they married. It was one of the last—although not the very last—time I allowed myself to be forced into pretending Brian and I could repair what had been shattered the year before.

"This movie is supposed to be great," Brian said happily, his arm casually strung along the backseat behind me. He apparently didn't notice the tension in my body, my heavy breathing, my hugging of the door next to me.

"I heard it's stupid," Melissa said, her voice taut and cranky. She had been pretty quiet the entire time, not saying much beyond hello after they picked me up.

Now we sat parked in the big lot of the theater, facing the huge screen, and the only real conversation was between the two men with Melissa and me. They kept attempting to draw us into it, but Melissa was in the zone where she didn't respond, and I was trying not to have a panic attack.

Light was fast fading, and soon the movie would be on, and I hoped Melissa was wrong and that it wasn't stupid, because this night was already dragging on too long, and I had way too much time to think about things—like how I wanted to scream every time Brian inched closer.

"Let's go get some popcorn or nachos, and some drinks," Mike said, putting a hand to Melissa's arm, and she pulled away abruptly, giving him a look of disgust. He pulled back and shook his head.

"I'll go with you," I volunteered, my intentions double-edged. I wanted to know what was wrong with Melissa, and I also wanted to get the hell away from Brian.

Mike glanced over at Melissa and she just shrugged her shoulders and looked out her window. He sighed heavily and opened his door, and I opened mine, glancing back at Brian, who had a scowl on his face, as though he had correctly interpreted my desire to escape from him, however possible.

"What's wrong with Lissa?" I asked Mike as we headed to the food shack.

"She's mad at me."

"Duh. But why?"

"Nothing. Just dumb stuff. She'll get over it." He didn't speak the rest of the time we stood in line, or while we ordered two big tubs of popcorn and Sprites for everyone.

By the time we got back to the car, I was about to crawl out of my skin, knowing the atmosphere in the vehicle would probably be worse.

I was wrong. Melissa was in the backseat with Brian, and he was holding her tightly. She cried profusely, her head down on his shoulder, and I could see anger fill Mike as he stared at them through the window. He finally yanked open the driver's side door and threw the food inside onto Melissa's seat, and then stomped off. I pulled my door open and stared inside.

Melissa gave a few gasps and then pulled away from Brian, wiping her eyes with the back of her hand. "It'll be okay," he told her softly, and then he moved to open his door and get out. "I'll go find Mike."

Melissa scooted out my door and walked to the front of the car, resting her butt against the side as she stared out at nothing. "Lissa, what's going on with you guys? Is it bad? You guys never fight like this."

She was silent for a moment, then finally spoke. "It's

just hard being married, Jannie. A lot harder than I thought it was going to be."

"So it's nothing serious?"

"No, nothing serious."

Maybe it hadn't been serious back then, but it had been a harbinger of things to come, and I had missed it, accepting Melissa's denials and not digging deeper. I faded off into sleep in the early-morning hours, still worrying about Melissa and what I had failed to see, and awoke to sounds from the kitchen.

I had slept in my jeans and T-shirt, despite Colt's offer of a shirt to sleep in—milestones sometimes come in small steps. When I entered the kitchen, Beavis following closely behind, Colt was padding around in pajama pants and nothing else. I felt my breath catch as I stared at his broad, bare chest, sprinkled with just the right amount of chest hair.

He saw where my eyes were focused and apologized, hurrying off to his room to put more clothes on, but I grabbed his arm and pulled him back.

"No, that was not panic you just saw."

"It wasn't?" he asked, his voice a deep-morning sultry scratch. And he moved a little closer into me.

"No, it wasn't," I said, but I backed up just a bit. Really small steps.

His cell phone rang, and he picked it up off the counter and answered it. The look on his face told me something bad had happened yet again.

"Mike Holt checked himself out of the hospital last night. Apparently, he is no longer a danger to society or to himself. Dammit, I should have known this would happen."

"So you don't think Brandon is responsible for Melissa and Ida?"

"Maybe Ida, but not Melissa. I'm sorry, Jannie, but I think your friend Mike did it. I think he killed her in a fit of anger and then hid the body."

Mike a murderer. It didn't seem possible. My mind flashed back to a time, when we were both six years old, and we found a bird that had flown into the large picture window my mother was so proud of. The bird was stunned, unmoving, and Mike had scooped the tiny creature up in his hands and carefully held it close to his chest.

"We should pray," he whispered.

I followed suit, fervently praying to our Father in Heaven to save the little bird who had not seen the danger in front of him, because it looked like the air all around him.

The bird died in Mike's hands, but not because of them.

How could Mike do something like this to the woman he had promised to love eternally? Colt's words—*"I'm sorry, Jannie, but I think your friend Mike did it. I think he killed her in a fit of anger and then hid the body"*—echoed some of my own deepest fears, but they still shocked me, hanging there in the air, finally said aloud.

"Why? Do you have evidence?"

"Well, we don't have the DNA evidence, obviously, or we would have arrested him. But with the mattress, well . . . Of course, now he's disappeared."

"Disappeared? I thought he just checked himself out."

"Yeah, but no one knows where he is."

The great lump in my stomach told me I was afraid of Mike—and this led my thoughts back to Melissa. Had she been afraid, too?

Had she been terrified?

CHAPTER EIGHTEEN

POLICE LOOKING FOR "PERSON OF INTEREST" IN DISAPPEARANCE OF MELISSA HOLT AND MURDER OF ELDERLY SUGAR HOUSE WOMAN, read the headline of the *Salt Lake Tribune* that Colt had tossed into my lap as we drove to the home of Debbie Talon's mother, where she was currently staying.

I sipped at the cup of coffee in the travel mug, also provided by Colt, and read the paper, learning that the newspaper knew the person of interest was Brandon Talon. The numerous threats he had directed at me were mentioned, along with my name and job—and the fact that Melissa had been my best friend.

"Please tell me you didn't give them this information," I said, almost mumbling, praying my mother was too busy this morning to answer her phone. While my parents subscribed only to the *Deseret News,* the church-owned paper, I was sure that they had the same information. The *Tribune* article cited an anonymous source.

"I didn't give them this information."

"My mother is going to go ballistic, imprison me in my

old room, make me quit my job, and arrange a marriage for me."

"You've got to be kidding."

"I only wish I was. Good girls do not have dangerous jobs. She should have grandchildren from me by now."

"Don't you have other siblings?"

"Yes, my brother, Jack. I have a niece and nephew, and Jack's wife, Karin, is expecting another one in September, but that does not get me off the hook. This will cement it."

He pulled up in front of the house where Debbie and her children were squirreled away, although not very safely, since Brandon wasn't exactly clueless about the location of the home. I opened my own door and stepped out, not waiting for Colt Singer, who didn't appear to notice. He walked up the front pathway with long strides, and I followed, knowing the state we'd find Debbie in. I'd been dealing with her for the past three years. Without Brandon, she could barely function. With him, she was in constant physical danger. It was lose/lose.

Colt rapped on the door sharply, and we waited, the neighborhood unusually silent for a warm summer morning. Other than the swooooosh-swooooosh of someone's automatic sprinklers, not even a bird call broke the ominous calm. I felt a trickle of moisture in my eye and reached up to wipe it away at almost the same time I noticed my heart was beating way too fast. Sweat beads on my forehead were the cause of the moisture, and my stomach began to churn. A panic attack, now?

Colt knocked again, and then looked over at me, his brow furrowing, his eyes closing slightly as he looked me over. "Are you okay? You are as white as a sheet."

The world began to seesaw, and I stepped back slightly then fell onto the grass with a hard thump, my butt hitting a sprinkler head. Sharp pain rolled through my body, but the world was still horribly akilter, and I didn't dare move for fear it would upend and I would never be able to straighten it.

"Jannie, what's wrong?" Colt asked, stepping toward me. "Should I call an ambulance?"

"No," I managed to get out from between clenched teeth. "Just give me a minute."

I breathed as deeply as I could muster, in and out, chanting *breathe, breathe, breathe* in my head, the way my therapist had taught me. Slowly, the spinning stopped and I felt a little steadier. After a moment, I shakily got to my feet, with help from Colt's big, warm hand, and I dusted off my behind, wincing as I felt the spot where I knew a nasty bruise would form.

No one had answered the door, and Colt alternated his concern between the house and me.

"I'm okay," I reassured him. "Not sure what brought that on. Usually, they only happen near churches or in situations where I might find myself in danger."

"Physical or emotional?" he asked softly.

I was quiet as I considered his question. "Both."

He shook his head and turned back to the door, this time ringing the bell several times and then knocking.

"This isn't right," he murmured. "Debbie's mother said they would be here." He went away from the door and toward the long skinny driveway at the side of the house. At the end of the paved drive there was a small garage, and he headed for it, me close behind.

He peered through the glass panes on the old garage door and said, "The car's in there. Something's wrong."

I glanced toward the side of the house, and the panic returned as I saw the red, bloody handprint imprinted on the bottom right panel of the four-paned glass window.

CHAPTER NINETEEN

Debbie Talon had lived her life as though it were predestined, much as we had been taught it was our entire lives. While I believed we could change the pathway we walked, I understood her. God and the church had sanctioned her marriage to Brandon. How did one walk away?

She never would.

Both Debbie and her mother had been brutally murdered, her two young children missing. Brandon had apparently come looking for me after he did away with his wife and mother-in-law. Perhaps he had tried to talk Debbie into dropping the restraining order and returning, and she had refused. I knew how he would plead and beg and promise to change. I'd heard the stories from her over and over again.

Debbie was not the first person to die at her husband's hand, and she wouldn't be the last, but she had been in my charge, and so I wept at the brutality. I sat on the front steps of the house and sobbed while policemen and medical personnel traipsed in and out of the house. Colt came out once to try to convince me to allow an officer to take me to his home, but I would not leave. I was still standing guard, even though I had failed miserably.

Somehow, I had known. The panic attack that came on before the discovery of the bloody handprint was a precursor for what would become one of the most brutal murders in the history of Sugar House. The handprint had apparently belonged to Debbie's mother, who was trying to flee through the kitchen toward the back door. She did not make it.

When my tears were spent, I got up and went to Colt's car, opening the door and retrieving my purse, which I had left in there when we arrived. I pulled out my cell phone and called Millie to let her know what had happened.

Colt came out of the house, his face grim and haggard, and stood beside me as I finished up with Millie.

"ME puts the death at sometime last night. Won't know the exact time frame, but I'm sure it won't exonerate Talon."

"I want to see her," I said, almost before I realized the words had left my mouth.

"No, you will not see her. It's time to let go and stop living other people's lives and start living your own!" His words were harsh, his tone strident, and I pulled away from him as he reached out to grab my arm.

I couldn't live my own life, for I had no life to live. God have mercy on me, how had I become this empty shell of a woman?

Against his better judgment, Colt dropped me off at the YWCA Shelter shortly before ten A.M. The sun was bright and harsh, and I squinted against it, angry today was so sunny, so beautiful. Three people were dead, apparently because Brandon Talon could not accept that his wife might finally be leaving him.

Except it made no sense. Debbie and her mother fit the pattern, of course, and Ida could be explained away, but what did Melissa have to do with it? And where were Debbie and Brandon's children?

All of these thoughts filled my head as I entered my workplace, nodding at Raymond, the day security guard who worked Fridays when Charlie was off taking his wife to the temple.

"Gotta note for ya," he said, the most I ever remember hearing him say at one time. He reached out with a big paw and handed me a crumpled piece of lined paper that had my name on the front, printed in a bold slashing hand in dark blue ink.

"Where did this come from?"

"Taped to the door when I got here."

Trepidation filled my chest as I considered the note. Who would do this—unless it was a message from Brandon Talon, perhaps a death threat, before he lost total control and decimated everything within firing range?

I slowly unfolded it, smoothing out the crumples, and read the printed words. "You wanted 'em, you got 'em. They won't be much good this way, but if I can't have them, no one will." It was signed with the initials *B.T.* Underneath the signature was a crude drawing of a Dumpster, complete with flies buzzing around and, most disconcerting of all, a small stick-figure arm sticking out of the top of the large container.

My heart nearly stopped in my chest as I pulled my phone from my purse and dialed 911. I couldn't remember Colt's cell phone number, and there was no time to spare. Breathlessly I relayed my information to the dispatcher.

Colt hadn't gotten very far, and he pulled into the YWCA parking lot with a screech. I could hear other sirens fill the air—a noise that was becoming all too familiar, especially in the past few days—and he was out of his car and striding toward me when I heard a loud explosion. Colt's body covered mine, and he knocked me to the ground as police cars pulled in and officers emerged, cautiously looking around.

"The Dumpster out back," I gasped, trying to breathe under Colt's weight.

He jumped up and pulled me to my feet, then ordered me inside the building as he headed to the corner, putting his back against the wall like I'd seen policemen do in suspense movies, drawing his gun from its holster and inching forward. I took a step toward him, and as if he knew I was going to do it, he turned and glared at me. I stopped.

Several other officers joined him on the wall, and he nodded and gave them a silent count of "one-two-three," indicated with his fingers, and they moved around the corner. I couldn't stay where I was. My ears were still ringing slightly from the sound of the explosion, and I couldn't imagine what horrible game Brandon Talon had been playing. Surely his children would not have been inside a Dumpster, and surely he would not have blown it up.

I couldn't stand it anymore and I hurried forward, rounding the corner and stopping at the sight of all the policemen gathered around a small, crumpled body.

"God, no. God, no, this cannot be happening. It cannot be happening."

A police officer heard me and turned toward me, gun

out, and I stepped back with my hands up, but I could only meet his eyes for a moment, so drawn was I to the small body on the ground.

Colt looked up and saw me, then said something to the officer next to him and rose, quickly making his way to my side.

"I told you to stay put."

"Please tell me that's not a child. Please tell me that's not Debbie's child."

"It's not a child, Jannie, it's a doll. Brandon Talon is having a lot of fun with us."

A doll. A child-sized doll.

That was the last thing I remembered.

CHAPTER TWENTY

I spent an hour on the cot in the small room that had become my new home, being nursed by my boss, Millicent Stone. I had a pretty good bump on the back of my head, garnered when I passed out before Colt Singer could catch me, and a headache to match the horror I felt.

Three people were dead, three people were missing, one man who was most likely guilty was locked up and refusing to speak to anyone without an attorney, and another man, whom I now believed was far from innocent, was nowhere to be found.

Nothing about the past few days had been easy, or real, and it continued to get worse and more complicated. I feared terribly for Debbie and Brandon's children. Even if they were found alive, they no longer had a mother or grandmother to care for them, and their father would likely spend the rest of his life in jail.

I could tell Millicent's fear was for me—I had become a walking magnet for disaster. Colt Singer had given her strict instructions not to let me out of her sight, and then with a brief squeeze of my hand, he had left to join a briefing and task force down at the Salt Lake City Police Department. The news media had gathered outside our building in full force, which had Millicent all aflutter. None of the other mothers or children could come or go, for fear that pictures would be taken and the men who many were hiding from would try to do the same thing Brandon Talon had apparently done.

"Millie, this is crazy. Just crazy."

"I know, love," she uttered soothingly. She rose from the side of my bed where she had sat, gently stroking my aching forehead. "I'm going to go make sure everything's okay. You stay here. Do not move from this bed. If you move, you're fired."

"Millie," I said weakly.

"Don't move."

"I won't."

About half an hour later my cell phone rang, and I sat up, moaning at the pain in my head. My purse was on the utilitarian white nightstand next to the bed, and I fished the phone out and answered.

"Hello."

"Jannie, it's me, Mike."

I was stunned to hear his voice.

"Mike, where are you?" I asked carefully. I didn't want him to hang up before I could get some information I knew would be vital to finding him. Despite all that had transpired, there simply was nothing connecting Brandon Talon to Melissa Holt. The only possible way he could have known about my relationship with her was by following—

and stalking me—and seeing her when she showed up at my house, but that seemed to be such a long shot.

I believed, despite all that had happened, that these were two very separate and distinct cases.

"I'm not saying. I have to find some things out, and I have to fix some things, before I can come back. But I heard that they think this creep Talon is responsible for Melissa's disappearance, and that it's linked to you. Good God, Jannie, if you did this to us—"

"Me? It has nothing to do with me. Brandon Talon could not possibly have known Melissa, or that she was my friend. I've hardly seen her, except for . . ." I stopped, realizing he had tripped me up, and I'd almost revealed something I didn't want him to know, if he didn't already know it.

"I talked to her on the phone every few months. We touched base, and tried to meet, but it was hard. Our schedules were different."

"She said you never called her anymore."

No, Mike, I thought. *It was she who didn't call me. Something was wrong, and she couldn't tell me, and I was too dumb to realize her distance was a cry for help.*

"We did touch base. Just not as much. But this has nothing to do with me."

"Well, I think it does. I think you're responsible, and by God, you're going to have to live with it for the rest of your life."

"Mike, I don't care what you think. You need to turn yourself into the police. They just want to question you. If you aren't involved, you'll be released."

"You're telling them it was me, aren't you?" His tone

became vicious and angry, and I cringed at the ugliness laced through his words.

"I don't know who did it, Mike. But up until this happened, you would have been the last person I ever suspected."

"And now?" His tone had softened some, and I made a decision then and there to do whatever I had to do to get him in police custody, at least until he was cleared—if he was cleared.

"I told the police you could never do such a thing, and they were wrong." I was a terrible liar, but I put every deceptive bone in my body to work. After all, I had been prevaricating in subtle ways, especially to my mother, for years. I wasn't exactly lying. I had a hard time believing Mike Holt, the man who serenaded Melissa while she laughed at him, could ever do such a thing. "You need to come to the police station and tell them you're innocent. As long as you are out there hiding, it looks like you're guilty."

There was silence on the other end, and when he spoke at last, his voice was low and tremulous but cold, so cold it sent chills up and down my spine. "You almost had me there, Jannie. Almost. But you don't trust any man, never have, not since Brian. You think I did it and wouldn't hesitate to tell anyone that. Bitch."

And the line disconnected.

Stunned, I pondered what had just happened, rubbing the back of my head gently, wincing when I felt the bump. The headache had eased some, thanks to Motrin and a cold compress provided by Millie, but this revelation about Mike—this other side of him—floored me. He hadn't been rational. He had been paranoid.

Was this what Melissa saw daily? And yet, he was confused. His wife had disappeared. He claimed she'd been having an affair. He'd tried to kill himself and was hospitalized. Could anyone be rational under those circumstances?

The fact he knew about Brian and me did not surprise me. Melissa knew, and she was married to him, and Brian and he were still tight. Of course someone had told him. But what I did find unsettling was that he had information about me that I considered precious, and sacred, and if he was just over the edge enough, he might try to use it against me in some way.

So which was it? Had Mike always been unbalanced, and I had never seen it, my closemouthed friend never daring to tell me what a huge mistake and misjudgment she'd made? Or had the entire incident simply set him off on a downward spiral?

The ringing phone gave me my answer.

"Jannie, it's Colt. Your friend Mike Holt was never headed to medical school. In fact, he never even graduated college. It was all a hoax. He failed all his freshman classes, and God knows what he's been doing every day since then."

CHAPTER TWENTY-ONE

I called Brian's office line without even thinking twice, twisted by two motivations. One, he needed to know this about Mike, and two, maybe he could tell me what the hell was going on.

Who was this man I had grown up with, the one who had married my best friend, the football star, the one that I sometimes—privately and jealously—wished loved me instead of my friend Melissa. He'd always seemed so strong, so sure.

But . . . no medical school? Not even graduating from college? If Melissa had known this combined with the credit card debt, Melissa who was always determined to stick everything out—well, I knew she might finally walk. This was too much to grasp. A huge swarm of lies, like angry wasps, all aiming for one target.

"Law office," chirped the young-voiced receptionist. I cursed. I'd rung Brian's direct line, so he was either in a conference or away, perhaps in court.

"Yes, this is Janica Fox. It's extremely important that

I reach Brian Williams. Can you tell me where I can find him?"

"Mr. Williams is in a meeting and can't be disturbed. I can make sure he gets your message as soon as he is finished," she offered politely. It would have to do.

The next phone call I placed was to my mother. My mother knew everything about everyone in our entire stake. My mother had to have known something was up with Mike and Lissa, and she'd never said a word. Now she was going to talk.

CHAPTER TWENTY-TWO

"Hello, Mom. You look lovely as usual." I joined her in a window booth at the Garden Room, high atop the Joseph Smith Memorial Building in downtown Salt Lake City. It overlooked the entire Temple Square and all of the city west of Main Street. It was beautiful and idyllic, and below I could see the many visitors to the square as they wandered in and out of the huge, black iron gates.

I could also see at least four brides posed in various places throughout the gardens of the actual temple grounds, having wedding pictures taken on the lush lawns where no one could walk but our church's most worthy members. They were sharing their wedding day, as all Mormon brides did, with many, many other brides.

I supposed this was not strange. There were only so many days in a year. But at the LDS Temple it almost seemed like an assembly line. You were given a time, your ceremony proceeded, and then behind you was yet another bride, waiting for yet another wedding, and getting ready to start yet another good Mormon life as a wife and mother and helpmate . . .

"Jannie, where are you? I've asked you the same question at least twice."

"Sorry, Mother," I answered, turning my attention back to her. It was close to 1 P.M., and I felt tired and raw, but my mother was her usual immaculate self. She had on a beautiful, light blue summer suit, with a strand of pearls draped around her neck, and her hair was immaculately coiffed. She wore tastefully light makeup, and I knew her shoes, although I could not see them under the table, would be the latest style from Nordstrom. My father did well in his business, and my mother had a reputation to uphold.

She looked me over, and I knew I did not fare as well in her perusal.

"Jannie, do you ever wear anything but jeans? How do you expect to get a husband dressed like that? And you really should wear some makeup. You look terrible. Are you sick?"

She leaned forward; her mother's instinct was to reach out and touch my forehead, to see if the fact I wasn't performing up to her standards was the result of a fever or some horrible plague.

I moved away so her fingertips only grazed my forehead.

"I'm fine, Mother. Just a lot going on right now, and I'm trying to find Melissa."

My mother's lips pursed, and her mouth made a little moue of disgust. "Isn't that the job of the police, Janica?"

Oh-oh. I'd gone from Jannie to Janica. Any moment now first-middle-last name status would start, and I'd feel like a five-year-old again, forever trying to please the demanding woman for whom I never quite measured up.

"Mom, what do you know about Melissa and Mike? You hinted you knew something was wrong, or that Melissa had done something, and I want to know what it was."

Best not to let her get started on me. That could take all day.

"Oh, Jannie, I know you're upset about Melissa. We all are. But, well, she wasn't living her life right, and if you aren't living right, and you listen to the whisperings of Satan, well, bad things happen."

"Enough of your vague insinuations, Mother. Just what was Satan whispering to Lissa?"

"Oh, the same old things he always says," she said vaguely. "Should we order?"

"Mother . . ."

"Oh, Jannie, I don't even want to think about it. It's what happens when you aren't on the up-and-up with Heavenly Father, and I've always loved Melissa like she was my own daughter, so it pains me"—at this point she put her right hand over her left breast, as though she were going to re-cite the Pledge of Allegiance—"to admit that she could do something like this."

"Like this *what*? What is it she is supposed to have done?"

My mother sighed deeply, but I was not deterred. Usually, Evelyn was doing the grilling. Today, it was my turn. I waited.

She sighed again then tightened her lips, a long-suffering look gracing her elegant face. I still didn't budge. Finally, she spoke.

"After Melissa disappeared, Mike went to his parents and told them he believed Melissa had been having an af-fair, and that she had run off with whoever she was involved with. They had a big fight, and he threatened to tell the bishop, and she screamed at him that she didn't care, that he wasn't enough for her. Mike left, and when he came back, after he cooled off, determined to try and make things work, Melissa was gone."

"So why didn't he just tell the police that in the first place?"

"Jannie, surely you can understand that. He was embarrassed. His wife, having an affair? It's mortifying. So he didn't tell the police everything, and it just escalated, and before he knew it, everyone was looking at him, and saying things like 'murder investigation,' and he just cracked."

"Mom, you don't have the whole story."

"I'm sure I don't, Jannie. I rarely do," she said dryly, with an implication that made my heart pound. But this wasn't about me and my constant dodging of the truth, at least as far as it related to her.

"Mike never graduated from college. He never even passed his freshman classes. He wasn't going to medical school. Lissa was killing herself trying to keep them both afloat, giving him money for books and school and God knows what else, and he was just out doing something else with it. What, I don't know. He was also running up credit cards and had them thousands of dollars in debt."

Finally, I had stunned my mother into silence. I could see this was something she never expected.

"Never graduated," she finally managed to say, then reached out and picked up her glass of ice water from the table, sipping it gingerly, her face ashen.

"Mom, surely you didn't believe so firmly that Melissa was bad that you never even considered whether or not Mike had a hand in this?"

But I saw from her face that it was true. Why did Mormon mothers love their sons so much, and have so little faith in their daughters, adopted or otherwise? My mother had watched Lissa, Mike, Brian, and me grow up and had spent countless hours in our company. Yet she had always taken Brian's side, and now it was apparent she was taking Mike's side, weighing in with the priesthood, the patriarchy.

It mattered not that I, as her daughter, was only a shell of what I should be because of this tendency. It mattered not that Melissa was missing. Surely I had done something to bring it on, to deserve my fiancé forcing himself on me months before we were to be married. *Stop, Jannie. You never told her.* But I was sure of her reaction. And surely Melissa had listened to Satan and done something wrong, which had led to her disappearance.

I stood, nauseated and sickened, and snapped the napkin I had been wringing between my fingers onto the table, with a loud slap.

"You don't get it, Mom. You never have. Melissa is gone, and no one is here to stand up for her, and everyone's believing Mike's lies, and you never stood up for me, either. You sided with Brian, never asked me what was wrong, or why I didn't want him anymore. Just more of Jannie's bad choices.

"Well, guess what, Mom. I haven't been to church in more than five years, and I have no intention of ever going back. There is nothing in this religion but destruction, at least for the women who live it, and . . . and . . ."

"Jannie," my mother hissed quietly, a large, fake smile on her face. "Sit down and quit making a scene."

"No scenes, Mom," I answered her. "No scenes at all.

Melissa may not matter to anyone else, but she matters to me. And furthermore, I hope she is out having an affair somewhere, with someone who actually cares about her enough to not lie to her."

With that, I turned and exited the restaurant, ignoring the stares of the other interested patrons wondering what family drama had just bubbled over into their lunchtime. The tears didn't come until I got into the elevator, and an elderly gentleman with a cane offered me his nicely pressed handkerchief and a pat on the shoulder. Tears poured down my face. I took it and dabbed at my eyes while he said, "There, there, dear. It will be all right," as though we had always known each other.

When we hit the bottom floor, I knew I had also hit bottom. My mother knew I wasn't going to church, my father and Jack would soon know, and they would come running to try to bring me back into the fold before it was too late and I became a daughter of perdition.

I could handle that. I really could, I told myself. What was the worst, though, was that my mother had given up on Melissa. Had others done the same? If so, she had little chance of being found, and in my heart I knew she had not run away with someone else. In my heart, I knew she was dead.

CHAPTER TWENTY-THREE

I sat at a restaurant across from Colt Singer and rubbed at the back of my head. It was nearly two P.M.; I had walked out on a lunch with my mother, after revealing my long-standing secret, and the day already seemed eternal. When I called Colt, he had confessed to having no time to take lunch and a desire to catch me up on things. Was that all he desired? I didn't know, but the last few days had made me determined not to waste one more minute of my life. I was going to live it.

"Soup here is good," he said, glancing at his watch, as he had several times already, and then back at the menu. It was a small diner located not far from the police station and the YWCA—a meeting point, of sorts. Despite the fact he'd said he had no time for lunch, we'd met at a place to eat anyway.

"Welcome, my friend," George Tsakis boomed as he stepped out of the kitchen, wiping his hands on his white apron. "Hello, lovely Jannie. Two of my favorite people, here at the same time. By coincidence? I think not."

"Hello, George," I answered almost shyly, embarrassed by his implications.

"Georgie, I'll have the usual."

"Me, too."

George gave us both a knowing look, asked me about my family's health, as he always did, inquired the same of Colt, as he also apparently always did, and then departed, a twinkle in his eye. George was one of the descendants of the immigrant Greek families who had come to Salt Lake City during the copper boom. His family had stayed here, not run off by the prevalence of the Saints, as they were strong in their faith, and even stronger in their family values, rivaling the Mormons in that respect. There was a very strong, thriving community of Greeks in Salt Lake City. Unfortunately, I sometimes saw their wives and daughters in jeopardy, too. I didn't think there was a community anywhere that domestic violence did not touch.

"So, you come here often?" we said in unison, and then burst out laughing. His was a full-throated meaty laugh that implied late nights, happy endings, and sultry sunsets.

I'd lost my mind.

"We have a lot in common, Janica."

I was startled by his quiet comment.

"We don't even know each other," I said.

"I know you were scarred by life a long time ago, and haven't been willing to get back into it since then. I know that I saw what life can do to people, and I've been living my life alone since then, too."

"Who are you, Colt Singer?" I whispered, our eyes locked. "What brought you here?"

"Justice, just like you. You've been looking for justice for years, for all that was done to you. You just give it to other people when you find it. Me, I've been trying to find justice for someone else."

"Who?"

George chose that moment to return to our table with salads covered in Greek dressing and feta cheese, topped with Greek olives, and steaming bowls of lemon rice soup. He smiled and winked and walked away.

"If you ordered the chicken shish kebobs, I am so out of here," I said, trying to lighten the moment.

"No, beef here," he replied, a half-smile quirking up one side of his mouth.

It was quiet for a moment while we ate, and then I stopped, put my soup spoon down, and looked at him. He looked up from his soup, and I asked again, "Who?"

"My mom. She put all of her faith in the world in my father, and he took that faith and used it to destroy her. He's not a nice guy, using a religion to commit his crimes."

I was silent, and my stomach hurt as I considered the little bit Colt had told me. *"He's not a nice guy, using a religion to commit his crimes."* What could he mean by that?

I picked up my soup spoon, not sure what to say but totally sure I could not stand to eat another bite.

He didn't volunteer more, which let me know he had relayed something deeply personal to me, but he wasn't going further. He had his reasons for doing it, and soon enough, I would know those reasons, but sharing time was over.

My cell phone rang, and I grabbed my purse and

pulled it out, glancing at the number before answering. It was Brian. "Hello."

"Jannie, I just got an urgent message from my receptionist saying you needed to talk to me. What is it?"

"Brian, it's about Mike. He called me this morning, and he didn't seem right. He seemed almost unbalanced, and he wouldn't tell me where he was."

Colt Singer's face hardened and his eyes narrowed, even more than when he heard me say Brian's name. I realized I had not yet told him this significant news, and I felt like giving myself the proverbial forehead slap. I was losing it. Too much was happening, and my mental processes weren't following through.

"Jannie . . ." Brian said, hesitation in his voice.

"Yes, Brian?"

"Mike is staying away at my request. I've called the police chief and arranged a time for him to go speak with the police tomorrow. I'll be present, along with a good friend of mine who is a criminal defense attorney. I'm sorry he called you. He's very upset right now. This whole thing with Melissa, with her betrayal, and everyone thinking it's something else . . ."

"Brian, you cannot seriously tell me that you believe Melissa did run away with someone? Are you kidding? You were her friend, too. What the hell is wrong with you?"

"Jannie, I know a whole lot more about this than you do," Brian shot back. "I've actually been a part of Mike and Lissa's life in the last few years, you know. You just disappeared, and ran away . . . from all of us."

I wanted to fight back, to say something awful, something wounding, but I couldn't. He knew why I'd left.

He'd apologized more times than I could count. I was the one who could not accept it, could not forgive, could not move on.

"Brian, Melissa would not cheat on Mike, and she would not run away with someone else without saying a word to anyone. She wouldn't. And Mike's been lying all along. He never graduated from college. He isn't going to medical school. It was all lies."

There was a silence; then Brian responded. His voice was composed and modulated, revealing no surprise. He already knew.

"All of which I am aware of, and which, apparently, the entire world will soon know, as well. Don't talk to the press, Jannie. They'll eat you alive." His emotions seemed to range from anger to compassion to concern. I couldn't keep track. It was dizzying.

"I'll be fine, Brian. Just fine. I just thought you should know. I have to go now."

I hung up before he could say another word.

"Mike will be turning himself in to the police tomorrow, with Brian and another attorney—a criminal defense lawyer—at his side."

Colt tightened his lips and nodded. "And he wasn't surprised at the news that Mike had been living a lie?"

"Didn't appear to be," I said casually, while a knot tightened in my throat. I reached out and grabbed my water glass and took a sip, trying to dispel the dry, growing panic that was building. My hands began to shake.

"You're getting freaked out again," he said calmly, reaching over and grabbing my wrist firmly. "Breathe. Just breathe. Put the glass down, put both hands on the table, and slowly breathe, in and out."

I did as he instructed, and gradually the growing panic dissipated, an uneasy calm flowing over my body as I followed the instructions of his melodious voice.

"I'm okay now," I said, after a moment had passed. "Thank you."

"What brought that one on?"

"Talking to Brian. It always does. It's inevitable. It's why he's so angry at me. I can't forgive him, because every time I talk to him I have these attacks, and I realize how fucking pitiful my life is, and so it goes, on and on, and—"

"Stop," he said with a chuckle. "You're going to get yourself worked up again. Hell, you're going to get me worked up. I don't believe I've ever heard you say the word 'fucking.'"

I blushed. "You haven't known me very long. But the truth is, I don't use it much."

"I do. Cops are notorious for their bad language. I'm among the worst offenders. But it has a different ring coming out of your mouth. It sounds almost, well, inviting."

My eyes grew wide as I considered the implications of his words, and I waited to see if the familiar panic would grow again. I definitely felt light-headed, and somewhat tingly, but there were no rats gnawing at the inside of my stomach, no army of insects trying to set up camp under my skin.

Colt Singer was different. He wasn't a good Mormon boy, and I was more at ease with him than I had ever been with anyone in my life—or at least since Brian and I had parted ways.

Small truths came at me in big ways. I didn't want my mother's life. I didn't want Melissa's life. I especially didn't want Debbie Talon's life. And if the truths I had been taught my entire life were the only pathway to righteousness, I would be paying an eternal price for exactly what I did want—the man sitting across the table from me.

CHAPTER TWENTY-FOUR

Colt promised to keep me updated about any events regarding Melissa and the murder investigations into Ida's and Debbie's and her mother's deaths. He gave me a kiss on the forehead and saw me to my car in the narrow parking lot of Tsakis Eatery, then shadowed me closely as I drove to the YWCA, as he had told me he would.

After I pulled up into my assigned spot, I shut off my car, grabbed my purse and got out, lulled by the fact that Colt Singer was watching my every step. I was surprised when someone grabbed my arm and pulled me into a big bear hug. I was not surprised when I heard a car door slam and rapid footsteps heading my way.

"Hey, sis," came Jack's voice, just before Colt Singer's voice said, "Are you okay, Jannie?"

I pulled out of Jack's embrace and stepped back, nodding at Colt, trying to tell him telepathically that I was fine and safe—at least physically.

"Detective Colt Singer, this is my brother, Jack Fox."

Jack was dressed casually in a short-sleeved red polo shirt and long shorts that covered his garments. He looked older than the last time I had seen him, not just by months but by years, with a few gray hairs popping out among the dark brown strands and worry lines creasing his forehead.

"Detective? I guess you're looking into Melissa's disappearance, huh. Sad thing."

"Yes, very sad," intoned Colt.

"I'm here to take you to Mom's, Jannie, so don't argue, okay? We need to have a family meeting. Dad called it. Nice to meet you, Detective. Good luck on the case. We really hope you find Melissa safe." His voice was sincere. I knew he meant it, but he was still being remarkably flip and forceful, just assuming that I would go with him. "I'll drive, Jannie. Mom and Dad are waiting."

"I have work to do," I protested, wanting one more minute, one more hour, one more lifetime to put this off.

"It'll wait," he said, an authoritarian lilt in his voice. He took my elbow and guided me toward his dark blue Taurus.

"Jannie, is this what you want?" Colt asked as we walked away.

"No, it's not," I replied, but followed Jack nonetheless. "It is, however, what I have to do. It's time to stop running."

Colt nodded in understanding and watched as my brother led me to his car and whisked me away to chez Fox, where all of my secrets would finally tumble out and my family would either lock me away forever or totally disown me. I didn't know which one would be worse.

On the way to our parents' house, Jack didn't speak. I finally broke the silence.

"You don't look good, Jack. What's going on?"

"Nothing. I'm fine."

"Things okay down at the Zoo?"

"Jannie, I don't like it when you speak disrespectfully of God's university."

"Jack, what the hell has happened to you? You never used to be like this."

"I grew up. Maybe you should try it."

"Why, so I can look like walking death, forty pounds too heavy, and ten years older than I actually am, like you do? No, thanks."

It was silent for another moment, and then Jack spoke. His words stunned me. "Karin doesn't want the baby. She's mad because she wanted to go back to school and get her master's, and now it is going to have to wait. She won't listen to me, or Dad, or the bishop. She said she's given everything up so that I can be the star for as long as she can remember, and now she wants her turn. But that's not the way it works. That's not the way it's supposed to be."

I heard the agony in his voice, and felt a small crack form in my own shield, the one I'd been carefully erecting since I first saw Jack and understood what was coming. Of course he was a chauvinist. He'd been raised by a card-carrying chauvinist and his adoring chauvinista, my mother, in a religion that was set up around the sanctity of the male priesthood, which only men could hold, and the sacred rite of motherhood, which only women could perform. My mother had often explained to me that men held the priesthood because women were mothers. That was our job. Fat and pregnant and having babies and wiping snotty noses and cleaning up poop and vomit—that was the pedestal to which I could aspire.

"Jack, why don't you support her? Let her go back to school."

"And just who, Jannie, is going to care for the kids?"

"Hello, Jack! Maybe you could help? After all, you have a really flexible schedule. Look at you now. Mom and Dad call and you come running, without having to explain yourself to anyone."

"Hey, it's summer. I only have a few classes right now."

"So why couldn't Karin have taken some summer classes?"

"Jannie, she's pregnant. Are you getting stupid or something? And who would take care of the kids?"

It hit me then, as he asked the same question he'd already asked. It had never occurred to him that maybe he needed to do his share in the child-rearing and raising. My father certainly never had. How could I expect Jack to know any better?

He pulled up to the house and gave me a dismayed look, shaking his head as he shut off the car and opened his door. Before he got out, he spoke again. "Geez, Jannie, you know I love you, but sometimes you totally perplex me. You know I love Karin, but this is the way it's always been. Suddenly I'm supposed to take over at home because she isn't fulfilled?"

"You aren't fulfilled, either, Jack. Don't you see that? It isn't just Karin. You don't look good. Have you ever thought about what might happen if you tried to meet Karin's needs, too? Instead of just doing what you think that God and the church has determined you are supposed to do?"

"When did you turn into this person, Jannie? I don't even know you anymore."

"I don't know myself sometimes, Jack, but I know there's more out there. It's just not as simple as they always told us it was. I know that the God I believe in doesn't want us spending all this time serving Him, then turning around to discover it's all gone. Our families, the time we could have spent with them, the precious memories . . . all gone."

I stayed seated, staring at the house where I had grown up, where inside the inquisition awaited. Where my mother wanted to know why I hadn't been going to church, and my father waited to deal out whatever punishment my mother deemed necessary, and where Jack would stand by and listen, just trying to help, just trying to bring me back into the fold.

I pictured myself running off down the street in the opposite direction of the house, Jack chasing after me, arms waving wildly as I fled faster and faster, away from the responsibility that awaited me.

Had Melissa felt the same thing? Melissa, who had been pregnant? Melissa, who might have just discovered that her husband was nothing but a pathetic liar? Running would be the natural instinct, just like I wanted to do right now.

I felt a jolt of hope rush through me. Maybe I was wrong. Maybe all my fears were mistaken and Melissa truly had left a situation that was no longer tolerable. She couldn't run to her mother, who was a whackjob. She couldn't run to me . . . why? I would have been there for her. I would have helped her. She might have gone to Brian, but he claimed no knowledge of her.

So where could she go? My hope dimmed a little bit as my car door swung open.

"Jannie, I love you, but I think you're wrong. Come on. Mom and Dad are waiting."

Let the hanging commence.

CHAPTER TWENTY-FIVE

My mother sat, primly, of course, in her favorite easy chair in the Mormon room of our house. Decorated in a tasteful mauve, which I didn't have the heart to tell her had gone out of style years before, it was full of homey sayings on plaques, and pictures of the temple and general authorities graced the walls. There were, of course, the photos of Jack and me throughout high school and, prominently placed, Jack and his family, with portraits of each new baby. On the decorative mantel of the fireplace was a cross-stitched homily: FAMILIES ARE FOREVER. Ugh.

I'd made it in my last year of Laurels, at Young Women's in church, hating every minute of it. I'd never been good at crafts or sewing, and the program where they had had us girls serve dinner to the boys—an apparent teaching lesson preparing us for our future—had been a disaster. Melissa and I had spent hours later giggling in my bed as we remembered how I had dumped soup down Brian's back and she had spilled an entire plate of spaghetti into Mike's lap.

She'd gotten better at it, at the service part of it, but I'd quit trying.

My father sat uncomfortably in the chair next to my mother. This was not his room, a small sitting room used exclusively for visits from the home and visiting teachers, the bishop, or any other church members who dropped by, hence its moniker, the "Mormon room." It had not been a part of the original design of our house. My mother had seen one in the *Ensign,* the church magazine, where the current president and his wife had been photographed, and she had to have one for herself.

She'd been the first to get one, and it had set a trend in the ward, almost to the point where the contractor who had erected it had to start turning down jobs so he could fulfill his church callings. My mother, the Mormon trend-setter.

This room belonged to Evelyn Fox. My father used it only when his church duties called for it. He much pre-ferred the ratty old recliner in the family room, where he and Jack had spent hours watching BYU football, even oc-casionally missing church for that most sacred of events, the Super Bowl. He didn't do that too often, since my mother wouldn't speak to him for weeks afterward.

Today, they waited for me. Jack sat down heavily in the only other comfortable chair, and left for me the Queen Anne chair, perfect for an inquisition. I remembered Jack's words just fifteen minutes before. "We need to have a fam-ily meeting. Dad called it." Nope. Not a chance.

My mother wasted no time.

"Jannie, we are very worried about you. What has hap-pened to you? You were so disrespectful to me at lunch, and then you said . . . you said . . ."

"Let me help, Mom. I said I hadn't been to church in five years. Give or take. Not sure exactly how long, but I haven't been inside a Mormon chapel since I ran out of the temple. Except, of course, for Melissa's wedding day."

"But Jannie, I don't understand why. Why would you do this?"

"I . . ." I didn't know what to say. Did I tell the truth? Did I even know what the truth was?

"Janica, your mother is upset. We really need to talk about this." My father's voice was deep, and even though he had been born and raised here, you could almost hear the burr of his Scottish grandfather when he spoke. I had always been able to easily picture him in his recliner, a pipe in his mouth, a sardonic smile on his face as he watched his grandchildren frolic about him.

But he had other expectations, other plans for his life, and so he sat upright and uncomfortable in the Mormon room, repeating what we all already knew—we needed to talk. But I knew he was not the instigator. He never had been.

"Janica, first thing you need to do is go talk to your bishop," my mother said. "Explain to him that you haven't been active, but that you know you need to get back to church, and to your teachings. It's easy to be led astray. I think it would be best, especially since the horrible events that have happened, that you move back in here. In fact, that's perfect!" My mother's eyes lit up like a child's at Christmas. "I'll call the bishop, have him transfer your records here, and you can go see him, and we'll get it all fixed. It'll all work out. I'll call him now."

"Mother," I interrupted. I was used to not being allowed to talk, but from somewhere inside me I finally found the strength to speak up, to say no. "I'm not moving back here. Don't call the bishop, because I have no desire to speak to him, or any bishop. I can take care of myself. I've been doing it for years. I'm sorry you're disappointed in me, but this is just the way it has to be."

My mother's mouth dropped open, and she settled back into her chair with a plop. My father just stared at me without comprehension.

"Hugh, do something. Say something," Mother finally managed. "Talk to her."

He didn't say a peep.

Jack spoke up. "Janica, what has happened to you? How could you walk away from the teachings you *know* are true? It's the only way to true happiness. You need to get on your knees and pray, because somehow you've been led astray. Somehow, you've lost everything that we were raised with, and you're going to be mighty sorry—"

"Oh, for God's sake, get off your high horse, Jack. Are you so goddamned happy, huh? Are you? You look like shit, your wife's fed up, and you must have gained forty pounds in the last six months. This is happiness? Give me a break."

Jack's mouth clamped shut, anger on his face, reddened by embarrassment and the knowledge he had shared something private with me and I had just spilled it. I tried to ignore the shame, pretty unsuccessfully. But he had tried to side with my parents in a fight that should be mine alone.

"Janica, where did you get that mouth? I did not raise you to speak words like that," my mother finally managed to get out. Her face was beet-red, too. My father's face was grave, his lips pursed together, something not unlike compassion in his eyes. My mother's face got redder, and

I feared I would have to call 911 as she suffered a heart attack. That would not have been easy to explain. Death by daughter's apostasy.

"Okay, enough of this," I said. "Here's the skinny. Your beloved Brian raped me shortly before we were scheduled to be married. I went to the bishop. He told me we were both at fault because I had been alone with Brian, leading him on, letting him go too far. He made us repent, go to see him once a week, and all that jazz, and we were so, so good, mostly because I couldn't let him near me after that. I couldn't even let him touch me. It hit me that day, the day I was in the temple. I couldn't do it. I couldn't live this life you expected me to live. So I ran. And I haven't looked back."

"Jannie, that's the past. You have to move on. I'm sorry this happened, but life is passing you by. Did you ever tell anyone, or ask for help?" My mother's eyes showed real hurt and compassion.

"Hello, Mother, have you been listening? I did tell someone. I told the bishop, the man *you* always told me to turn to. I also told you just what he said."

"Jannie, when did this happen? Did he hurt you? Oh, my God," Jack muttered, his head in his hands. "I should have been there. I didn't protect you. I'll kill the son of a bitch . . ." He half rose from his chair, then sat back down as my mother glowered at him.

My father said nothing.

"Jack, this wasn't your deal. You were away at college by then. You didn't know, and you couldn't help, and I handled it my way. I'm fine, only I don't have any desire to go into churches. Oh, hell, the truth is I *can't* go into churches. So there."

"Have you seen someone, Jannie?" my mother asked, delicately edging around the type of person I would have to "see" to get help. The kind of person that someone like Melissa's whackjob mother would have to see but mostly refused to.

"I see someone weekly, Mother, and I'm doing fine. I'm sorry to hurt you, but I don't really have any desire to go back to church. I don't embrace it. I suppose there is good and bad in it, but I can find good and bad anywhere. Since I really can't tolerate going inside one, I choose to find my good and bad elsewhere." I stood up and backed away from all of them. "Now I need to go. I have things to do. I won't be coming to live here, I won't be coming to church, and please don't send the bishop or anyone else after me. I'm doing fine. I'm getting better."

I was. Really I was, I convinced myself, as I jogged out of the house without another word, running down the street away from my childhood memories as fast as I could, just as my first inclination had been when Jack and I pulled up.

CHAPTER TWENTY-SIX

The reality of what had just happened, when it finally hit me, destroyed me. I ran until my side ached and sweat poured down my back and trickled from my forehead over my nose and onto my lips. It was a hot July day, even in the late afternoon, and several people walking through the neighborhood gave me odd looks as I passed them. No one else was jogging in the heat, and I was a strange sight in my Levi's racing down the street.

I'd been so desperate to escape that I'd left my purse, along with my phone and all the other contents—including my gun—inside it. God forbid my mother should open it and find the gun. That really might give her a heart attack.

The stitch in my side got worse, and I was finally forced to stop, panting, sweat and tears mingling. I gasped and tried to slow my breathing, my heart feeling as if it were going to jump right out of my chest and onto the pavement below me. I heard the rush of a car and slam of the door and looked up to see Mike Holt headed toward me; and my first instinct was a leap of joy to see an old friend, and then memories came back, and the harsh look on his face made me step back, first one step, then two. I couldn't run anymore. I could barely walk.

"Jannie, we need to talk. Get in the car."

"Mike, I am not getting in your car. I don't know what's going on here, but you weren't terribly nice to me on the phone so I'm not real comfortable with you right now."

He sighed and moved toward me. I took another step back.

"Jannie, please. I just want to talk to you, to explain. This whole thing is crazy. Melissa walks out on *me*, abandons *me*, cheats on *me*, and everyone is all worried about her. Now the police want to talk to me, and Brian tells me he thinks they'll try to charge me with something, even though there's no evidence of anything. Nothing, not one shred."

My mind traveled to the bloody mattress that Colt Singer told me had been found earlier in the week, and the new mattress that was found on Mike and Melissa's marital bed, but I didn't say anything. I knew that nothing had come back from the crime lab on the mattress, and it would take a while as they tried to find traces of Melissa's DNA on the personal things she had left behind. I also didn't want to tip Mike to the fact that the police knew he had bought a new mattress.

Colt had confided to me that the police chief was leery to even sign the form to allow the expensive DNA testing without more proof that Mike had something to do with his wife's disappearance. The pyramid of lies he had created was what Colt hoped would change the chief's mind and encourage him to push getting the DNA results even earlier.

"Mike, I'm sorry, but I don't know you anymore. I don't understand you."

He stayed where he was, and so did I, still dripping

sweat and fighting to breathe. I needed this calm time in case I did have to run again. In case my childhood friend had become the worst of all things—a murderer.

We stood staring at each other for a moment, and then he shook his head.

"You're right, you don't understand. Melissa wanted to marry a doctor. She always said, 'I'm not going to be my mother. I'm not going to marry a man like my father.' And I'd play along. 'Well, I'm gonna be a doctor. I'm gonna be so successful, and you can be a doctor's wife, and have a beautiful home, and raise our kids, and we'll go on vacations to Hawaii.' And she believed me. I was just talking, but she believed me, so when I started college she was always nagging me to move faster, to take more credits, get done faster. I was behind anyway, because of my mission. I was older than most of those college freshmen, and it was just too much. I couldn't do it. The day I got my grades, I just stared at them, and I knew I couldn't keep going."

My mind spiraled back to another childhood memory.

Mike and I, lying on the trampoline in the backyard, near dark. We were both ten.

"What are you going to be when you grow up, Mike?"

"I dunno. A fireman, I think. Or a policeman. What about you?"

"I'm going to save the world. I'll be a scientist, or maybe a great doctor."

"Sheesh," he scoffed. "Why would you want to be a doctor?"

"Well, doctors make lots of money, and they cure people, and—"

"Doctors make lots of money?"

"Of course," I told him in my most officious, impressive tone. I was just guessing, of course. Dr. Johnson, who was in our ward, had a really big house with a swimming pool in the backyard. I didn't care so much about the money. I just wanted to change things: to save people.

"Maybe I'll be a doctor," Mike said.

"Do you want to be a doctor?"

"Well, not really, but it would be nice to have a swimming pool."

The hand that grabbed me belonged to Mike, no longer ten years old, big and solid, and most likely responsible for the death of my friend. I fought him off as his grasp brought me back to the present, and I knew that Mike had never really aspired to this. It had been someone else's goal. Mike the doctor. Not his. But why had he gone along?

"Four years later, Mike? Four years later you were finally forced to tell the truth? What were you doing all that time? Where were you? And where was the money that Melissa thought was going to pay for your tuition?"

He didn't answer. The silence grew, and just as my breathing became regular the panic started to set in. *Not now, not now,* I willed myself. *Breathe, in and out, just breathe.* I heard Colt Singer's voice in my head and obeyed it, breathing deeply, until the panic ebbed. I pulled out of Mike's grasp and stepped back, preparing to run, when he took another step toward me.

He moved and I turned to bolt just as I heard a car engine zoom up and a door slam, and Mike turned and ran, jumping into his car and slamming the door and driving off just as Jack grabbed me and held me. I collapsed into his arms, a sweaty, sobbing heap. He picked me up and carried me back to his car and put me gently in the passenger side, then stood outside to make a phone call, which I assumed was to my parents. He'd left the engine running, and the cool air hit my wet skin with a sharp pang that made me shiver. When Jack hung up, he got into the car and sat, holding my hand as I sobbed.

Ten minutes later, Colt Singer pulled up. Jack had not called my parents but instead had called the police.

CHAPTER TWENTY-SEVEN

"Are you okay? Did he hurt you?" were the first words out of Colt's mouth. "I'm going to kill the son of a bitch when I find him," was the next thing he said.

He pulled me into a tight embrace against his chest, and I could feel his heart beating through the thin dress shirt he wore.

After a moment, I pulled away, uncomfortable with the stirrings I felt while in his arms, and also bothered by the fact he felt so . . . safe. I was headed down a dangerous road with Colt Singer, at least where my heart was concerned.

"He didn't hurt me. He did grab me, but I think he just wanted to talk. He seemed scared, and confused, and . . . He seemed like a man who is being charged with something he didn't do, Colt."

"Or a man who is trying to cover his tracks and convince people he's innocent. This guy is a habitual liar, Jannie. He's been lying to everyone for years."

I was quiet while I considered this. He did lie. He lied to the one person he was supposed to be totally honest with.

How could I believe anything he said? And yet I wanted to. He was a part of my childhood. How could all of this have gone so wrong?

"I can't issue a warrant for his arrest if he didn't hurt you, Jannie." Colt was quiet as he spoke those words, and I knew he wanted to have something, anything, to give him license to arrest Mike.

"If he killed Melissa, he hurt me more than I will ever be able to deal with, but physically, he didn't, Colt. He just wanted to talk."

"Fine, but I'm calling Williams and setting him straight about what his client is—and isn't—allowed to do. Please give me his number." His voice was low, and quietly dangerous. I told him the number and he punched it into his cell phone.

When he was connected with Brian, I watched his face stiffen and tense up. "Williams. Detective Colt Singer. Your client? Tell him to stay away from Janica Fox. He is not to go within a mile of her, or I will have him arrested for assault, stalking, and whatever other charge I deem necessary." Colt was quiet for a minute while he listened. I could hear Brian yelling on the other end of the line, although I could not make out the words. "Threatening you? Why no, Williams, I'm not. Just a piece of good advice for your client. You want to have a hope in hell of defending him, you better make it clear to him what he needs to do. Stalking the missing woman's best friend is not a good idea. Although it seems you don't really understand that no means no, either. I suggest you both figure it out."

Then he disconnected and put his phone in his pocket.

"You probably shouldn't threaten Brian. He's got a lot of connections."

"Yeah? So do I. He's a scumbag hiding behind a religion and a thousand-dollar suit. A scumbag is still a scumbag, no matter where he goes to church and what he hears. He wants to mess with me, he'll find out that I don't make distinctions."

Jack watched both of us from his car, and Colt walked over to him and shook his hand. "I'm going to take care of her, all right? I won't let her get hurt, even if I have to handcuff her. She's a little headstrong."

"A little?" Jack said, an amused look crossing his face. "Jannie, is this what you want?"

I nodded my head, my throat tightening up as I considered my brother in front of me, and the concern he had shown for me after learning about my rape and the distress it had caused me for so many years.

Jack came to me and hugged me, tight, a bear hug, and I almost expected him to give me a noogie like he used to when we were kids. But he didn't. "I want you to be okay," he said after he let me go. "Please be okay. Let this man protect you. I'll call Mom and tell her what happened so you don't have to do it. And I'm sorry, Jannie. I'm sorry for what Brian did to you."

"Don't get any ideas," Colt said to Jack, a stern warning plastered on his face. "Stay away from Williams, okay?"

"Who, me?" Jack asked blithely. "No problem. If I even got close to him, I'd probably strangle him, so I think I'll let you do your job. My kids don't need their dad in jail." Then he got in his car and drove off.

It was nearly five, and Colt motioned me over to his car, and I got in, grateful for the blasting air-conditioning. Colt took a few minutes to finish the paperwork on the incident with Mike, so it would be documented, and I leaned back in the seat and let the cool air caress my body. I opened my eyes when I heard a click and saw that Colt was talking into his radio, informing dispatch he was done investigating and telling them he was going off the clock.

He drove me to his house, where he urged me inside. I complied without resisting. I was bone-tired, weary, sore, and sad beyond belief. I knew my mother, and I knew her well. Why it was always such a shock when she reacted the way she did was perplexing to me.

My father could always be counted on to follow her lead.

I dropped to the sofa and stared ahead unseeing. I heard running water and looked up to find Colt walking toward me holding a T-shirt, a black pair of sweats, and a towel.

"You need a tub."

"A tub?"

"Yep. A tub. My mom taught me all about it. It's different from a bath. It involves extremely hot water, very little thought, and usually, bubble bath and all sorts of female scented things. However, I'm sorry, I don't have bubble bath. Fresh out. Last girlfriend took it all with her in a huff."

"Oh, this is the not-good-Mormon boy, Moroni, you warned me about?"

He gave me that same impatient look he always did when I called him Moroni.

"Come on," he said, pulling me up and guiding me toward the bathroom. "I know it's a warm day, but I suspect you're cold. Get in. It's hot, but not too hot. Soak as long as you want. There's a towel." He pointed to the top of the toilet where he had placed a fluffy white towel.

He walked out and closed the door, and I complied, shedding my clothes, not even bothering to lock the door.

He wouldn't walk in. I knew it. He wouldn't come near me until I gave him permission.

Two wounded souls. Together, can they make a whole, healthy soul?

Jannie, you are losing it.

I climbed into the tub and sighed, the heat stinging and turning my skin red then soothing the aches, both physical and mental. I felt safer in Colt Singer's house than I had in years. It was going to be hard to get me out of here.

I stayed in the tub nearly an hour, Colt knocking twice and inquiring politely whether or not I had drowned. I assured him I was quite well. Finally, I pulled my weary body from the tub and stepped out, first rubbing dry, then wrapping the towel around my head before I pulled on the sweats and then the T-shirt. I didn't have clean panties, and years of my mother's training had made it impossible for me for to put on the same underwear I had been wearing before my bath, so I quickly washed them with some gel hand soap and rinsed them out, hanging them on the shower curtain. There was nowhere to hang them discreetly, and since they were a nice pair of bikinis from Victoria's Secret, I refused to be ashamed. A girl must have clean underwear.

I did the same with my bra, which reeked from my impromptu jog, and then I pulled the towel off my head and fluffed my hair. It poofed up for just a moment, and then fell back limply into straight, long locks. The many different colors of blond in my mane were the only really unique thing I had going for me. My brother Jack had a glorious red, curly mane, attributed to our Scottish ancestry. In my younger years, I had ached to be different, to have a bit of that curly hair, but in recent years I had been thankful to blend in with all the other Utah girls. The only bright spot, ancestrywise, for me, was I inherited the porcelain complexion of my mother, who attributed her roots to Scandinavia, England, and a few other places I could never remember. She knew every link of her lineage, and spent hours doing her genealogy. Undoubtedly, she would now hope to completely erase me, her only daughter, out of the family tree and family history. I knew I had proven a disappointment.

I searched Colt's cupboards, and felt like a Peeping Tom or nosy nelly, but I was not stepping out of this bathroom until I had brushed my hair, tangled from being rubbed so vigorously with a towel. I found a hairbrush in the drawer of the cabinet, and when I had done the best I could with my hair, I hung the towel up on the rack, made sure I tidied the bathroom, and then walked out.

The smell of food hit me full force, and my stomach began to grumble, reminding me it had been at least four hours since I had eaten. The kitchen was empty, and a small door was ajar, leading into the backyard. A small brown brick patio was home to a barbecue grill, several chairs with comfortable-looking cushions, and a large cooler.

Beavis jumped up and rushed me excitedly, sticking his nose in my crotch. "Look, buddy, I thought we had a deal," I said, pushing him away, and rubbing his head. He complied eagerly, more than willing to give up the crotch-sniffing if it meant petting. Every time I stopped scratching behind his ears, he would impatiently nudge my hand with his head, reminding me to carry on. I didn't see Colt, but knew he couldn't be far, as the barbecue was merrily smoking away.

I sat in the chair and Beavis settled by me, sitting on

my feet, tossing his head every time I stopped scratching.

Colt's backyard was a bit of a jungle, with overgrown grass, weeds where a garden should be, and way too many trees for such a small space.

"Admiring the view?" he asked, coming out of a door that led into what I guessed was his garage.

"You need a gardener," I told him.

"No shit," he said with a chuckle. He walked over to the barbecue and lifted the lid, the smell of hamburger wafting over invitingly. He picked up a spatula resting on the wood sideboard of the grill and flipped the burgers expertly. "Just a few more minutes and then the food will be ready. Want a beer?"

He fished one for himself out of the cooler and set it down, then looked at me. I shook my head, a short abrupt motion.

"You've never even *tasted* beer, have you?"

"I have, too," I said, a little offended he thought I was so . . . so . . . Mormon.

"When?"

"One time Mike and Brian got it, and they tried to get me and Melissa to try it, and I took one sip and thought I was going to throw up. Melissa *did*. We'd always thought it looked so good, you know, they make it look so good on those television commercials, and man, it was so nasty. Melissa swore she was sick for a week after." I smiled as the memory came back, and then the thoughts of her caused my spirits to fall again.

"Well, it's an acquired taste," Colt said, as he sat down in the chair next to me. "Beavis likes you."

"He does," I agreed. "We made a deal. No crotch-sniffing and he doesn't get sent into exile."

Colt just smiled and shook his head.

"So how did you acquire a taste for beer?" I asked him.

"College, I guess. I joined a fraternity. Drank too much. Partied away my four years. Sobered up when real life took over."

"You partied through college but still managed to graduate," I said.

He knew I referred to the fact that Mike had not even gotten past his freshman year, apparently without doing any partying at all.

"There's a lot more wrong there than just lack of good grades, Jannie."

He was right. I didn't know what had transpired in the years since Mike, Brian, Lissa, and I had graduated from high school, mostly because my own grief had moved me away and I hid behind it. And Melissa would never come to me with her pain. I always had to go to her. I'd failed her, there.

"Time to eat," he said, and stood and held out his hand to pull me up. Inside, we sat at the kitchen bar and ate messy cheeseburgers without speaking. I was surprised by how hungry I was, and I devoured every bit, wiping my face with the napkin repeatedly.

Finally, I sat back. There was nothing left on my plate to eat.

"Just call me a pig," I said, repeating my mother's favorite words whenever I had enjoyed a little too much party cake, or ice cream, or even Sunday dinner.

"You are no pig," Colt said, a rough edge to his voice, and then he grabbed my plate, stacking it on his, and headed to the sink, rinsing both off and tucking them neatly in the dishwasher.

"All this and he cleans up, too."

"Who do you think is going to do it—Beavis?"

"I kinda assumed that's why you had him."

He laughed at my lame joke and continued to tidy the kitchen, wandering out to the deck to clean up the area out there. When he was done, he came back in and opened the fridge.

"I can make you something slightly alcoholic that will take the edge off all you've gone through but will taste like candy."

"Candy, huh?"

"Well, maybe not candy. Punch."

"Okay, fine," I said, the thought of "taking the edge off" very alluring at this point. I had forsaken it all anyway, given up my life, outed myself to my mother and father. Slowly, I was also settling into the fact that perhaps it had never been right for me. Maybe I was missing a Mormon gene. I'd never enjoyed church, never enjoyed the eternal lessons and hours spent at the ward house.

He settled me on the sofa, drink in hand, and turned on the television to a crime show, then gave me a chagrined look and changed the channel to *American Idol.*

"This one's always good for a laugh."

I drank half the drink, which tasted like punch as promised, and faded off into a peaceful slumber without dreams.

When I woke up it was pitch-dark, and my heart was pounding. The room was unfamiliar, and I knew I was in a bed. Colt's bed, apparently. I threw my arm out and groped around on the right and then the left, and there was no sign of him. There was also no noise, save the heavy breathing of my now faithful companion, Beavis, sleeping on the floor beside the bed.

I stood up, and Beavis lifted his head and stared at me.

"Lay down, boy. Just going to go use the potty," I whispered. I padded out of Colt's room, still wearing the sweats and T-shirt, and walked into the bathroom, relieved myself, then quietly made my way into the living room, where I was sure I would find Colt sleeping on the couch. He was not there.

I looked around the house, and then heard a noise from the front window. Looking over I could see a shape, and I inhaled sharply, unable to control my breath. Someone was sitting there, facing the window, not moving.

The thump-thump of my heart drowned out all reason, and I slowly began to step backward, to run, to get away. I turned and ran smack into a firm chest and screamed so loudly I barely heard the dog baying and barking along with me.

"Jannie, shhh, shh, it's okay, it's me." Colt's voice comforted me, and a light switched on. He held me close, and when I stopped shaking, I looked over to discover the shape that had looked like a person had been nothing more than a large standing mirror.

"Oh, God, oh, God help me, I am never going to be normal, never," I sobbed into his shirt, crying and shaking while he held me tightly.

When the storm subsided, he led me to the couch and wiped the tears off my face gently with his fingers. "You are going to be normal. You're a scared woman, in a scary situation. We don't know what is going to happen next. Everything is totally unpredictable."

"I've been living my life this way for more than five years, Colt. I don't know if I can ever get better."

"Yes, you can. It's time for you to let go and let yourself get better, though. You can, and I'll help you."

The jarring peals of the phone interrupted our conversation, and he looked at his watch.

"Couldn't be good at this time of night," he said as he picked up the handset. "Hello?"

He listened to whoever was speaking on the other end, grabbed a notepad and pen from the side table, jotted down an address and then said, "I'll be right down."

He hung up the phone and turned to me. "Jannie, I have to go. I'm calling a police car to watch the house."

"What is it? It's about Melissa, isn't it?"

"No," he said tersely. "It isn't." Then his expression softened. "Will you be okay?"

I was quiet for a moment. "I don't want you to go. I know you have to, but I don't want you to. I just wanted you to know that."

"I do have to. The patrol car will be out front. You hear a peep, you dial 911." He handed me the cordless phone then hurried into the bedroom to change, coming out dressed in black jeans, a black T-shirt, and a SWAT jacket, wearing a ballcap with the same logo emblazoned on it.

"What's going on, Colt?"

"It's not about this case. Just a domestic situation gone bad. A man holed up in a house with his kids, threatening to shoot if anyone gets close." He headed out the door, all business, and then turned back. "You will be okay, right? You can handle this, Jannie?"

"Yes, I can handle this."

"Okay, don't open the door. Don't answer the phone,

unless the caller ID says it's my cell phone or the cops. I'll be back as soon as I can."

As soon as the door was firmly shut and I saw the headlights of his car brush past the front window, I ran to the bathroom and changed back into my mostly dry underwear and bra, then pulled his sweatpants and T-shirt back over the top of them. Despite what he'd said, I knew he was lying. He'd seen the most vulnerable side of me and decided to protect me. And I'd taken a big step by admitting I wanted to be protected, at least by him. But hiding what was happening would not save me. I knew that now. I was telling the truth when I said I could handle this. I would be there when Melissa was found.

I pulled the notepad over and lightly rubbed the next sheet with a pencil until I could see the address he had written down. I stopped in my tracks as I realized I had no vehicle. But I couldn't let that deter me, especially now I had made this decision.

I headed to the back of Colt's house, flipping on the back light then turning it quickly back off, remembering the patrol car he'd promised out front. Probably wouldn't see the light from that angle, but it was best to be sure.

I edged my way in the dark past the barbecue grill and the chairs, bumping my shins on a chair and silently cursing, until I reached the garage door. A nudge on my knees nearly sent me spiraling back into panic, until I looked down and saw Beavis.

"You are truly a butthead," I said, and then ordered him back to the patio to lie down. He was not happy with me, information he imparted by putting his tail between his legs, but complied with my request.

I tried to open the door to the garage, but it was

locked, of course. Colt was a cop. I headed back inside and stared around until I saw a key holder attached to a cabinet, and I rummaged through until I found three keys that looked like they would fit the garage door.

I crept back outside, and Beavis once again jumped up excitedly, his short memory forgetting he had just been admonished to lie down and stay. I ordered him to the ground again, and he put his head down on his paws and looked disconsolate.

I tried the first key in the lock, but it didn't fit, so I stuck it in the pocket of my sweatpants and tried the next one. This one turned the lock and I stepped inside—to discover it was pitch-black. There was absolutely no light, even from a streetlight shining through a windowpane, and I immediately realized the garage was windowless.

Taking a chance, I felt along the wall for a light switch, and when I found it I flipped it on. The bulb was bright, and I blinked against the harsh light.

Colt's garage was neat and orderly—and entirely empty, save for a mountain bike hanging from a hook embedded in the ceiling and a shiny black BMW motorcycle. I briefly considered trying to find the key to the motorcycle, then laughed aloud at my folly. I hadn't a clue how to drive one.

I reached up and wrestled with the mountain bike until I got it down from the hook. I got on, realizing I could just barely reach the pedals. If I was forced to stop short I'd be in deep trouble, but unless he had a skateboard hidden somewhere (something I highly doubted), the bike was my only choice. The address on the pad was only about ten blocks from here, and if Melissa was there I was going to be, too.

Since the garage door faced the front of the house, I didn't dare open it and go out that way. I eased the bike through the side door and then over to the fence, looking for a gate that would lead out of the yard. There wasn't one. Toward the back of the yard, I could see a board was slightly loose, and I peered through, making out a brief alley before another fence. Colt's house was one of those Avenues homes that had an alley running behind it.

I pushed and pulled at the board, but it wasn't budging, and after my third sliver I took another route. I boosted the bike up and over the fence, trying to hold on to it so I could drop it gently. No luck. It clattered loudly on the pavement on the other side, and I cringed as Beavis came running, barking loudly. A loud knock told me the noise had also caught the attention of someone else—most likely the officer who was watching the house—and I quickly scrambled over the fence, apologizing silently to both Colt and the dog.

The bike was scratched but still working, and I mounted and took off, pedaling as hard as I could, jumping every time a dog rushed a fence and barked viciously. I settled into a routine. There were no lights flashing behind me, no threats to "stop or I'll shoot," and I flew through the luke-warm summer night air, headed to the address where Colt had been called to oversee a crime scene.

"Please, God, don't let her be dead. Please, God, don't let her be dead," ran through my head in time with the swish of the bicycle wheels. "Don't let her be dead."

The address belonged to a small corner grocery store embedded in the middle of a neighborhood filled with old homes and Salt Lake history, and I cursed, thinking perhaps I had read it wrong. I stared around, and the flashing red and blue bouncing off a fence caught my eye. I headed in the direction of the light, turning the corner of the store and walking onto a full-blown crime scene.

The overhead spotlights were set up over a Dumpster, and several crime scene techs were inside, combing through the contents. I did not envy their job.

"Hey, you, what do you think you're doing?" a rough voice called, and an older, heavyset policeman, uniformed, headed toward me.

"I'm just her . . . I'm just . . ." Words failed me. What was it I was doing?

"Oh, Jannie, you just can't help it, can you?" a familiar voice said, and I turned to see Colt standing by my side.

"You know her, Singer?" the other cop asked.

"I know her. She has a vested interest in the case."

"Hmmph." He raised his eyebrows but didn't comment further.

When the officer had turned and walked away, Colt gave me a searing look.

"Save it," I said impatiently. "My mother can cut steel in half with her looks. I'm hardened to it."

"Jannie, this is a crime scene, and you are not supposed to be here . . . and speaking of that, how the hell *did* you get here?"

"Um, bike?"

"Bike? You had a bike? You were at my house, how could you have . . . Oh, good Lord, tell me you did not drive my motorcycle over here?"

I almost didn't answer, just because I was enjoying the mixture of emotion on his normally impassive face—it was something comparable to rage and utter astonishment, and fear for his beloved motorcycle.

"I said 'bike.' I took your mountain bike. I do have some bad news about that, though. I sort of dropped it when I was trying to get it over the fence."

The relief over the fact I hadn't stolen his motorcycle eased the pain of the mountain bike accident, and he shook his head.

"You are very strange, Jannie Fox."

"And you lied to me, Moroni Colter Singer. What is going on here? Is it Melissa?"

"No, Jannie, it's not Melissa."

"It really didn't have anything to do with her disappearance?"

His hesitation told me that wasn't true, either.

"What are you looking for here?"

"We already found it. We're just making sure that we didn't miss any crucial evidence."

"You found what?"

"Not what, Jannie. Who. We found Debbie's babies."

CHAPTER TWENTY-EIGHT

Why is it, when people are forced outside of the norms of acceptable society, say, when they choose to take the life of someone they love, someone they profess to care for, that they then dump the person in a place next to yesterday's garbage? Does it make them feel better about their choice to snuff out a life, to end a soul's worldly journey, if they pretend it was nothing more than trash all along?

"Oh, I was just going to throw it away, anyway."

I stood on one side of a two-way mirror that looked into a room where Brandon Talon was proclaiming his innocence, over and over again, both to the murder of his wife, Debbie, and her mother, and to the murder of his two children. The killing of his four family members had taken place at roughly the same time, according to the ME. Brandon claimed he knew nothing about any of them. The police were not falling for his story. Even though he looked clean-cut and respectable, the kind of boy you take home to your Mormon mother, he did not have an alibi. He sat in the room with a sullen look on his face, arms folded tightly into his body. I turned away and walked from the room, sitting in a chair down the hallway from the interrogation room. I'd heard enough today to last a lifetime.

I waited an hour or so, until Colt came out of the interrogation room and motioned me to follow him. I knew Brandon Talon would follow shortly, and despite the fact he would be shackled, I had no desire to be seen by him, or even be anywhere in his vicinity.

Colt drove us back to his house in silence. I figured he was still mad I had encroached on his crime scene, against his wishes. Maybe I'd have to pay for his bike. His words, when he spoke, were not what I expected.

"You're really brave when it's someone else's ass on the line."

"What do you mean by that?"

"You're fearless if you think it's Melissa, or some domestic violence victim you're protecting, but when it comes to yourself, you'll just curl up and die and never live at all. The only thing you're afraid of is living, Jannie."

"That is ridiculous," I gasped, hurt by his accusation. "I am not afraid of living. I know I'm the walking wounded, but I'm trying to get better."

"No you're not. You're masking it by not living your life, by hiding out, so to speak, but then you put yourself in extreme danger if you think someone else is going to get hurt. You aren't afraid at all to die. You're just afraid to live."

"That is the most insulting thing anyone has ever said to me."

"Is it because you're afraid if you enjoy life, outside what you've always been told enjoyment is about, that you might go to hell? Or is it just because you don't want to disappoint those people around you who expect so much and give so little back?"

"You don't know me well enough to talk to me this way, Detective," I said, a harsh sob caught in the back of my throat. I refused to let it escape.

"Actually, I think I might understand you a lot better than you understand yourself."

"You're an arrogant asshole. Please take me to the shelter."

Without a word, he turned his car in the direction of the shelter and pulled up to the front, watching as I knocked and rang the buzzer until the night guard roused from his deep slumber and, recognizing me, unlocked the door.

"Good night, Jannie. I hope to see more of you, if you ever decide you want to be real again," Colt said through the open window of his car.

I let the glass door slam and click loudly back into place, and I didn't turn as I made my way through the hallway and around the corner, not collapsing, not sobbing, until I was in my small room, lying on the now-familiar cot.

A soft whisper told me Millicent had entered behind me; I recognized her scent—Zest mixed with the cigarillos I knew she secretly smoked at night, a window ajar in her bathroom.

"Hush now, Jannie, it had to happen sooner or later, now, didn't it?" she murmured as she stroked my hair.

I cried a little more then resolutely sat up.

"What's that?" I asked, as a brown suitcase propped up against the end of the bed caught my eye.

"Clothes from your apartment. Detective Singer had them gathered up and sent."

Detective Singer.

"Better now?" she asked.

"No, not better."

"He broke through, didn't he?"

I stared at her. "Who broke through? What do you mean?" But I knew exactly whom she meant. Playing dumb rarely worked with Millie.

"Your detective. I knew someday someone would come along who would realize that you'd given up on yourself, and be mad at you for doing it. I've prayed for it, in fact, for years. I even light candles for you at mass, not that you believe in that."

"I don't know what I believe in anymore. I don't know that I ever believed there was only one truth, and one right, and one wrong. The people who think they are right are doing just as many bad things as they claim the others are doing. Religion doesn't except you from anything, Millie. It just means you walk around wearing a shield of armor that's made of nothing more than paper. You don't realize it until it's too late."

"Did I ever tell you about the time I was working in El Salvador?"

"No," I said, warily. Millie had a tendency to drink a little brandy in the evenings with her cigarillos, and I knew from experience she could become quite a storyteller at those times.

"My best friend, Sister Amelia, and I had been serving at this school, in the poorest, most horrible conditions of the jungle there. The children were just beautiful, just the most precious things you will ever see. The light in those eyes, despite their living conditions, was so bright you could see straight to heaven and all the way back through them.

"But one day, one bright sunny day, it was my turn to go to the market. It was a fair haul—four miles downhill and then four miles back uphill, through the jungle, so it took the better part of the day.

"I got back near nightfall, and the school was silent. Absolutely quiet, not a peep, no chickens cackling or goats bleating, and I knew something was wrong. I crept inside and found Sister Amelia lying on the dirt floor, blood flowing from her head. She died two days later. Bandits had come, taken all the livestock, the sheep, the chickens, and then beaten her and raped her.

"I left El Salvador that same week and never went back."

"That's horrible, Millie. God, I had no idea you had gone through something like that."

"We all go through some things like that, Jannie. Everybody has a story. Everybody's parents messed up and subsequently screwed them up, and everybody got hurt by another person they loved when they didn't deserve it. I'm not different or special. God had already given me my calling, to care for those who could not care for themselves, and I took it. It brought me here.

"But you—you haven't got the calling. You are here hiding. And sooner or later it's going to backfire, and you're going to be very, very angry. And I just hope that happens sooner, rather than later.

"Well, you get some rest. There's only a few hours until dawn. Night, dear."

She quietly left my room and shut the door, and I was alone again, realizing that twice that night I had been told I was afraid of living.

But how was I supposed to rectify that?

CHAPTER TWENTY-NINE

I awoke after a couple of hours' sleep with a sure knowledge that had evaded me for years. Or had I been avoiding it? My father had known about Brian raping me, and had never said—or done—a thing.

Part of the reason I had been hiding for so long, behind my fears and panic, was the horrible knowledge that my family would be so, so disappointed in me—that I could never live up to what they expected because I was damaged goods. And whatever my father knew, my mother knew. Only Jack had seemed surprised, and angry.

They knew, and the world had not come to an end.

The fact that I had not seen this—had not realized this—made me wonder about my own ability to deceive myself. Why was I refusing to live, and move on?

I groaned as I sat up, and pushed my tangled blond hair away from my face. Looking at my watch, I saw it was nine A.M.—Mike and his attorneys, including Brian, should be at the police station now, meeting with Colt Singer and the other officers on the case.

My heart ached just a little as I thought of Colt. Had

I chased him away forever? I didn't want to face that right now, so early, so I moved on to wonder about Mike. What would he say? Would they arrest him?

I wanted to go down there, to force my way into the room, to listen to him either tell the truth or lie about the fate of my best friend, Melissa. With a start, I realized that somewhere along the way I had become convinced of his guilt. I knew he had probably killed her because he couldn't live up to her expectations. Melissa had to have been terribly angry when she discovered his deception, and when her ire was raised, she had a terrible temper. But she was never violent.

For Mike to go this far? To not let her walk away and start her life over? It just didn't fit. How could you kill someone you loved? I would never know that answer.

Since I knew I would get nowhere at the police station, I instead focused on my own life, or lack of it, and what I needed to do to fix it.

I should be angry about the fact my mother and father knew about Brian and still embraced him. Instead, I was depressed. Maybe, just as Mike was able to deceive Melissa, and I was able to deceive myself, they, too, were incapable of seeing the damage this had done.

I got up, thinking about Colt, and his pronouncement on my pathetic behavior—and it was pathetic—and tidied myself, then stumbled down to the YWCA kitchen to make some coffee.

While the smell of freshly perked coffee began to fill the air, a *blub, blub, blub* sound issuing from the machine, I returned to my room and gathered up fresh clothes and undergarments.

I made my way to the community showers, then dressed

and fixed my hair. Now showered and dressed, I sat at the table waiting. Waiting for the courage to walk out the door and live again. Waiting for the courage to go see my father and find out just exactly how he and my mother could reconcile what had happened to me and never say a word.

I drove to my father's office building in the new downtown Wells Fargo building. His insurance firm had moved there last year, and my mother extolled the virtues of the new location while privately decrying the fact that my father's building had two nightclubs and a restaurant that served liquor conveniently located on the first two floors.

After parking in the underground garage, I got onto the elevator and hit the seventh-floor button. I wasn't sure whether the quibble in my stomach was from the launching elevator or because, for the first time in my life, I intended to confront my father.

But confrontation had never really been necessary before. The few times he had caught me doing something wrong, especially when my mother wasn't aware of the transgression, he had handled it in a manner totally different from her. He had not been angry at all.

I remembered when Melissa and I had met at age eight, when her parents moved into our ward, and after a few childish, awkward starts, had become best friends. Weekends and sleepovers were always at my house, because her mother was what young Melissa described as "sicky."

Our hanging out was innocent enough, until the day we stole a six-pack of Coca-Cola from the neighbors who were "jack-Mormons." In our minds, Coke had the allure of the unknown and the forbidden, on the list of things we were not allowed to imbibe because it contained caffeine, something that violated the Word of Wisdom.

"It's there on their porch," Melissa whispered as we walked by for the fifteenth time. "They've forgotten it." Mrs. Carson, who wore sleeveless shirts and short shorts, much to the dismay of the sisters in our ward, had just returned from the grocery store and unloaded her car, leaving behind the Coke.

"You do it," Melissa urged me, pushing me forward down the walkway.

"I can't steal it. My mother will kill me."

"It's not really stealing, is it? She's forgotten it."

"Yeah, but she'll remember when she walks out and sees it."

"Not if it's not there, silly!"

We argued back and forth for a minute, before Melissa suddenly rushed forward, snagged the Coke off the porch, and turned and dashed down the street, me following her at top speed, staring nervously behind, waiting for Mrs. Carson to come out yelling and screaming and police sirens to pierce the calm afternoon air.

We rushed into my house through the back door, slammed it behind us, and jetted up to my room, where Melissa quickly shoved the contraband under the bed, just as we heard my mother's footsteps following us.

"What on earth are you two up to?" Mom asked as she walked into the room, eyeing both of us suspiciously. "You ran through the house like you were being chased by demons. And I've asked you time and time again not to slam the door. Jannie, you know better!"

"Sorry, Mom." I dropped my head to hide the guilt

I knew must be plastered across my face like a neon sign. What would she do if she discovered the Coke? Knowing my mother, I had a feeling the fledgling friendship would be cut short, and quick. "We were having a race and—"

"Through the house? Goodness, Jannie! You two could have broken something."

"Sorry, Sister Fox," Melissa piped up. "We'll quit running around."

My mother gave us one more funny look, as though not convinced of the truth of the story, and then shook her head and turned and walked out. We both collapsed in giggles on the floor of my room, and laughed until our stomachs hurt. Then the guilt set in.

I was fearful when I took the first sip of the warm Coca-Cola, which had always been forbidden in our household. It poured down my throat and I choked a bit, probably on my guilt. But it didn't taste dangerous. In fact, it was sweet, and bubbly, and made my noise tingle, and when Melissa burped loudly we both cracked up again. We each drank two Cokes and then burped again.

"What in the world?"

We looked up to see my father standing in the doorway, watching us imbibe the forbidden Coca-Cola, and the laughter stopped in my chest, but a burp I was suppressing did not. It came out loud, louder than any that Melissa had managed to utter, and I stared at my father in shock.

His lips twitched, and it took a minute for me to realize that he was fighting back a smile. "Where did you get the Coke, girls?"

We were both silent, and I considered the trouble we were in. Not only had we stolen, but we had stolen Coca-Cola. It was a double sin.

"It was my idea, Bishop. I did it. We saw it on Mrs. Carson's porch and we took it. I'm sorry," Melissa said.

Another twitch of his lip.

"That's stealing, girls."

"Yes, Bishop," Melissa said.

"Yes, Dad," I said, bowing my head in shame. My mother was going to kick my butt.

"You probably ought to take your allowance and give it to Mrs. Carson, don't you think, Jannie?"

"Um, yes?"

"Yes, I think so. Probably tuck it in an envelope, and leave it on her doorstep."

"Um, okay."

Then he smiled. A big smile. "When I was your age, I stole a Coke from a nonmember, too. It sure tasted good. Better not tell your mother."

I knew why he said that. Because then there would be no Melissa and I anymore. She would be weeded out as one of the undesirables. And I would never get a chance to tell my mother, "But I could have said no."

My father turned and walked out. And it was never mentioned again.

I got out of the elevator onto the plush seventh-floor offices of Fox and Fox, although in the past few years, since my grandfather died, only one Fox worked in there. My father had always hoped Jack would work with him, but Jack had his own vision and mission, one that had involved all things LDS. How could they not be proud of him?

I walked up to the receptionist sitting behind the massive granite desk. I'd only been here twice before, and both times had been brief visits.

"Hello, I'm here to see my father," I told her, not wasting time. "I'm Janica Fox."

"Oh, you're Hugh's daughter? I'm afraid he's not here right now. Did you have an appointment?"

An appointment? Perhaps that was what was necessary to be a part of his life. If I had just made appointments growing up, maybe I would know my father a little better now.

"No, I don't have an appointment. Can you tell me where he is?"

She looked a little embarrassed, and it made me cringe. I was his daughter, for God's sake. Why would she hold back this information?

"Well, he's having lunch with a client and then he had a seminar this afternoon. I don't expect him back until tomorrow, probably around noon or so."

I looked at the clock on the wall behind her. It was only ten-thirty in the morning.

"Lunch? It's early for lunch."

"I'm sorry, Ms. Fox. I can leave him a message you dropped by."

"No, thank you. I'll catch up with him later."

I turned and left, choosing to take the stairs instead of the elevator to work off some of the frustration I was feeling. When I reached the second level, I pushed through the doors and onto the mezzanine floor of the building. Walking forward briskly, I stopped cold at what I saw.

My father, well dressed in a three-piece suit, exited the elevator directly in front of me, an attractive forty-something woman behind him. She was petite and blond, wearing a white linen suit, three-inch power heels, and an air of élan. Either he had been in the office even though his receptionist said he was not, or I had missed him by mere seconds as he headed down the elevator.

Despite the fact they were less than twenty yards from me, he didn't notice I stood there gaping. The two did not speak as they hastened to the escalator, and without a conscious decision, I found myself following.

My father was a businessman. He dealt with both men and women every day in his workplace. He was also a stake president, spiritual leader of hundreds of Mormons. Why did the sight of him with this woman make me so uneasy?

They exited the front doors and got into a white limousine parked on the side of the street. My father in a limousine with another woman? My father in a *limousine*?

My gut instincts suddenly kicked in, and I raced back into the building and down the stairs to the underground parking garage. I got into my car and sped through the garage, barely stopping to pay the attendant, who gave me a strange look and took his time opening up the bar that blocked my way.

I headed north up Main Street, the same direction the limo had been headed, and cursed when I couldn't see it. I pressed even harder on the gas pedal just as the light in front of me turned yellow. I started to hit the brake when I caught a glimpse of the limo turning west up ahead on North Temple, so I glanced right and left, didn't see anything coming, and floored it.

The noise was horrible, an implosion of sound, the crash of metal and horrific screeching, and a terrible pain in my face and nose told me there *had* been a vehicle where I had not seen one.

Stunned by the impact, I felt the pain in my face begin to subside, and I realized the air bag had inflated and hit me hard in the face and chest. While I was sore and scared, and slightly spacey, I didn't feel more serious or severe pain. As the air bag slowly deflated, I tried to look around and was aware of the sound of more crackling glass and screeching metal, and then heard the big roar of an engine.

The grill of a large truck was the first thing I saw when I turned my head left; then it began to pull away, slowly at first, then more rapidly, and I could see people running toward my car. The driver of the black truck, whom I could not see, pulled farther back, gunned the engine, then whipped around my car and sped off, going east. I heard shouts go up as people yelled at the driver to stop, and one of the first to arrive at my car, a sixty-something man in an elegant three-piece suit, glared briefly in the direction of the fleeing vehicle before he turned and asked me if I was okay.

"I'm fine. A little shook-up, I think, and bruised, but fine."

I could hear the roar of sirens in the distance, and I shook my head to try to clear it.

"Boy, you're lucky that wasn't worse," the man said to me. "That was one big truck. That was kind of strange. You ran the light, and he was stopped, and then it's like he just gunned it when he saw you. Weird."

"The light was yellow," I protested weakly.

The man chuckled. "Pretty dark yellow."

The paramedics arrived and took over, seeing to my cuts and bruises and shining lights into my eyes and asking me numerous questions until they were finally satisfied I was okay to be released. After they were done, a traffic officer put me into his car and questioned me about what had taken place.

"Several witnesses say you ran a red light."

"It was yellow," I protested lightly, my argument losing steam in the face of "several" witnesses.

"Well, the witnesses say red. But here's the weird part. The truck that hit you, described as a black Dodge Ram four-by-four, 2004 or 2005 model, was completely stopped and parked at the side of the road. The driver pulled out onto the road and gunned it, heading straight for your vehicle. Then he fled the scene."

"That's strange," I answered, as though he might have just told me that the grocery store was out of milk. Maybe four or five days ago it might have been strange, but each morning I woke up to more and more pieces of my life out of alignment. Why should today be any different?

How did this happen, Jannie? Well, you see, I was following my father and some woman in a limousine, and they got away from me, and I was trying to speed up to catch them. Apparently, someone did not want me to do that.

"Yes, it is strange. Do you know anyone who drives a black truck?"

I thought back to the men I knew—and considering my cloistered life, there weren't very many—and shook my head. "I don't."

He asked me for some more pertinent details, gave me a warning for running the red light—"It was yellow," I insisted again—and then asked me who I wanted to call to come get me.

"Oh, I'm okay to drive," I said. "I have some bruises and cuts on my face, but that air bag really did the trick. Kudos to the safety people at Honda."

He gave me a funny look and pointed in the direction of my car, which was being loaded up onto a flatbed. The entire left side was completely smashed in, all the windows broken. The damage was so severe I wondered how I had escaped with so little injury. I wouldn't be driving that car for a very long time, if ever again.

"Oh," I said, feeling as though the wind had been knocked out of me. Who would I call? Considering the situation that had gotten me in this predicament, I decided to cowboy up and call Colt Singer, even though he was mad at me and I was so confused about my feelings toward him that it was entirely possible there was some anger there, too.

But Colt could help me find answers. I wanted to know where my father was going, and whom he was with. Colt Singer could help me find out.

CHAPTER THIRTY

"Hello, Trouble," Colt drawled as he poked his head into the police car where I had been sitting out of the hot summer sun, waiting for him to show up.

"Funny, ha-ha."

"You're okay?"

"Cuts and bruises. I'll be okay. I need your help."

"Oh?" One of his dark eyebrows cocked upward in inquiry, and I stifled my irritation. I was not going to fight with him or be pulled into silly mind games. I needed to know where my father had gone.

"Yes. I was following my father when this all happened. The light was yellow, and I thought I could make it—"

"The light was red," the officer who had interviewed me, who was filling out paperwork, threw in helpfully.

"It was *yellow*." I motioned for Colt to move, and I got out of the police car and politely thanked the officer for allowing me to wait there, out of the heat.

Colt directed me over to his car, and we got inside.

"So, why were you following your father?"

"Well, I clued in on something he and my mother did—and said—when I was with them at the house. You know, the day they ambushed me with Jack? Anyway, when I told them Brian raped me, neither one of them flinched, or moved a muscle. No reaction at all. Colt, they knew. They had to have known, and they never said anything, never offered to help, or get me help, just kept encouraging me to get together with Brian. What kind of shit is that? What kind of parent is that?"

I was fuming; the anger hit me hard and solid, and I realized it was the first real anger I had felt toward anyone or anything—besides Brian.

"And so you came down here to question your father? Why now? And why not your mother?"

I was silent for a moment, as I considered his question. *Why now?* I suspected he already knew the answer to that. I was finally admitting to myself I knew the answer, too.

But I decided to avoid the most pointed of his questions, and segued into answering the first and third. "Well, my mother is the queen of circular logic. She can talk her way around any problem or situation, and in twenty seconds the fault and blame is back on you. You end up defending your actions, even though that wasn't how it started out. I wasn't in the mood. It's too much work. My relationship with my father is much simpler. It barely exists, so there's less baggage to climb around before I finally get the answers I need."

Colt placed a call to dispatch and asked them to run the plate of the limousine, which I had hurriedly memorized before taking off to get my car and trying to follow my father and his mysterious companion. While we waited for the information, he asked me what I hoped to gain by tracking down my father.

"You could learn something you don't want to know, along with all the things you want to know."

"I'm aware of that."

"But are you sure you're really prepared for that? There's nothing as devastating as learning about the betrayal of a parent."

"You say that as if you know. How come I don't know anything about your family? Were you betrayed by your parents? Or one of them?"

His lips thinned but he didn't answer, and I considered the short time I had known this man. I'd grown close to him, accepted him when other men made me fall apart, even fallen slightly in love with him—all without knowing a thing about him.

"I don't know you at all, Colt Singer. I just realized that. You are a virtual stranger to me, and I share things with you like we are long-lost pals."

"I don't share much about myself."

"No kidding."

He sighed heavily. "What do you want to know?"

"For starters, family. You said you're from a Mormon family. Do they live here? Do you see them often? Are you close? Brothers and sisters?"

"My family is from Idaho. I was raised in Boise. I got a football scholarship to the U and have been here ever since."

"You played football for the U?"

"One season only. Blew out my quad. That ended my dreams of going pro. The only other thing I ever wanted to do was be a cop. Like my dad."

"Your dad is a cop?"

"Was a cop. That was when he was playing on the right side of the law."

"Um, Colt? This is like pulling teeth. Your father is a criminal now?"

The squawk from the radio interrupted our conversation, as the dispatcher had the information Colt had asked her to find. After he wrote it down, he turned back to me.

"Do we finish this now, or go find your father?"

I desperately wanted to know what my father was up to, and also find out why he knew about Brian and me, but never said or did anything. But even more, I wanted to understand this enigmatic man who had become my constant companion and the one person I could turn to for help no matter the circumstances. My father would have to wait.

"I want to understand you. Tell me."

"My father and mother were high school sweethearts. Married shortly after graduation. I came along almost nine months after that. They were mostly happy, or at least my mom thought they were, until the day my dad came home and announced that the church had strayed from Joseph Smith's teachings, and that we needed to go back to the fundamentals. My mother thought he meant going to church more often, or reading the *Book of Mormon* every day, but she was in for a rude awakening.

"Along with working for the local force, my dad had a part-time job at a lumber mill so my mom could stay home with me, and he made a delivery to a polygamist compound in a remote area of Idaho, on the border of British Columbia. Next thing my mom knew, he had our house up for sale and was planning on moving us out there with them.

"Mom was fairly mild, had always been a good, obedient daughter, but she had no intention of moving away from family and friends, and she sure as hell had no intention of living a polygamous lifestyle."

"Good heavens."

"Yeah, well, it gets better. My mom called her dad up and told him what my father was up to, and Gramps got his shotgun and came to the house and told my father to get out. Seems my father had always had a wandering eye. He had just found a way to make it work for him.

"Mom divorced him, he never came back, and she raised me alone. End of story."

"And you never saw him again?"

"No, he never came back or tried to see me. Then he was shot, trying to kidnap some guy's fourteen-year-old daughter and bring her to live with him at the Idaho compound. That was the year I turned fourteen, too."

I felt the blood drain from my face as I considered Colt's story compared to mine. How mild and stupid it must appear. It certainly seemed that way to me right now. "Colt, that's awful. Oh, I'm so sorry I made you tell me. You must hate retelling it."

"I do hate retelling it. And I'd appreciate it if you wouldn't repeat it."

"You don't even have to ask. But where's your mom, now?"

"She's here, in Salt Lake City. It was embarrassing for her, living there where everyone knew about her nutty ex-husband and his taste for young girls, and the shootout with the law. So my grandpa moved her up here, paid her way to nursing school, and bought us a little house. She still lives there. She's content now. She retired last year, and she travels with her friends, and the only thing she doesn't have that she wants—at least according to her—is grandchildren."

"So you have the pressure, too."

"Yes, somewhat. She would never pressure me to marry someone I didn't love, though. I know she wouldn't."

"Well, you're lucky there."

I remembered what Millie had said to me, about everybody having a story, everybody having a rough life, with tales of sorrow and pain to tell. The difference is how you choose to live your life, and how you choose to deal with what you are handed. It was time for me to step up to the plate and live.

"Are you ready now? Asked enough questions?" he asked me.

"Yes. I guess I'm as ready as I will ever be." And I meant it.

"You better be, because this is not leading us to a good place. The limousine is a rental, of course, and it's procured by the day. Your father's firm rented it. The itinerary is Wendover."

"Wendover, as in Nevada?"

"You know another Wendover?"

I was silent as I tried to digest all this information. While my father often entertained clients, even those from out of town, he maintained a strict stance against partaking of the evils life offered, including alcohol and gambling. To take a client to Wendover would violate every principle he had ever professed to hold true.

"I need to rent a car," I said.

"No you don't. I'll take you."

"You have work to do."

"Don't you?"

"Millie will understand."

"Will she?"

"Yes." I hoped she would. I thought she would.

"Give me two hours to clear some things up, and then I'll take you. If they are headed out there, it will wait two hours."

A part of me wished I could wait ten hours, and not find what I suspected I would. I wanted to be a little girl again, faithful and trusting, never questioning the faith of my father and mother and those before them—and mostly, never believing they were capable of doing such despicable things.

It was too late to turn back the clock. If I had that ability, I could save Melissa, stop her disappearance, which had started out abruptly and turned into a slow fade because no one knew where she was, or what had happened to her.

Thoughts of Melissa made me remember Mike, and his meeting with the police this morning.

"What happened with Mike? Did you end up arresting him?"

"He never showed."

CHAPTER THIRTY-ONE

The limousine was parked in the lot of the Mandalay Bay Hotel and Casino, just over the Utah state line. Colt and I pushed through the doors of the casino, and I immediately wished I had worn a jacket, for even in the midst of a high-temperature summer, it was kept chilly.

We quickly covered the gambling floor and found no sign of my father. Sometime in the recent past the casino had switched from slot machines that poured out coins to a coinless system, and something seemed to be missing without the *ching-ching-ching* of jackpots being paid out.

Colt gestured and led me to the check-in desk for the hotel, where he flipped out his badge and declared it an emergency. He needed the room number of Hugh Fox.

"No, I'm sorry, there is no room," the Hispanic female clerk told him several times, fear in her eyes.

"Look under Fox and Fox," I suggested. Still no room.

We turned, and prepared to walk away when a blast of memory hit me. "Do you have a room under the name Jack H. DelMar?"

When I was growing up, my mother had invented a

code name for us, should a stranger ever come up to us and try to steal us away. If he didn't know the code word—my brother's, father's, and grandfather's first names combined—we were to run like the wind and scream for help.

We hit the jackpot with that name. Room 602. The clerk looked relieved to see the last of us. I suspected she would be in serious trouble should her superiors discover she had willingly given out a room number. She was probably more worried about the trouble with the police.

We took the elevator up to the sixth floor, and the panic began to settle on me as we neared. I took deep breaths, slowly, in and out, trying to calm myself. Colt reached over and grabbed my hand and held it tight.

"We don't have to do this," he said.

"Yes we do."

I knocked on the door of room 602 and heard the light tinkle of feminine laughter, and my stomach dipped and waved dangerously.

"Yes, who is it?" came my father's familiar, steadied tones.

"Room service," I said expertly, with a hint of an accent. Colt gave me a wondering look as we heard the locks disengage and the door opened.

My father stood there in nothing but a robe, his face lined but more carefree than I had ever seen it before. Behind him, in a pink negligee, was the woman I had seen him with, leaving his office. As soon as recognition set in, the light went out in his eyes, and he dropped his head in shame.

"Jannie? Jannie. What are you . . . How did you? Oh, my God."

"Wow, Dad. I simply don't know what to say. Look at you. Here in a hotel room, with a woman who is most decidedly not your wife, wearing nothing but a robe. Aren't you going to introduce us? You remember Colt Singer? Colt, this is my father, Hugh Fox, the esteemed stake president of the Canyon View Ward, and his, well, his . . . just exactly what *are* you?"

I directed the last part of my question at the woman in pink, who quickly ran to the bed and pulled on a robe that didn't cover much more than her nightgown.

Nobody spoke for a minute, and then I turned and walked away, Colt following on my heels. My father did not come after me.

CHAPTER THIRTY-TWO

"I warned you about what you might find," Colt said as I sobbed into his shoulder while he drove back to Salt Lake City.

"How could he? How could my father do this? To my mother, to me, to Jack . . . to the ward? To the church?"

"Do you really think he's doing this to the church, Jannie?"

"Yes, dammit! He made a commitment. He's the stake president, for God's sake."

"It doesn't matter. He's a man first, and men are easily led astray."

"Not Mormon men. Not men of moral conviction. If you live your life right, you can fight off the temptations of Satan, and . . ." My voice caught and I couldn't say any more.

"You don't believe that, Jannie, and you know it."

"I did. That's the really sad part. I did believe it, for so many years."

For much of the trip back, I obsessed over silly things, like what my father had done with his garments. Had he taken them off, folded them neatly, and put them away in a drawer, then conveniently forgotten about the vows he made? Had he removed them before the trip? Somehow, garments were not conducive to sexual intimacy, and I couldn't imagine anyone getting hot and heavy . . . Oh, God, the whole thought made my stomach ache.

How could someone go through the temple, learn the signs and tokens, and then just abandon all of it? Even I, the queen of questions, had given it more weight than that.

Colt dropped me off at the shelter and promised to pick me up later to go rent a car, since mine had been to-taled. Right now he was checking the people I knew for anyone who might have a black truck, including any friends or relatives of Brandon Talon. Apparently, the license plate had been obscured—conveniently—by mud.

Millie took one look at my face and ushered me into her office, shutting the door and pulling me into her arms.

"More bad news, eh, Jannie?"

"When it rains, it pours," I answered dully.

"Your mother has called here six times. She's frantic to reach you."

I pulled my cell phone out of my purse and saw that the battery had gone dead—I hadn't thought to charge it for a very long time. I took the stack of messages from Millie and crossed the hall to my office, opening the door and flipping on the light. I sat heavily in my chair and set my cell phone in the desk charger. It beeped success at me, and I picked up the desk phone and dialed my mother's number. It would do no good to try to avoid her. Six times meant she was serious, and would soon hunt me down.

"Hello?" The voice that answered sounded old and tremulous.

"Mother?"

"Jannie. I need you to come home."

"Mom, I'm right in the middle of some—"

"Jannie, please. I need you to come home." She began to sob.

"Mom?"

"I need you. I need you here. Now."

My father must have told her; somehow, in between the time I saw him and the time I returned home, he had called her and told her. Confessed even.

"Millie, this is never going to stop. I have to go," I said, poking my head into her office. "My mother is a wreck. Please don't fire me."

She just shook her head and shooed me away.

I called a cab from my cell phone and waited anxiously out front until it arrived. We drove to my parents' house, the cabbie trying to make idle conversation without success, as all that had happened roiled through my head. When we arrived, I quickly paid him, and then exited the cab without bothering to shut the door, bolting up the front stairs and through the front door into the entryway.

"Mom?"

There was no answer, but I could hear noises from the direction of the kitchen, so I headed that way.

"Mother?"

I rounded the corner to see Jack standing in the kitchen, holding a frying pan in one hand and a saucepan in the other.

"Jack, what are you doing?"

"Answering the 911 call, just like you," he said, still considering the two pans.

"What are you doing with the pans?" I asked, wondering

if he intended to bean my father when he chose to once again walk through the door—if he did come home.

"Well, I was going to make her something to eat."

"Does she want something to eat?"

"I don't know. That's what she always did for me when I was feeling bad."

I shook my head and fought back a laugh. "She needs ice cream. Check the freezer. I'll go talk to her."

"Thank goodness," he said with relief.

I found my mother in her bedroom, on her bed, sobbing into one of her large, decorative pillows that were there "just for show." This pillow would never be showworthy again, covered in black mascara as it was. She wore white sweatpants, a T-shirt that had to have been left behind by Jack, and her hair was frizzy and sat bolt upright on her head, as though she had been asleep for a week.

"Mom, it's Jannie."

She ignored me, wailing into the pillow. I felt like a foreigner, an alien—I did not know this woman. Or perhaps it was just that I was seeing my mother as a human being for the first time.

"Mom, talk to me." I sat on the edge of the bed next to her; she looked so tiny and frail right now. She cried for another minute, then sat up and put her arms around me and pulled me close, sobbing some more. A brief muscle ache in my lower back and higher, just below my neck, reminded me of the violent car crash I had endured shortly before I found my father with his . . . the only words I could think of were vile and disgusting. The ache reminded me that, finally, I was alive.

"He's leaving," she finally said, her voice little more than a whisper. "He didn't even have the courtesy to tell me in person. He called me to tell me he's leaving me! He has someone else."

My heart dropped. Did she know I had tracked him down in Wendover? Would he have taken this drastic step had I not confronted him?

"Mom, when did he call?"

"Just an hour ago. He has someone else, Jannie. He violated our temple marriage. He violated our sacred vows. How could he? I'm married to him for time and all eternity. How could he? What about his calling? What will the ward members think? How can I ever show my face outside this home again?"

"You don't have to resolve all of that right now, Mother. Let's try one thing at a time. He's leaving you. He told you that?"

She sobbed into my T-shirt, soaking it with her tears, and then straightened up and met my eyes.

"He's leaving. He said he will be back tomorrow morning at ten to pack some things, and he wants me to be gone. To make it easier on *both* of us. Like that's going to happen."

"Maybe it's the best thing, Mom, at least until you guys figure out what to do."

Her eyes brightened. "I know what to do. I'll call the bishop. That'll show him. He will surely talk some sense into him."

She tried to reach across me to pick up the phone, which was sitting on the bedside table.

I reached out a hand to stop her. "Mom, don't. You need to give this some time. You aren't thinking straight right now."

"But I just don't believe he did this. That he would

have an affair. My husband . . . an affair? I don't understand."

"You may never understand, but right now you need distance. Don't make any rash decisions. You may want him to come home, and then what do you do if you've told the world what a heel he is?"

"Jannie, you don't seem the least bit upset or surprised. Why is that? Did you know this was going on? Did Jack know, too? Did everybody know, and were you all just laughing behind my back? Look at dumb old Mom, thinks her husband loves her and is committed to her, and a good faithful Mormon man, and he's out screwing around . . ."

"Screwing" was the harshest word I could remember ever coming out of my mother's mouth, and it caused my eyes to widen.

"Did you know, Jannie?"

Resolve filled me. I would never lie to my mother again, no matter how hard that might be. "I found out today, Mom. I followed him to Wendover. That's probably why he told you, because he wanted to do it before I could. I went to his office to talk to him, and he was leaving. He didn't see me then, but I saw him with . . . a woman. So I followed him to Wendover and confronted him."

"Oh, you saw her." Her voice grew flat, tiny and insecure. "It's true then. I thought maybe . . . I mean. I was hoping. Oh." I wasn't the only Fox with the capacity to lie to myself. "Is she . . . is she pretty? And young? Is she prettier than me?" She began to sob again, and I cursed my father for his mess, and for leaving me to try to clean it up.

"She's not prettier than you, Mom."

"But she's younger."

"Yes, she's younger."

Jack walked into the room, and his eyes grew wide as he watched the woman who had raised us, who had always been the epitome of self-control and manipulative reason, collapse on her bed.

He rushed over, handed me the bowl of ice cream and a spoon, and rushed out again.

"Here, Mom, it's ice cream. Ice cream is magic. It cures everything." I recited the words she had said to me as a child, whenever the monsters under the bed grew too big and the power of prayer too weak to dissolve them. At these times, we resorted to magic. Today required magic.

She sat up and took the ice cream.

CHAPTER THIRTY-THREE

It was around seven when Colt picked me up at my mother's house, as I had called and told him where I would be. I left her there with Jack reluctantly standing guard. He was not happy with my decision to leave, but as I explained, I had other worries right now. I had Melissa, who was still missing. I also had the murders of Debbie and her mother and children.

Colt drove me to a Hertz in downtown Salt Lake City and escorted me inside without saying much. I didn't know if he was still mad at me, or consumed with the case, but it made me uncomfortable, and I wanted to lighten things up a bit.

"I'd like an armored vehicle, please. Do you have a Hummer?" I asked the clerk behind the desk, who was young, blond, wan, grossly pregnant, and before I'd asked for a Hummer, bored out of her skull.

Behind me, I heard Colt's deep, throaty chuckle. So far, I'd made two people's night slightly more interesting. I was on a roll.

The clerk stammered out that they didn't have any

Hummers, but she could call around to try to find one. I laughed and compromised with a dark blue Chevy Blazer. It was big enough that I felt more powerful, more capable—and strangely safer. Odd, how a vehicle could do that.

"Did you find a black truck?" I asked Colt as he followed me out to the SUV I had rented.

"Not yet. Nothing registered to Mike, any of his family members, or his attorneys—including Brian. Also, nothing registered to any of their close friends. I guess it could be some weird, unrelated incident, although I doubt it."

"Has Mike turned up yet?"

"No," he said sourly, a scowl marring his handsome features. "Family says they haven't seen him. I know they're lying. Not sure what I'm supposed to do about it, though."

"I'm not sure why he'd disappear, unless he's trying to clear his name before he turns himself in. It just doesn't make any sense."

"Not much about this case does."

I climbed into the Blazer, and before I could shut the door he leaned in and gently brushed my lips with his, a gentle caress that caught me by surprise, and then in turn I caught him by surprise, as I pulled him closer and deepened the kiss. I felt hundreds of unidentified emotions run through me, along with a few I knew by heart that had always terrified me, and finally I pulled away.

"Don't start a fire you can't put out, Jannie," Colt said in a low, slightly breathless voice.

"I always wanted to be a Boy Scout. I never thought it was fair only boys got to be in it. I could go for a few merit badges."

"I was a horrible Boy Scout. Got kicked out. My mom finally gave up."

"But I bet you were good at starting fires. Don't they have to teach you how to put those out, too?"

Colt smiled widely, dimples I had somehow missed before showing up on both sides of his mouth, and he reached for my chin with one hand and tilted my head up so I was staring at his face. "I'm getting tired of worrying about you. Will you please go to the shelter and stay there? I need to figure this case out, and I keep getting sidetracked by your antics. Let me do my job and solve the crime, Jannie. That's the only way I can keep you safe, and I can't do that if you keep showing up at crime scenes, or investigating on your own and putting yourself in danger."

He slammed the door after that speech and stepped back, waiting for me to pull out. I waved and drove off, trying to interpret the bubbles that were roiling around in my stomach. I laughed out loud, amazed that I had managed to flirt. I had flirted with him, and it came so naturally. He watched me leave, but I wasn't fooled. He would be checking on me. He seemed to care about me, even though he had not tried to make one move to force me to submit to him. I didn't know where this was going, but I couldn't wait to see.

CHAPTER THIRTY-FOUR

The next morning, I faced the mountain of paperwork piling up on my desk. It took the better part of the day to work through the cases. At three P.M., I leaned back in my chair and stretched, just as Millie came into the office. She was holding a manila file folder and wore a frown.

"Jannie, remember Elise Donovan?"

I thought for a moment, trying to place the familiar-sounding name, but nothing immediately jumped to mind. "Elise, Elise . . ." I tapped my finger against my forehead.

The phone on my desk rang as I thought.

"Jannie Fox," I answered.

"Jannie, it's Brian. Look, I need to see you. I need to talk to you about Mike."

"Brian, I—" Millie gave me a look that said she needed to talk to me right then, something she didn't do very often, so I cut Brian short. "Brian, I have to go. I'm in the middle of something here, so unless you know something about Melissa's disappearance, I really need to go. I'll call you later."

"But Jannie—"

"Gotta go, Brian." I hung up the phone, and turned my attention back to Millie. She'd been more than patient with me recently, and I still had a job to do. If I didn't do it, I might soon find myself without work, and my carefully built independence would crumble. I'd call Brian later.

"Elise Donovan. Oh, wait," I said, as the face came to me. "Important husband, something in the city council? She was here for just a few days with her two kids?"

A mousy blonde with bland, unremarkable features and a small, timid voice floated through my memory, although it was a vague memory.

"Right, well, Mr. Donovan is claiming we violated his civil rights by not allowing him to see his children when his wife stayed here, and he has filed a lawsuit. I need you to pull together all the paperwork, proving we did everything by the book. We have a meeting with the attorney first thing tomorrow morning. I'm sorry to spring this on you now, so late, but it's as much a surprise to me as it is to you. Okay?"

"Yes, Millie, don't worry. I'll take care of it."

She handed me the file and left my office without another word, a sure sign she was very concerned about this suit. Should someone succeed in shutting us down, all the women we saw every year would be in jeopardy. Millie had made this her life's work, and she wouldn't give it up easily.

I left my desk and walked briskly down the hallway to the stairs, taking them up two flights to the top floor, which was only used for storage. It was always empty and silent up on this floor. We didn't use it much, so all the air-conditioning vents were shut off, to save money. It was stifling hot, musty, and oppressive. For some reason, to-day it almost seemed ominously quiet.

I walked quickly down the hall, the slap-slap of my shoes on the tile floor sounding like gunshots breaking through a massive wall of silence.

I entered the records storage room and went directly to the large brown file cabinet that held the records alphabetically from D to F. I pulled the top drawer out, and it opened slowly, creaking loudly.

I shuffled through the files until I found the name Donovan, and as I pulled it out I heard a loud thump in the hallway. I jumped and my heart began to pound as I considered who could be out there. No one ever came up here except Millie or me, and on occasion, someone we had hired to move things into storage for us. Another, softer thump made me back into the space between the two file cabinets as I considered my options for escape. I still held the file, but it shook as I froze and listened. Logically, I should just call Millie's name, except she had sent me up here, so why would she follow? Was there something pressing she had thought of? But she would come right to the room. I waited, heart pounding, listening for noise, but heard nothing. My breath sounded ragged to my own ears, and way too loud. If someone really was there—could my own fears be getting the best of me?—I needed to be quiet, stealthy.

There were no windows in the records room. Even if there had been, it was on the third floor on the opposite side of the building from the fire escape.

The shelter was old, and it often made settling noises. Especially late at night when there was no other ruckus to mask the sounds. But it had never thumped before—at least to my knowledge.

I listened and heard nothing, so I weighed my options. Did I continue as though nothing had happened, as though I were paranoid? Or did I proceed as if there were a killer on the loose who wanted me dead—and was this a true fact? It was hard to know anymore.

I waited for what seemed like hours, until my legs began to cramp and sweat poured down my face. The heat was stifling, and I felt my body begin to sway, just slightly, back and forth, an uncomfortable rhythm because I feared it would lead to noise and sound, and even though I had heard nothing for what seemed like hours—and what had probably been ten minutes—I was still terrified.

You're being ridiculous, Jannie. You're just jumpy because of everything that has happened.

When I heard no more noise, I decided to shake off my terror and get back to my office, and away from the desolate third floor and my rampant imagination.

I stepped cautiously and quietly into the middle of the room and toward the open door. I stood there a minute after I reached it, listening, heart still pounding in my ears like I was standing next to a drum corp.

I heard nothing but my own body's reaction to the surge of fear.

I took a deep breath, my heart began to slow, and the roar in my ears diminished a little. Garnering as much courage as I could muster, I peeked my head around the corner and looked right and then left. I saw nothing but the empty corridor. Thankful it was summer and thus not even close to the darkening of twilight, I forced myself out into the corridor. With a burst of adrenaline I was unable to control, I broke into a run. When I reached the stairs, I felt a surge of relief and I shoved the door open and screamed as a tall, bulky figure reached out toward me, a gun in the right hand. A second, smaller figure stood behind the first.

CHAPTER THIRTY-FIVE

My scream echoed down the empty corridor and I turned and sprinted back toward the records room, just as I heard a voice yell, "Whoa, Jannie, it's me, Charlie, and Millie's with me."

I collapsed into a heap on the floor, and sobbed. I felt Millie's gentle hand on my shoulder, and she struggled to pull me up, Charlie on the other side of her tugging to bring me to my feet. "Shhh, Jannie, it's okay. I'm sorry we scared you," she said.

I forced myself to calm down and pulled away from both of them, wiping at the tears that were now drying on my face. "You two . . . You . . ." I finally managed a dry laugh past a huge lump that sat in my throat. "You scared the shit out of me."

They looked at each other, unease in different degrees crossing their faces, and I straightened up, my back taut, hair standing up on my arms.

"What is it? Why did you come up here after me, anyway?"

Millie stepped forward, concern etching even deeper lines in her already heavily creviced face. She reached out to me and grabbed my arm with her gnarled hand. "We came up because we found something. Something on your desk."

"Millie, what is it? Just spit it out."

She took a deep breath. "It was a piece of paper on your desk. I went back in to your office to see if you were there yet, and saw it. We left it on the desk, because it's probably going to be evidence. You should probably come see for yourself."

"A piece of paper? Millie, why are you so worked up over it? What did it say?"

She motioned me to follow, so I did, wondering what I would discover back at my desk. My one safe haven seemed to have been violated. Where would I go now?

◆ ◆ ◆

LEAVE IT ALONE, OR YOU WILL SEE MELISSA MUCH, MUCH SOONER THAN YOU WANT.

It was on plain white paper, printed off a computer, with no identifying marks. I stared at it, and then shook my head. "Did you see anyone come in here?" I asked Millie.

"No, but I was in my office."

"Nobody that wasn't authorized came through that door, Jannie," Charlie asserted, his chest slightly puffed out, as though this note were going to be his downfall—someone getting through on his watch.

"You should call the police, Jannie," Millie said, a slight quiver in her lip betraying how unnerved she was.

"Maybe it was in my purse, or on the bottom of it, or something, and . . ." I struggled to think of a way the note could have gotten onto my desk, but it all seemed a reach.

All three of us jumped when my phone rang.

"Jannie, this is Brian. I really, really need to talk to you. Please don't hang up. It's about Mike."

I rolled my eyes and asked him to hold, then covered the speaker end of the phone with my hand. "I'll call Colt as soon as I'm done here. You two go back to work."

"I'm calling reinforcements in," Millie said, grim lines around her lips. "We need more security. Charlie, you better get back to your post. I think I'll stay in here for now, with Jannie."

I sighed. "Millie, it's not necessary. Whoever it was is long gone. They would have seen Charlie and made their way out of here. Fast."

"Fine, but leave your door open. And don't get mad when I check on you every five minutes. And I'm calling the police."

I knew there was no arguing with her, and frankly, I was freaked out enough I would gladly welcome the investigation.

"All right, Brian, what is it," I said into the phone.

"We've got to do something about Mike, and the fact he's hiding out. He called me a little bit ago and he swears he didn't do this. But he doesn't dare turn himself in, because the police have been hot on his trail. After the Salt Lake City police botched the Elizabeth Smart case, he's worried they have an agenda and will do everything possible to convict him."

"The police are not going to pin something on Michael that he didn't do, Brian. And Mike's just making himself look guilty. Why didn't he show up at the assigned meeting? Didn't you tell him that he's digging his own grave here . . ." I stopped, as the unfortunate cliché I had used tore into my stomach. Maybe the grave he had been digging had not been his, but my best friend's.

"Jannie, I don't know. He's not listening to me because he's scared. I told him that I'll do whatever I can to help him, but he's like someone I don't know anymore. I'm worried. I'm really . . ." His voice faltered as I imagined he wondered if he was saying too much to me.

"What is it you think I can do, anyway?" I asked, wanting to keep him talking.

"That's something it would take too long to explain over the phone. And you seem to have forgotten that Mike was your friend, too. It wasn't just Melissa. It was the four of us."

I sighed heavily. "Brian, I don't feel like I know anything or anyone anymore, including Mike."

"Why would you say that?"

"Because everything has changed. It's all different now. Melissa might have been pregnant, and now she's missing. Mike and you have both said things about her that I just don't believe, but I don't have the truth to back it up because Liss isn't here to defend herself. And most of all, because I moved away from all of this a long time ago, and I'm angry because maybe I really didn't know her anymore. I'm pretty sure I didn't know Mike like I thought I did."

"You never know how people will react in different situations, Jannie. But you're right about not knowing Mike like you thought. You don't know him at all. You never have. Neither did Melissa."

"Oh, please, Brian, you make him sound like a complete stranger. He grew up across the street from me. He was like a brother to me. And yet everything he is doing right now is so wrong . . . so foreign to his nature, or at least what I thought was his nature. The Mike I remember would not run from the law. And he damn sure wouldn't hurt his wife."

"No one really knows Mike, okay? Not like I did. Not even Melissa. I knew him . . . I *know* him better than anyone else. That's something that neither you nor Melissa seemed to see—you never *knew* the real Mike. He isn't capable of doing things on his own, or making decisions on his own. I did it for him all through high school, and I've continued to try to do it now."

"Brian, come on. Where the hell is this coming from?"

"I'm tired of it, okay? I'm tired of everyone acting like Mike is the big hero, the big football star, the future doctor. He wasn't even smart enough to pass his ACT test! I had to tutor him for hours just so he'd get a high enough score to get admitted into college. Is this stuff really such a surprise? Why couldn't anyone else see it?"

Where *was* all of this coming from? I was shocked and a little confused. I knew Brian had spent a lot of time helping Mike with schoolwork, but I figured it was just . . . What did I figure? Had I somehow missed the fact that Brian had been the one getting Mike through?

"How could he get into medical school if he could barely do well enough on the ACT test to get into college?"

"He couldn't and didn't. That was just him fooling himself. He wanted it for Melissa, okay? She wanted to marry a doctor, and even when I told him he would never be able to do that, he wouldn't believe me. He figured he could bluff his way through, like he'd always done."

I was silent in my shock. I'd never questioned whether or not Mike would be able to make it through college, let alone get accepted into a medical school. Of course, I knew now that he hadn't made it past his freshman year, but before . . . before I had always thought Melissa had the perfect life ahead of her, the perfect boyfriend, the perfect future husband, Dr. Michael Holt.

Brian continued. "He's scared and worried right now, and afraid he'll be railroaded if he turns himself in. You have to admit, that detective you seem so fond of acts convinced that Mike is guilty, even though they have Brandon Talon in custody. Mike isn't capable of taking care of himself. He never has been, so I have to do it. And if that means protecting him from that cop—"

"Colt Singer is a good cop. He would never railroad anyone." I couldn't hide the hint of anger in my voice, and also couldn't deny to myself the instinct to protect him. "And as a lawyer, you should know better. Please tell me you aren't advising him to hide, Brian."

"Of course I'm not advising him to hide. I'm a damn good lawyer, Jannie. I would never do that. But, whatever. You've always been naïve about how things work and the realities of life. I guess it shouldn't surprise me that you think *your* detective wouldn't do anything like that."

My detective? Was it that obvious?

"Brian, has anyone ever told you that you are a complete ass?" I had never before spoken to him like this, choosing instead to just run away.

"Janica," he said, his shock evident in his voice. "I'm not . . . I . . . You know what, I don't even know why I called. I never know why I call, but I do. I keep hanging on, hoping you'll realize how much I care about you, and how much I miss you, and every single damn time you just end up pissing me off, and I promise myself I'm going to walk away, and then I go through it all over again!"

His breathing was heavy and I heard the hurt there. I felt the familiar guilt spear through me. Despite the fact I was angry at Brian, and had been for years, I never quite forgave myself for hurting him.

"Brian, I'm sorry. Let's not do this. Let's focus on Melissa, and finding her. The way you've talked about Mike, you almost make it sound like, well, like you think he could be guilty. Like maybe he couldn't handle things when it got too tough. Is that what you're saying?"

There was silence for a moment. "No, that's not what I'm saying. I don't think Mike hurt anyone. But I need to see you in person to explain more. We can meet somewhere public, so you feel safe. I know you think I'm so terrible."

"Brian, I do not think you're terrible. But you can't deny what happened, and I will never forget it. It changed me, okay? There is only so much I can put behind me. I'll meet you, though. Let's talk about Mike."

I wanted the information he had to give, and he wouldn't tell me over the phone. It would require some give on my part so I reluctantly agreed to meet him at the China Nite restaurant on State Street around seven. It used to be "our place." When he suggested it, a wave of nausea rolled through me—I hadn't been there since before the rape—but I was tired of running. I was going to face this, get past this, and move on.

I finished up a few last-minute things then left. I poked my head into Millie's office and she immediately looked up. "I'm headed to my room, Mill."

"I'll walk you," she said wearily, a tired look on her face.

"Not necessary. Did you call the police?"

"Yes, they are on their way. But I don't want you wandering off alone, and—"

I whipped open my handbag and pulled out the gun I always carried. "I'll be fine, okay?"

"Goodness," Millie said, shock crossing her face at the sight of the gun. She knew I had a permit to carry a concealed weapon, and thus must have known I actually *had* a gun somewhere around or on me, but the look on her face told me the reality of my gun-toting had never really occurred to her. I'd certainly never pulled it out in the shelter before.

"Don't worry. I've trained with it. I won't hurt myself or anyone else, unless they are after me."

She shook her head as I put the gun away, and muttered something that sounded like, "Never thought I'd see the day."

She returned to her desk and began working on papers that I knew must be the quarterly financial report. Since this was mind-numbing and brain-bending work, I didn't want to bother her anymore.

Not far from Millie's office, I turned the corner and entered a stairwell up to the dorm ward, where the bedrooms and Millie's sleeping quarters were located. Surprisingly enough, most of our boarders had checked out, and we only had one or two mothers, with a few children, staying with us. We'd be filling up again soon, as it was close to Mormon Pioneer Day, and like all holidays, it brought out the worst in abusers. But right now, instead of the usual sounds of cries, televisions playing, and kids shouting, it was so quiet I could hear the sound of my feet as they slap-slapped-slapped on the tile floor.

It was almost unnaturally still, and I felt a cold prickle of fear begin at the base of my spine and then move upward. *Ridiculous, Jannie,* I told myself. *If someone got in here—* Whoever *had* gotten in here was long gone. *This is a secure facility. No one is here. No one is here.*

I pulled my handbag closer to my stomach and put my hand on the clasp, so if necessary I could get to the gun inside.

Who was I afraid of?

Mike Holt. The shiver that racked my spine told me yes. I was terrified of Mike. I believed the note had come from him. I shook it off and resolutely continued until I reached the small room that had become my temporary home. I was appalled to realize I was almost afraid to turn the handle and open the door, and I shook my head and looked both ways to make sure none of our boarders were around and would see me, and then I opened up my purse and pulled the gun out.

I unlatched the safety, and then I reached for the door handle and turned it, throwing the door open and moving quickly into the room, settling into a shooting stance as I scanned the small space, which was couched in shadows as the sun headed toward the west, and the room was on the east.

A shape in the corner made me tighten my grip on the gun. A shape that had never been there before. I'd expected to find nothing, but I was wrong. "Who's there? Don't move. Don't move a muscle, or I'll shoot," I ordered, my voice high-pitched and shaky.

The shape swayed slightly and then moved rapidly toward me. Fear froze my mind as it hurtled toward me. I felt my trigger finger pull against the metal, felt it biting into my finger, never quite pushing it hard enough to hear the sharp click, as the size of the shape registered in my brain.

The child brushed past me as I watched in shock, dropping the gun to my side, blood fleeing from my face and brain as the little boy ran away.

Breathless and dizzy, I leaned against the door and watched as the boy, maybe four or five, a shock of dark hair sprouting out of his head, ran away down the hall, giving me glances over his shoulder, enabling me to see the tears pouring down his face. I'd scared him as badly as he had scared me.

He turned into one of the dorm rooms that housed families of three or more, and I heard the door slam.

I began to shake as the reality of the situation settled in. I could have shot and killed a small boy. I'd almost pulled the trigger. I could still feel the metal, could almost imagine the indent from the pressure.

I picked my purse up off the floor, quickly latched the safety and threw the gun inside, then closed it and leaned back against the door.

I wasn't sure I could ever touch the gun again.

I took a minute to regroup, then I put my hand on my heart and shook off the terror that had gripped me. I'd have to talk to the boy's mother. I hadn't been around much in the past few days, so I didn't know our new admits, but those who were sheltered by the YWCA were expected to respect each other's privacy. That meant not going into other rooms, although perhaps he had just been playing a game of hide-and-seek, or discovery. After all, this was hardly an ideal place—or situation—for a young child to find himself in. While the children and their mother might be safe, at least temporarily, it was hard to say what the future would hold.

I walked back into the room and then stopped cold. There, on the bed, was a shoebox, one I hadn't noticed before, in my fear and the heat of the situation. Had the child left it behind? Was it filled with the treasures of a child—small rocks, toys from fast food restaurants, and other memorabilia? Or even worse, something alive, like grasshoppers or bugs, or a garden snake? Why had the little boy been in my room, and why had he left this box? In the past few days, I had not had good experiences regarding shoeboxes.

I walked to my bed and picked up the box, shaking it lightly. It made an odd thump, thump, thump, as though something small and solid were inside, but it didn't move unless I shook it, so I decided that whatever was inside was not capable of moving on its own. I opened the lid cautiously and peeked inside, puzzled by the small golden ring I saw.

I threw the lid on the bed and reached in to pick up the ring, and then the buzzing in my ears and the shaking in my hands started. It was a beautiful but small diamond solitaire, princess cut, with diamonds on both sides. I'd seen it before. Many times. Wrapped around it were several strands of thick, curly hair.

It was Melissa's wedding ring. Most likely, it was also Melissa's hair.

CHAPTER THIRTY-SIX

"Why were you in Ms. Jannie's room?" Colt Singer asked the small boy for the tenth time, and he just shook his head and put his thumb in his mouth, sucking harshly on it. Tears still poured down his face, and he wouldn't meet Colt's eyes.

Moving in closer, bending down next to the boy's chair so they were almost eye to eye, instead of looming over him, Colt waited for the boy to sneak a glance his way, and then he smiled broadly.

"You aren't in trouble. Your name's Hayden, right? Hayden, we just want to know what happened. Can you tell me if someone asked you to take something into Ms. Jannie's room?"

Hayden stopped crying and his eyes darted furtively around the room. We were in a conference room where we often met with domestic violence victims to go over instructions or to explain how the shelter worked. Hayden was seated in a chair that was much too large for his small body, his legs sticking out over the edges, nowhere near the floor.

"Hayden," I said, "are you thirsty? I'll get you a Sprite from the machine. Want a Sprite?"

"Want beer," he said in a small voice.

"Whoa, pardner, you're a little young for that," Colt said, an uneasy chuckle in his voice, but I'd been around enough shelter kids to know the lingo.

"Root beer it is," I announced, and then pulled seventy-five cents out of my pocket and walked over to the pop machine, listening as the coins fell into the slot with metallic clanks. I pushed the button and waited until the root beer can hit the bottom with a clunk.

I opened the can and gave it to Hayden, who immediately put it to his mouth and slurped from it noisily.

"Now, Hayden, can you tell us who asked you to take the box to Jannie's room?"

"Same guy," he said, in between slurps.

"Same guy? Same guy as what, buddy?" I was surprised how gentle Colt could be, although I shouldn't have been. I'd seen a little bit of this side of him, this deeper, more compassionate side, from the moment we met.

"Same guy as the note."

So Hayden had been responsible for the note, too. That eased up my fears a little bit. At least the person stalking me—*Mike?*—hadn't been able to get inside the shelter. Yet.

Carolyn Hemp, Hayden's mother, sat in the corner, watching the whole interview and ordeal without saying a thing. She didn't intervene or interrupt. She didn't look like she cared at all, except her legs were jumping and she kept biting her fingernails.

"So the same man who gave you the box also gave you the note, and told you what to do with it?"

"Yup." Hayden slurped at the root beer again, and then

smiled shyly at me, a slight foamy mustache from the soda gracing his upper lip, his dark brown eyes twinkling in delight at the sweet taste of the drink.

"Did he offer to pay you to do it?"

Hayden set the soda can down on the table and scooted forward a little bit, so he could jam his hand into the front pocket of his jeans. He moved his fingers around until he found what he was looking for, and then pulled out a rolled-up dollar bill.

"He gave me this. Do I have to give it back? He said it was mine, long's I did the job right. He said it was a present for the pretty lady. That pretty lady," he said, pointing to me.

"Actually, I have a better deal for you. I'll give you this," Colt said, standing up and taking out his wallet. He pulled out a crisp five-dollar bill and motioned to the police officer standing in the back of the room, watching the interview. "Get an evidence bag," he instructed him.

Then he moved forward to Hayden. "This, Hayden, is five dollars. That's four more dollars than you got there."

"I don't think so," Hayden said with distrust on his face. It probably looked just the same. "This one has a better picture."

"This is more money."

"Looks the same to me."

Colt turned to me, frustration in his eyes.

I moved forward and knelt by Hayden. "Hayden, guess what? You like Matchbox cars?"

He nodded his head eagerly.

"With one dollar, you can buy one car. With five dollars, you can buy five. Detective Singer is giving you five dollars. It's a much better deal. Lots more cars."

"Will it buy more food for the baby?"

My heart nearly stopped as I considered the small child in front of me, already fiercely paternal and protective of his baby sister, Callie, whom Millie had fed a bottle and taken to the room for a nap before the interview started. He was putting Callie's needs in front of his, even when lured with Matchbox cars. No doubt, he would be faced with this again in his life, I thought, as I looked over at his unconcerned mother.

"Yes, lots more food."

"Okay, you can have it." The uniformed officer had returned with an evidence bag and he moved forward and took the money from the boy's hand with his own gloved hand, and placed it in the bag, sealing it firmly.

Colt handed Hayden the five-dollar bill and it quickly disappeared into his pocket, alongside who knows what other treasures hiding there.

Carolyn Hemp's dull eyes had sharpened remarkably at the sight of the money, and Colt didn't miss her sudden interest as she moved forward and watched her son pocket the cash.

"Now, how did he give you the money?"

"I was playing in the water and he just came up. He showed me her picture, and told me to follow her where she goes and just put the stuff there, and then he would come back and give me more. But he said I couldn't tell anybody, so I guess he's not coming back, huh?"

"No, probably not," Colt said.

"Oh, well. That happens lots." This little boy had already seen too much in life.

"Can you tell me what he looked like?"

"Like you. A man."

"Was he tall? Short?"

"Like you."

"Blond hair, brown hair?"

"Like you!" he said loudly, emphasizing by pushing his finger at Colt.

"Okay, like me. Can you think of anything else to tell me, Hayden?"

"No. Can I go watch 'toons now?"

"One more thing. Do you recognize this picture?" Colt showed the boy a photograph of Mike, taken in an idyllic setting that I knew was Memory Grove, Melissa by his side. The little boy just looked at the picture and shrugged.

"So, you can't tell if that's him."

"I don't know. Maybe."

I watched Colt's shoulders deflate. "Okay, thanks for your help, Hayden. I have one more question. How did you know which room was Miss Jannie's? And where her office was?"

He shrugged his small shoulders and told us he'd been watching. "You're out late a lot," he said to me. "Can I go now?"

"Yep, you can. Stay out of Jannie's room and office, okay, buddy?"

"Okay," he agreed, scooting off the chair, feeling his pocket to make sure the money hadn't slipped out when he wasn't looking, and then reaching over to get his soda from the table, scooting out the door.

Carolyn Hemp stood, but Colt shook his head at her and motioned for her to sit back down. She glared at him, but obeyed. She was a harried woman in her early twenties, although she looked older, and was rail-thin. Her drug-addicted boyfriend regularly beat her but never before as violently as this time. She was still sporting signs of that severe beating as she watched Colt question her son. Both eyes were black and her lip was cracked at the side, still slightly bloody, and swollen. She wore a short-sleeved shirt that displayed her many bruises and her bony arms.

Millie had fed the baby a bottle and put her to sleep in a crib, then returned to the room. She sat silently. I knew that expression. Most would not recognize it, but I had worked with Millie too long to not know exactly what she was thinking. This mother would not save her children. She might talk the talk, for a day or so, but mostly, she was trying to pay her boyfriend back. Soon her master would call her and she would return. Motherhood took a second seat to serving that master, and that master was methamphetamine.

We saw our fair share of meth moms. We tried not to judge them, but since the results were almost always the same—they returned to the abuser over and over again until the state took their children or the abuser took their life—we chose to distance ourselves and not get attached.

Carolyn Hemp was not in love with her boyfriend. She *was* addicted to the drug he provided her with.

"Carolyn, please tell us again how a strange man approached your son while you were walking around the block and somehow you didn't see it?" Colt couldn't hide the disgust in his voice, at least not totally.

"He wouldn't come back in. I had to take care of the baby, she was crying, and so I didn't notice what he was doing."

Colt stared at her without speaking, and she squirmed and tried to look away, but he forced her to make eye contact.

"You were getting drugs, weren't you, Carolyn?" he said to her, without further preface.

"What? I was just taking care of my kids," she said, a faux look of disgust on her face.

"I'm not stupid, Carolyn. You were hooking up, weren't you?"

She wriggled uncomfortably in her seat, and looked away from Colt's piercing eyes.

"Was it your boyfriend? The one you are hiding from here? The one who gave you those bruises?"

She didn't speak, her lips clenched tightly together.

"Don't really care all that much about these kids, do you, Carolyn?"

"I do, too," she said, finally forced into speaking. "I love my kids. I'm a good mom."

"You're such a good mom that a complete stranger walked up to your son and handed him a box, told him to deliver it to someone you really don't know, and you didn't even see it."

Her eyes closed up tightly, and her face became stone, her mouth a hard slash. "Kid's everywhere. I can't control him."

"Why didn't you see the man who handed him the box?"

"My baby was crying. I had to try and get her to calm down."

"More likely you were buying drugs, huh, Carolyn?"

"I was not!"

"The boy was twenty feet from you, and you didn't see

him by the side of the road, almost in traffic? It would take more than a crying baby to do that."

"How the fuck would you know?" Carolyn said to him, harshly. "You a mom? You know what it's like to have two screaming brats hanging on you all day? I was taking care of the baby. I didn't see him or the man you think gave him the box."

Colt shook his head in disgust and let her go back to her room.

I knew Carolyn would clear out before nightfall. This was no longer a safe haven. It had become that way the moment she knew we were on to the reason she was so skinny, the children so raggedy and poorly fed.

"Well, I'm going to make sure she gets settled in okay," Millie said. I knew that meant she would make sure the children had eaten and been taken care of. The mom wouldn't give it a second thought, especially if she had scored some drugs.

"Well, that was a bust," Colt said after Millie left the room. "The description Hayden gave was vague as hell. And without the photo confirmation, we have nothing to go on. Man about my height, no beard or mustache, my hair color, just average-looking. Could be one of a million men roaming around this city."

"Could be Mike," I said thoughtfully. "That picture is about five years old. He's changed a lot since it was taken. Aged."

"Most recent one we could find. I realize it still could be him," he answered, "but if he's trying to prove his innocence, he's doing exactly the opposite—delivering the note and a ring and some of Melissa's hair to you. And why? Is it a warning? Shut up, or this could happen to you?"

"Maybe he's trying to prove that Melissa walked away, and she left this behind. He can't really get close to me, so he resorted to trickery to give me this, as a message."

"Pretty damn vague message."

"Yeah, it could mean two things—either Melissa left it and him behind, or she's no longer alive to wear it."

Colt invited me to dinner, but I had already committed to meet Brian and talk about Mike. I told Colt I was going to try to do some laundry and catch up on some bills. He gave me a funny look that made me wonder if he instinctively knew I was up to something, and then told me to stay in and be careful.

I could be careful, but I had an appointment and would not be staying in.

I drove to the China Nite with pins and needles shooting through my nervous system. I did not want to be there, with Brian, but it was a public place, and he certainly wouldn't try anything. It seemed so silly, really. Brian had gone too far, in the heat of passion. Chinese food would not bring that response about. But still, I couldn't quite relax in his company. I was sure I never would.

I saw his Lexus as I pulled into the parking lot, and I unconsciously cringed, then steeled my shoulders and turned off the ignition, forcing myself to go inside the restaurant, to breathe. The world tilted alarmingly as I tried to walk to the entry, and I stopped and made myself once again take deep breaths.

"Hello, table for one?" the Asian hostess asked me.

"No, I'm meeting someone." I scanned the aisles and found Brian seated at one of the booths about halfway through the restaurant, his arm thrown casually over the back of the plastic bench. He was dressed in a white sport shirt and, I assumed, jeans, although I could not see below his waist. He waved at me and then smiled, a look that turned my blood to ice. It was just like we were dating again. Why had I agreed to this?

Melissa. It's for Melissa.

I forced a fake smile onto my face and headed toward him, scooting into the bench across from him and picking up a menu to busy my shaking hands. "Hello, Brian."

His smile faded as he looked at me closely, seeing the bruise and the cuts from the accident. "What happened to your face?"

"Minor car accident. I'm okay."

"Jannie, are you sure . . . ?"

"I'm fine."

He shook his head and then said, "We'll take an order of dumplings, and two Sprites," to the waitress, who came over as soon as she saw me sit down. "I think I know what she wants, but let's give her a minute to look at the menu. It's been a while since we've been here."

"I don't want a Sprite," I told him obstinately, angered that he would step in and try to take over my life so completely, based simply on the fact we were sharing a meal.

"You always drink Sprite," he replied, confusion gracing his handsome features.

"I haven't had a Sprite in at least three years," I said. "You don't know me anymore, Brian. This is not the past. I came here to talk to you about Mike, not step back into the way things used to be."

His face fell, and I watched confusion, then anger, then

sadness, travel across his features. "Can't we just have a simple meal, and not be angry, for once? Please?"

"Fine," I answered, a hard edge to my voice that belied the guilt I felt in my stomach. I could not let him get to me and I needed to be strong, but I knew if I didn't play nice, I would not get the information I had come here to try and retrieve. I made myself smile. This was for Melissa. "Do you come here a lot?"

"No, Jannie, I don't. It's too hard. Too painful."

"Brian, why don't you move on?" I was surprised the words came out of my mouth. This was not going well. This was not the way to get him to tell me what information Mike had wanted me to know.

"I can't," he said, surprising me. "I love you. I always have, and I can't just walk away. I've tried. It doesn't work."

I was touched by the honesty in his voice, and once again the guilt settled in. Brian and I had dated for a lot of years. I had allowed him certain "benefits," especially once we were engaged. But that one thing—penetration—had never been allowed. And after it happened, I realized that all the things they told me, all the things they said were true. "One step just leads to another," my Young Women's leader used to say. "You think 'just this one thing won't hurt,' but you're wrong. Because it's always one thing. Just one step further."

And they'd been right. Each step we took was just one step further, until we'd gone too far and couldn't go back. Until Brian pushed my dress up around my waist and tore my panties off, and held me down while he unzipped his own pants and pushed himself . . .

"This was a mistake," I gasped, as the panic settled in

and I felt the familiar symptoms, nausea and pounding heart, begin to control me. *Breathe, Jannie, breathe*. I forced myself to think of Melissa, of her alone and scared somewhere, wanting someone to help her.

"Why are you shaking?" Brian asked me, concern on his face. "Jannie, what's wrong? Why do you look like that? You're so pale, and you're trembling. What's wrong?"

He'd never seen me like this, didn't know the physical reaction I endured whenever I saw him, or whenever I went near a church. I had never told him, just used to run away.

"I'm okay, I just need a minute," I said, trying to breathe deeply and not let the horrible feeling overtake me.

"Dumpling," the waitress announced in a singsong voice as she set a platter of appetizers on our table. "Here Sprite."

"I don't *want* Sprite," I said, my voice nearly a scream. "I want tea. Green tea."

"You want tea?" The shock in Brian's voice registered through my trembling haze of panic, and I began to calm, his dismay at the fact I had ordered a drink containing caffeine calming me for reasons I really didn't understand.

"Yes, I want tea. Green tea. Thank you." The buzzing in my ears subsided, and the panic faded.

After the waitress left to fetch my tea, Brian studied me, shaking his head, not speaking, his mouth a thin, tight slash. I didn't give him the satisfaction of offering justification for my decision, even though he was clearly waiting for an explanation. In the years following high school, Brian became a senior member of the card-carrying Word of Wisdom police, Lissa and I had used to joke. We got the biggest kick out of trying to slip him caffeinated beverages, or ordering them ourselves, just to set him off.

"What did Mike want you to tell me about Melissa?" I asked, reminded by my musings of the real reason I was sitting across from him.

"Well, I'm worried. First of all, Mike tells me one thing about Melissa, then another. He can't really seem to keep his story straight. He claims he's innocent. Jannie, I want to believe he's innocent, but . . ."

"I don't think he's innocent, Brian," I said. "I think Lissa figured out what he was up to, and she'd had enough. She was done. She was tired of the lies." I thought about telling him about the journal, and what Melissa had written there, but decided to keep quiet. After all, Brian would be a part of the team defending Michael if he was charged.

"I cannot handle this. It's all a pack of lies. I don't understand why all of this has happened to me. Where did it come from? And why? All of my life I have striven to be a good person, to read my Scriptures, to follow God's plan for me. I had a temple wedding, and I go to church every Sunday. So why has God handed me this travesty? What did I do to deserve it?"

"Jannie, don't jump to that conclusion. I admit things look bad, but don't you think it's possible that Melissa might have been having an affair? That she might have left with this person? After all, you didn't really know her anymore."

"I don't believe she had an affair, and it pisses me off that you are suggesting it!" The anger burned in my chest as I defended my missing friend.

"People do things, things they wouldn't do in other circumstances, when they are upset, Jannie. You, of all people, should know that. You work with women who do that
on a regular basis. Once Melissa discovered that Mike
wasn't going to school, and that their whole life was built
on a pack of lies, who knows what she would do? Who
knows how she would react? Do you know how you would
react?"

I considered his question carefully, and remembered
thinking that I had always been slightly jealous of Melissa
for having Mike. For one-upping me, just a little bit. Look
how it had turned out. What kind of person was I?

"I don't know because she didn't tell me, Brian, but I
don't believe she left with anyone. I think Mike killed her."

Seconds later, just mere seconds, my cell phone rang. I
remembered that in the aftermath. That the two events—
my declaration of Mike's guilt and my friend's fate, and
the phone call that confirmed it—were only seconds apart.

"Jannie, it's Colt. I'm afraid I have bad news. I came
down here to the shelter to tell you, but of course, as
usual, you are not here."

My stomach dropped, and I knew. I knew in that instant that it was over.

"You found her."

"Yes, we found her body. I wanted to deliver this news
in person, but since we appear to have a leak in the department, in just seconds it's going to be on every news
station. It was a freak thing we even found her. A homeless couple was Dumpster-diving behind the fast food
joint on 300 West and found the body. It was found earlier
today, but we believe fairly strongly that it is her. We're
waiting on analysis from dental records, but it would help

if you could come and try to ID her. I feel like crap asking you to do this."

Seconds, in just seconds.

Melissa was dead.

CHAPTER THIRTY-SEVEN

No one knows what goes on behind closed doors. I knew that was a line to an old country-western song, a genre that always seemed to spotlight the vagaries of human nature and now, apparently, also described my best friend's life. I hadn't known how bad things had been for Melissa because somewhere along the way I got too caught up in my own plethora of problems and stopped paying attention to her or hers.

I had not been a good friend. I would never get another chance to be one.

I made plans to meet Colt at the morgue, where I would attempt to identify the body. Her mother had already been admitted to the hospital, collapsing as soon as the news was delivered. Her father had also collapsed, and was with his wife at the hospital. Apparently, they had requested that I follow through and make the final identification.

Was this a punishment, meant to show me what a coward I had become? Was this God's way of telling me my life had become too self-involved and, as a result, my best friend was now dead?

Cut the melodrama, Jannie, I told myself sternly. This was going to require me to be tougher than I had ever been before.

"Lissa's body has been found," I explained to Brian, who had been watching my face with a stoic expression on his own. "I need to go down there to identify her. Her mom and dad are both in the hospital. I'm sorry. I have to go."

I stood up, and Brian followed, throwing bills on the table to cover the food we had not eaten. He followed closely as I almost ran to my rental vehicle and tried, clumsily, to insert the key into the lock. His big hand closed over mine, and he turned me to him.

"Jannie, I'll take you. Please, you are a mess. You shouldn't drive. I'll take you."

I realized that his hand was on mine, and I waited for the shaking and panic to come, but it didn't happen. Instead, I felt a small warmth—tiny, flickering, but warmth. He'd loved Lissa, too. We had both loved Lissa and Mike, and now one was dead, apparently at the hand of the other.

"Okay," I acquiesced.

We didn't speak as he drove the rental SUV—which I had insisted we take rather than his own Lexus—to the morgue. I didn't intend to be abandoned anywhere again, dependant on someone else to take me where I wanted to go.

Colt visibly flinched when I walked into the morgue with Brian close behind, and I stopped, cocking my head, considering his reaction. What did this mean to him? What was his real interest here? Had this just been an attempt to get close to me, to try and solve the case? No, I knew it wasn't. His reaction was proof.

He didn't ask any questions or make any comments. Instead, he explained that I would not actually be standing next to the body but would instead view the remains on a television screen.

"This is not pretty. The body is fairly decomposed, having been exposed to the elements for nearly a week. Also, it's been hot, which adds to—"

He stopped speaking as I began to sway, feeling the blood drain from my face as I considered the condition Melissa's corpse must be in.

"I'll do this," Brian said, stepping forward, grabbing my elbow firmly. "Jannie shouldn't have to do it. I know Melissa just as well as she does, so I'll do the confirmation."

For a brief, fleeting moment, I considered letting him do just that, but finally my courage took hold, my guilt, my desire to do right by Lissa.

"No," I said, shaking his hand off my elbow. "I'll do it. I'll be fine."

We left Brian in a waiting room area, glaring at us as we walked away.

"Making amends? Coming to terms with the past?" Colt asked quietly, as he guided me through a door.

I felt a brief spurt of anger roil in my stomach, then decided to ignore it. He was angry. He had some sort of interest in me, although I didn't know what it was, really, yet. I wanted to think it was more than just the case. I really did.

"I met with him because he said he wanted to talk about Mike. I thought maybe we could put our heads together and come up with a way to convince Mike to turn himself in. But this . . . finding Lissa's body . . . He's probably going to run."

"He won't get far. He's not smart enough."

The rub was, I had always believed otherwise, mostly because I wanted to, because other people told me that Mike Holt was the ideal Mormon boy. Just like Brian.

Colt led me into a room, sparsely furnished with some chairs and a table and, mounted high on a wall, a television that was obviously connected to a video feed.

"Are you ready for this?" he asked, concern tingeing, and slightly softening, his harsh tones. His voice seemed to bounce off all the walls of the room, coming back at me in quadruple force. How could I ever be ready for this?

He picked up a phone receiver from a base that was fastened to the wall, and waited a moment before telling someone on the other end to go ahead. There was a brief pause and then white lines arced through the picture tube of the television set. Those cleared and I saw a table, and a form underneath a tarp or sheet. Standing next to it was a medical technologist. The tech was dressed in scrubs from head to toe, and appeared to be a man, although slight of figure. He looked up at the camera, then slowly undraped the body, revealing the head and shoulders of a bloated corpse.

Despite the condition of the body, I knew the instant the drape came down that it was Melissa. Her hair was unmistakable. Her facial features, swollen and bloated, and in some cases rotting, were still recognizable.

My friend, my best friend, was dead.

I was not strong. The floor came up to meet me.

* * *

The paramedics tended to the bruise on my head and urged me to get an MRI. I refused further medical treatment. It was just another bruise, to match those I had received from the car accident, and every other event in the past week—all those events that had slowly, methodically, destroyed the shield I had set up around my life and forced me to live again, while my friend—my best friend—lay dead on a cold metal slab.

Brian, apparently upset when he saw the emergency crew come into the building and into the room where I was, had pushed his way through and was screaming something about lawsuits and reckless endangerment, especially since Colt wouldn't let him anywhere near me.

I finally waved the medics away, and told Brian to please leave, I would call him later. I needed more information from Colt, and of course I had no real desire to be in Brian's company.

"I don't have a car, Jannie," he reminded me, his sarcastic tones brutal, the old Brian, the one I had spurned, back in place of the understanding, caring Brian who had driven me to the morgue. Colt Singer's presence did not help that. In fact, I knew that it accounted for a great deal of Brian's hostility, but frankly, I didn't care. I did not understand my relationship with Colt yet, and might never, but I had known for years that any feelings I had for Brian were long gone. He would come to accept this, eventually. He had to, because it was not going to change.

I didn't know how Brian had gotten home, only knew that he had left in a huff when I told him I needed to talk to Colt and that he should leave. He'd been holding on to my keys, since he had driven, and I asked for them as he was retreating, shoulders taut. He turned and tossed them through the air, and Colt reached out and snapped them up, glaring at Brian's callousness.

Now I sat across from Colt in a conference room, nursing a cup of bitter coffee in a Styrofoam cup. Neither of us had said much since the paramedics left. I sensed anger emanating off him like the waves off a hot tarry road on a smoldering summer's day. He was mad that I'd been with Brian. Brian was mad I was with Colt. I didn't understand this sudden, strange triangle I was the point in.

Was Colt angry because he cared? Or was it disgust that I would allow someone who had abused me physically back in my life, just because we shared a common denominator—my dead friend.

"How did you find her?" I asked finally, wanting to break this unwieldy silence.

"I explained that. Homeless couple going through the Dumpster ran across the body. It's lucky, actually, because the garbage was scheduled to be picked up later today. Then she would have been brought to the landfill, and God knows how long it would have taken to find her, if we even ever did."

Garbage. Like Debbie Talon's babies, Melissa had been discarded like garbage.

I began to weep. Colt came to me without comment, pulled me into his arms, and held me tight while I sobbed. We sat in hard metal chairs, scooted close together, and I wept out the indignities of my life while he held me.

When I could finally speak, I uttered words harsh and relentless, anger and guilt twisting my gut.

"I betrayed her. I locked myself up in a fortress, and

wouldn't let anyone near me, and by doing that I betrayed her."

"You didn't betray her, Jannie. You were just doing the best you could in light of a bad situation. Your guilt is what's keeping you out of churches, and causing your panic, isn't it? It's not really Brian, even though he forced you to have sex. It's because you can't handle the guilt. You think you did something wrong, and you can't face what you are sure are the eternal consequences of that action."

He just held me, not waiting for an answer, and I wished I could believe him. But I knew the day I chose to hide away from reality, that very day, I had betrayed Melissa. And now she was dead. I wasn't sure how I was supposed to go on. However, I *was* sure that I would.

CHAPTER THIRTY-EIGHT

I called my mother first. In the depths of her misery, the life she believed she'd been living shattered into pieces around her feet, I knew she needed something to keep her going.

For the first time in her life, Angela Holtzbrick had something to really justify her deep depression and unstable mental condition. I wondered, briefly, if this would work the opposite effect, as it did to most people, and snap her out of her fragile state. My mother didn't have a lot of respect for Angela, but she did have a great desire to be in control and to be needed. Here was a situation where maybe she could help.

"Mom, Melissa's body has been found," I told her after Jack put her on the phone, though not before he whispered that I better get my "skinny ass back here and help me, or I am so going to kill you."

"Oh, no, Jannie, no. I can't take much more. I can't. This is horrible." She actually moaned, and I winced.

"Mom, you need to go to Angela and Pete. They are both in the hospital. They need help coping with this, and frankly, I can't think of anyone who could do a better job."

"Cut the crap, Jannie. You think I've wasted my life, never working, just serving the church. I'm not stupid. I know how you look at me."

"Mom, I have never said that, and I don't think it. You are good with people, especially in times of need. You know how to comfort them, and that's a gift. These people need you, and you need to get off your bed and stop feeling sorry for yourself and move on with your life."

I winced again. Like mother, like daughter. I was dishing out advice to my mother that I should have taken myself, years before.

"Jannie, I know you're angry with me. I know you're mad because we've kept Brian in our lives, even after *it* happened, but you have to understand, the bishop explained it to your father, and well, it sounded like you were . . . like you . . ."

"Not now, Mother. Now is not the time. If you and I are ever going to have a relationship, we will have to discuss it, but now is not that time." I softened my voice. "Mom, you need time to deal with what you've been handed, and I really think helping someone will at least take your mind off what's going on with Dad. Will you do it?"

I heard a deep sigh and then she agreed.

In the background, I heard Jack shout, "Hallelujah!" My brother, the king of subtlety.

Now that someone was dealing with Pete and Angela, I turned to Colt and asked him what was next.

"I've already sent uniforms to the Holt residence. We've been keeping an eye on their house since Mike disappeared.

No sign of him. But they need to know that Melissa's body has been found."

"If they had their television or radio on, they already know." I pointed to the television in the conference room where we sat. The local station had interrupted all regular programming and had been blaring the news of the body's discovery. Police had not yet confirmed to the media that the body belonged to her, but they had been making educated guesses since the newscasts began.

"Colt, is there any chance—any chance at all—that Brandon Talon did this? That it was really about me, and what he saw as my interference in his life?"

"I don't think so, but we haven't ruled that out yet. The mattress DNA came back with both Melissa's and Mike's DNA on it. No surprise there. The blood was Melissa's—again, no surprise, especially considering the discovery today. Basically, what we know is that she was killed in her home, on her mattress. The mattress on their bed now is brand-new."

"Wouldn't someone have noticed Mike buying a new mattress and moving it into his apartment? Mattresses are not small."

"Nobody appears to have seen it. We've checked credit card receipts and sales slips from everyone who sold mattresses in the two days it would have been purchased, and nothing there, either. Either he paid cash and walked out, or he didn't buy it."

"But his DNA is on the mattress you found discarded, so it was their mattress. Which means she was killed inside her apartment instead of leaving, like he says she did."

"Yes, she was killed there. We have blood spatter, too. We need to find Mike and arrest him to find out the rest, but it looks like Brandon Talon killed his wife, mother-in-law, and children, and that Mike killed Melissa. It's just a coincidence you were tied to both."

"What about Ida?"

"We don't know. Either of them could have been involved in that one. Brandon because he was angry with you because of your interference with Debbie, and Mike because he was trying to get evidence back."

"And Mike is still out there."

"Yes, which means you are not safe."

"Why would he want to kill me, Colt? Tell me that?"

"Why did he kill your neighbor? I think he was caught trying to retrieve incriminating evidence—the box. And he didn't succeed. We have the journal, and we have the pregnancy test."

"Which aren't really damning evidence," I pointed out.

"Apparently, he doesn't know that."

My cell phone rang, and I answered it, shocked by how weary I felt, how hard it was to reach into my purse and grab the phone, to click the on button, to put it to my ear.

"Hello?"

"Jannie, have them check Melissa. Have them check her out."

"Mike? What are you doing?"

Colt stood up as soon as I said Mike's name.

"Don't try to keep me on the line, Jannie. I know you're not on my side, but I didn't do this. Have them test her body. Check her out. She was pregnant, and I'm placing bets that baby was not mine. Have them do the tests."

With a click, he disconnected.

I shook my head and hung up. "He said to check her for pregnancy. He claims the baby wasn't his. But he said she ran away. He doesn't seem surprised that they found her body. He knew she was dead." I sighed.

Colt told me to wait while he talked to the medical examiner. I sat with my head in my hands, trying to reason out all that had happened in the past few days. I jumped when a hand touched my shoulder and I looked up to see Colt had returned.

"It's been a long day," he said. "It's nearly eleven P.M. Let's go. I'm taking you to my place. You aren't safe."

"And Mike keeps touching base with me, so you want me close in case I find out more."

"Yeah, that, too."

CHAPTER THIRTY-NINE

Beavis was thrilled to see me back. He shook his tail with such enthusiasm I was afraid it was going to fly off and break something. Colt led me to his bathroom, handed me a towel, and instructed me to get in.

"I'll get you some sweats and a T-shirt. You should probably just bring your suitcase here, because I intend to keep you safe until this is over."

I turned the water in the shower on as hot as I could stand it, and then took off my clothes. I stepped into the spray and gasped as the hot needles of water pricked my skin. I turned around and let the water pelt my back, trying to ease up the tension in my muscles, tension that had been there since I first got the call about Melissa's being missing.

A cold object brushed against my leg and I screamed, and backed up into the shower wall, turning to see Beavis's nose poking through the shower curtain, his body a blurry, distorted yellow object.

"Beavis! You scared the shit out of me. How did you get in here?"

"He followed me," came Colt's voice from the doorway, and I instinctively covered up my nakedness, even though I knew he couldn't see much through the flowered curtain. "Sorry, Jannie. I was bringing in some clothes for you. I wasn't spying on you, I promise. Come on, Beavis, out! Leave Jannie to shower in peace. I swear he would get in there with you if he could. Of course, I'd do the same thing."

With that I heard the door shut, and I was glad to be hiding behind the shower curtain, even though I was alone again. A warm flush settled in my stomach and lower, and I considered the events of the past few days.

In one week, I had witnessed the murder of my best friend, another murder of an abused woman and her family, the murder of my landlady, and the betrayal of my father, and it was like a light bulb had come on in my head.

I had stopped living after Brian took my virginity. Although I could never get that back, it *was* time to take my life back. Most instrumental in that would be granting myself forgiveness for the sin I believed I had committed.

Could I do that? I had to. I owed it to Melissa.

There had been no violent force, really, that night that had scarred me so badly. I hadn't screamed for my life, or tried to gouge out his eyes or grab his balls and squeeze— all the things we'd been taught we should do if someone ever tried to rape us. Right up until the moment it had happened, in fact, I had been there, too, with him, a part of it. Ignoring the warning sound of my mother's voice and all the voices of my church leaders past, speaking in what must have been tongues in the back of my head.

I was jarred from my reverie by the realization the water was growing chillier, and I moved forward to shut it off and pushed the shower curtain aside, reaching for the two fluffy towels Colt had left for me, both sitting on a stool by the side of the shower. I wrapped one around my body and the other around my head, turban-style, and looked down to see my hands were shaking.

There was a knock at the door, and Colt asked, "Are you okay? Coming out anytime soon?"

"Be right out," I called back.

I took a moment to calm down, but knew that now I was dealing with the past it would not go away until it was resolved—or at the least, until I could come to terms with it.

I dried off and pulled on the sweatpants and T-shirt. Again, I was pantyless, so I washed those out, along with my bra, and hung them to dry. Poor Colt was going to see a lot of my underwear if the situation didn't change drastically.

I wandered out to find him sitting on his couch, bare-chested, muscles rippling in his arms as he read a magazine. He wore glasses, which I had never seen him do before. In the boxer pajama pants, shirtless, hair casually mussed, and spectacles, he looked different, older, and, most alarming of all, extremely attractive. His chest was solid, hard, his muscles flexing as he moved—even minor movements—and I knew I wanted this man, and it bothered me immensely. I had finally come to the core of my emotional problems, my emotional phobias, and now my mind was telling me it wanted to do things with a virtual stranger I had never thought I would allow myself to do ever again.

"Sorry we scared you," Colt said, after he looked up and saw me watching him. "Are you hungry?"

Beavis sat at his feet and thumped his tail on the hardwood floor, giving me that doggy smile that offered unconditional love.

"No, I'm not hungry." For food at least. To be touched, to become human again, to connect with this man—for that, I was starving.

"Why are you staring at me like that?"

I looked away and blushed, and he stood up and came toward me. I backed up slightly, afraid that if I touched him, or let him touch me, I would explode and everything I'd been in the past would scatter into pieces in the universe. He kept coming, and reached out to me and pulled me close. His bare chest was warm, and I allowed myself to melt into him, to put my arms around him and let him hold me tight. His obvious arousal should have frightened me. I pulled back slightly, as he pressed against me, then forged ahead. I'd convinced myself—for years—that it was the male organ that had caused all my problems. Of course, I couldn't fool myself any longer.

"I'm sorry. I know this is not what you need, or want, but I can't control the way I feel around you," he whispered into my hair, his voice low and husky, his scent musky and male, and exotic. "But now is not the time to push your boundaries, Jannie." He pulled away and tilted my head up with his hand on my chin, the other arm still holding me around the waist. "You need to learn to trust me before this goes any further."

"Maybe I'm ready now. I feel like I'm ready now."

He pulled away just slightly, and I felt alone and cold, even on a hot summer night.

"No. Now isn't the right time," he said, obvious regret

tingeing his voice, along with sultry heat that lowered its timbre.

He went to pull completely away from me, but I stopped him, holding him tight to me, feeling his heat, his arousal, his utter maleness.

"No, you're wrong. I am ready. At least, I'm ready for you," I said, my voice barely a whisper.

He bent down and kissed my neck lightly, feathery kisses, starting at my ear and working his way down the side of my throat to my shoulders, pushing aside the too-big T-shirt I had donned, to get to the skin underneath. He made his way back up my neck to near my ear, then whispered, "You aren't ready for me, because I want you so bad it hurts. And you don't need that right now."

His words stirred feelings inside me I'd never thought I would—or could—feel.

"I do need that right now. I do need to be desired that much. I want to start my life tonight."

"Jannie, I warned you, I'm not a nice Mormon boy. Once we start, we won't stop."

"I don't want a nice Mormon boy. I want you."

He lifted me off my feet and carried me, bride-style, into his bedroom, placing me on the bed. There was no light in the room except for moonlight streaming in through the shutters, and Colt didn't stop to remedy that. He joined me on the bed, moving toward me and pulling me into a tight embrace, his arms warm, bare, and muscular, brushing against the skin on my arms and causing electrical charges to go off inside my body.

He was watching me, gauging my reaction, I could see, the moonlight illuminating half his face as his hands roamed around my body, never quite touching the most sacred and sensitive parts, but coming damn near.

"You're playing with me."

"That's part of the game, babe. Sex is part game, and part deadly weapon. Lucky for you, you have total control over it. You get the deadly weapon part, and I only control the game."

"It feels pretty serious to me," I whispered.

"I can lighten it up." His voice was soft and low. "I have handcuffs. You like handcuffs?"

His comment caught me totally off guard and I laughed out loud, suddenly giggling so hard I could barely control it.

He smiled, and I could see that was his intent. At least I hoped. I was definitely not ready for handcuffs.

He leaned in again and kissed me and I closed my eyes and lost myself in the moment, enjoying the heat moving from my toes up into my stomach as I arched against him. He grabbed the T-shirt I wore and pulled it up from the bottom, slowly exposing my bare breasts and nipples as he lifted it over my head and threw it to the floor.

"God, you are beautiful. Beautiful." He stroked first one breast, then another, lingering over the nipples as I felt pleasure flush my body. He leaned down and kissed first one, then the other, then flicked at the right one with his tongue. I shivered, and he pulled back.

"Are you okay? Please remember, the secret word here is 'no.' All you have to say is 'no,' and I stop."

"Don't stop."

"That's not the secret word."

"Dammit, I said don't stop!" I almost yelled, and he laughed and leaned back down to continue his exploration of my breasts. My breath grew ragged as he laved my nipples and breasts, and I felt a tightening in my loins I'd never experienced before.

He lifted his head from my breasts and expertly stripped off the sweatpants, leaving me wearing nothing, as my underwear had been hung to dry in the bathroom.

I felt a wave of shame, and a brief desire to cover my body, and then I pushed it away, like a pesky cobweb. This was obviously what God had intended for my life, and I wasn't going to turn away now.

Somewhere in the back of my head I knew my mother was screaming, "God? That's Satan, Jannie." I'm sure Brian was there, too, but I closed off that part of my mind that belonged to the past and went with the pure emotion of starting over, starting a new life, opening myself up to someone for the first time—at least willingly.

Colt stripped off his shorts and my eyes widened as I stared at his arousal. "I think there might be a problem," I said in a whispery voice.

"What?"

"That," I said, pointing to his engorged member, "is not going to fit inside me."

"I think you'll be surprised," he said, then pushed me gently to the bed and ran his hand over my stomach, down to the triangle between my legs and lower, spreading my legs gently with his hands and stroking the innermost private part of me. He was gentle at first, then a little harder and stronger, as he felt my response, finally putting two of his fingers up inside me and moving until I cried out for him to stop, tension building inside me.

"Come inside me. Come to me," I said, and pulled him down on top of me, as he removed his fingers and positioned himself over me. The edge of his penis nudged gently at my opening, pushing in a little, then backing out, then further the next time, until he filled me completely, and I was amazed at what my body was willing to accept from this man. Would my heart be as open?

He moved inside me and sirens went off in my head as my body responded to his, totally. When the orgasm shook me, filled me, consumed me, I felt tears running down my face.

Colt stopped still and stared at me, concern etched in his eyes. "Did I hurt you? I'm so sorry. You should have said something, you should have—"

"Shhh," I said, putting my finger on his mouth. "You didn't hurt me. You made me real. You made me come. Now, come inside me."

And he did.

Later—much later—he grabbed my hand and led me into the kitchen. Beavis tagged behind, tail happily wagging, his two favorite people holding hands near midnight on a hot July evening.

The *cr-aaaackkk* of lightning startled both of us, and we jumped, and then laughed. The inky sky outside the kitchen window filled with lightning bolts as a summer storm sizzled across the Wasatch Front.

"Are you hungry?"

"No," I said, as I leaned into him, stepping on my tip-toes to touch my lips to his. He returned the kiss, and I savored the taste of him.

"You are hungry," he said against my lips, and I pulled slightly back.

"I guess I missed out on a lot of life. I wasted a lot of

time. You, and Melissa, made me realize that." All it took was Melissa's name, and I felt my mood drop.

"You have to eat. I know seeing Melissa's body was a huge shock, and it wasn't a pretty sight, but you've got to keep your strength up." I didn't need to tell him I was suddenly remembering, feeling, more deeply than I could have imagined, the loss of Melissa, and the shock of seeing her body.

"I can't."

He pulled me to a bar stool and scooted it out, and I sat, as he stood behind me and rubbed my shoulders. We had dressed in what we'd been wearing before our romantic interlude, and his hands were firm, but gentle, through the T-shirt.

We were both quiet for a moment, his hands trying to rub away all the tension that had reentered my body, when he spoke.

"Do you have regrets?"

"No. None. You made me live again, and realize they were wrong. I believed what they said. I should have fought for my life, I should have died before I did something like that. I believed it. I couldn't forgive *me*. I thought I was being punished, so I just shut myself up in a shell and refused to live. You were right when you said that."

"What did you mean, you should have fought until you died?"

"You have to know what I mean. You were raised Mormon, too. The endless chastity lessons, the talks on keeping your virginity, and what a precious gift it was, and how little you were without it."

"Yuck. That sounds terrible. I think they didn't exactly

treat us the same way they did the girls. We always wondered what you were doing in your meetings."

I reflected back to the time spent in Young Women's, and almost cringed, especially as one particular lesson came back to me.

"One time they had us all dressed in white wedding dresses, and they paraded us up and down and then had us write down what we wanted in a husband. I guess wearing white was supposed to drive home that if you weren't virginal, you couldn't wear white. They took our pictures and framed them with the temple in the background, and then gave us this whole chastity lesson, underscored with the quote from Spencer W. Kimball about how it was better to be dead than to lose your virginity."

"What the hell? And we thought you girls were getting together and learning how to cook or something like that. That is some wacky shit. And what do you mean, quote about how it was better to be dead?"

"You don't remember it?"

"God, no, I think I'd remember something like that."

"I can't remember it by heart. We can probably find it on your computer, though. Unless you have some church stuff hidden around here somewhere."

"Nope, fresh out of church stuff. It never really suited me. I have a few things you might consider anti-Mormon, but, hey, let's not go there tonight." After Colt said this, he led me into the other room where his computer sat in a corner. He sat down and booted it up, logged on to the Internet, and then directed me to sit in the chair. It didn't take long for me to Google the quote and find what I was looking for on an LDS Web site.

Also far-reaching is the effect of loss of chastity. Once given or taken or stolen it can never be regained. Even in forced contact such as rape or incest, the injured one is greatly outraged. If she has not cooperated and contributed to the foul deed, she is of course in a more favorable position. There is no condemnation where there is absolutely no voluntary participation. It is better to die in defending one's virtue than to live having lost it without a struggle.

"Damn," Colt said, leaning over my shoulder, so close I could smell his male, musky scent. "Somehow I made it all the way through eighteen years of church without hearing that one!"

"Well, I heard it, and others, and I took them to heart. My mother embroidered them on pillowcases and put them in my room. But when it happened with me . . . with Brian, I didn't really fight back. It was almost an afterthought, you know. Here we were making out and suddenly it was just going too far, and he wouldn't stop. And I didn't scream, or fight hard enough, or . . ."

Colt gently pulled me up from the chair by the shoulders and turned me to face him. "Dammit, Jannie, it doesn't matter. You said no. You told him to stop."

He pulled me in to his chest and held me tightly as he spoke. I could feel the words vibrating through his skin. "Were you mad at Brian, Jannie, or you were mad at God?"

I considered his question. "I was mad at both of them. I still am. I suppose that's part of the problem. How can I go to church, even go inside a church, when I'm so damned angry at the God I was taught to give the ultimate respect? And I did something awful, so He's probably just as mad at me."

Colt sighed and pulled away from me, still holding on to my arms and looking down at me. "Boy, we sure did inherit some twisted beliefs, didn't we?"

"I don't know. I don't know that much about other religions. But I do know that this one—being a Mormon— became something I just couldn't deal with anymore. And I mean physically, as well as mentally. You never told me why you don't go to church. It sounds like you don't believe."

"I stopped going when I was eighteen, for about a month, when I was working out of town on a road crew, and I just never got back to it. But the truth is, Jannie, I never really believed it. I mean, there's good in it. The whole Christian values thing. But, the whole story is just . . . I'm not sure where you are with this, but you need to know where I stand. So much of it is so silly, but it gives my mom a lot of comfort. She loves it. Sunday is her favorite day in the week. She takes trips to Nauvoo and all those old Mormon hot spots with her friends, and she loves it. It works for her. It just didn't work for me. I'm trying to be respectful of her beliefs, and the beliefs of all the people around me, without violating what I believe."

I considered what he said, and thought about my own mother. Her entire life was wrapped up in religion, but in her case it was about stature in the community, about how she appeared to other people. At least it had been, until my father fell off his pedestal and cracked wide open.

"I don't really believe that Mormonism is the only true religion," I ventured, feeling the words roll across my tongue as large and hard to speak as though they were huge boulders. It was blasphemy, and yet I knew it was true.

"Well, that is certainly a big step, and on that note, let's eat," Colt teased, and stood. I rose and followed him back into the kitchen.

I was relieved he didn't feel the need to force me further, to explore my own apostasy, despite the fact I knew it had actually begun years before.

He went over to the cabinet and opened it. His telephone pealed sharply and he sighed and answered it.

"Singer . . . Now? Why now?" He listened for a moment and grimaced. "Fine, I'll be right there." He hung up and looked at me with a solemn expression. "Apparently, Brandon Talon has decided to confess to the murder of his family. He also claims he has information for us about your landlady's murder, but he's holding on to that card hoping to make a deal."

"But he would only do that if he wasn't the one who killed her, right?"

"One would presume that."

"What could he know about it, if he didn't have anything to do with it?"

"I don't know, but I guess I'll find out. I'm calling a squad car to watch the house, but I have to go in."

"No, don't call a squad car. I think I need to check on my mother. She hasn't been doing so great since my dad dumped her. He was supposed to move his things out today, so I should go see her."

"I'll drop you off."

"No, Colt. I will drive myself. I appreciate your concern, but I really need to get on with my life, okay? I'm sure I'll be fine."

"Mike Holt is still out there."

"I'm not a threat to him. Whatever was in that box, he has to know by now that I either gave it to the police or at least told you about it. And that's all I know. Why would he come after me?"

"Because he's sick and twisted? Because his mind isn't working right?"

"He's not going to do that." I stepped forward and put my hand on his shoulder. "I'm going to be okay. If it makes you feel better, I'll call you when I get there."

He tightened his mouth and stared at me, then gave in. I could tell by the slackening of his shoulders.

"I'm not trying to take your independence away, Jannie, but please don't do anything stupid. Please. Go to your mom's house, lock the door, and stay there."

"I will," I promised.

When I arrived at my mother's house, the lights were all blazing. As it was nearing 1:30 A.M., alarm boiled up in me, and I parked the SUV in the driveway and bolted to the front door, where I used my key to let myself in.

"Mom? Mom, are you in here?" I ran down the hallway calling her. Why would every light be on? My mother was an early-to-bed and early-to-rise type, so it made no sense.

I couldn't find her in the living room, or in my father's den, and when I reached the family room my panic was building to a blood-pounding crescendo. There, on the floor, were all of our photo albums, pictures spilling out of them onto the creamy white carpet. A pair of scissors lay on the floor next to the albums, and sprinkled throughout the living room were circle-shaped bits of photo paper. As far as I could tell, she had cut my father's head out of every picture he was in with us.

"Mom, where are you?" I yelled, now desperate to find her. Those albums were her pride and joy. She had spent years putting them together, a loving testament to her perfect Mormon family, living in a perfect house, in a perfect neighborhood, located right smack-dab in the middle of Mormon country.

I found her in the kitchen, sitting calmly at the table, sipping a mug of hot cocoa. "Oh, hi, Jannie. What are you doing here so late?"

"Mom, couldn't you hear me calling you?"

"Um, yeah, I guess I did."

This was a very strange reaction.

"Mom, why didn't you answer me?"

"Well, I thought maybe it was my imagination. You haven't had much use for me for years, so I thought maybe I invented your voice in my head and was just trying to convince myself that you were here looking for me."

I moved around the table and forced her to make eye contact with me. What I saw in her eyes told me she was on something, some kind of medication. *Angela!*

"Mom, what did you take?"

"Oh, nothing much. Angela gave me something for the anxiety. I took her home from the hospital, you know, and got her settled in. Apparently, Pete has had a heart attack. Mild, but he'll be hospitalized for a while. Somehow it slipped out that my husband was a scum-sucking, bottom-dealing cheater, and she offered me something to help me sleep."

"Mom, what did you take?" My mother had spent her entire life using herbal cures and never taking anything stronger than a Tylenol, except for the times she had spent in the hospital having first my brother and then me.

"Oh, I don't know. It's something that starts with a *z*, I think. Anyway, it made me feel so nice and cozy, I decided to go through our old photo albums, and then I made myself a cup of cocoa."

"How many did you take?"

"Just two, dear. I do think I'm ready for bed now, though."

She stood, woozily, and staggered a bit, turning to head toward the hallway that led to the stairs. She wore threadbare red flannel pajamas two or three sizes too big and a pair of fuzzy pink slippers. I was alarmed. The pajamas must have been my father's, and the slippers looked like an old pair I had left behind when I moved.

"Aren't you a little warm, Mom?"

"Oh, I was so cold, that's why I made the hot cocoa." She took a few more shuffling steps forward and then lurched a bit. I rushed to her and led her out into the hallway and up the stairs to her room.

"Do you have more of those pills, Mom?"

"In the bathroom," she said, idly motioning with a limp-wristed fling of her hand.

I tucked her into bed, and she moaned a bit, then flopped from one side to the next.

"Get some sleep, Mom," I said.

"Jannie?"

"Yes?"

"Why did this happen?"

So much had happened, I wasn't sure which "this" she was referring to, but I was going to take a guess and assume she meant my father's infidelity and betrayal.

"Bad things happen, Mom. They happen to everyone, no matter who you are."

"It wasn't supposed to be that way. I did everything I was supposed to. My whole life I've lived like I was supposed to, paid my tithing, accepted the callings, went to church faithfully. It wasn't supposed to be this way."

Her words made me recall what Melissa had written in her journal.

I cannot handle this. It's all a pack of lies. I don't under-stand why all of this has happened to me. Where did it come from? And why? All of my life I have striven to be a good person, to read my scriptures, to follow God's plan for me. I had a temple wedding, and I go to church every Sunday. So why has God handed me this travesty? What did I do to de-serve it?

"Mom, I don't really know why. I just know that you can do everything you think is right and still bad things happen. It doesn't mean you are bad. It just means you're human."

"That's not what they teach us," she said, her voice a lazy, slurring drawl. "That's not what they've always said. If you live right, Satan can't come into your life. You're supposed to be blessed when you do the right things."

"Maybe it was all just a myth, Mom. Something some-body made up to get everyone to live a certain way, or do a certain thing. Because the bottom line is, people are just human, and everybody screws up, and innocent people get hurt."

There was a silence and I thought perhaps my mother had fallen off to sleep, so I stepped quietly to the door, but as I walked out, I heard her speak again.

"Jannie, promise me you aren't leaving the church. Promise me. It was bad enough learning that you hadn't been in years. I can't take that, on top of everything else. This is all your father's fault. He's the one who said we had to ignore the whole thing with Brian. After what the bishop told us, we figured it was both of you. It's his fault. Don't leave because of him."

Her words stunned me, even though I had already learned they knew about my assault and why I wanted nothing to do with Brian.

And in that instant it all became clear. I had already parted ways with this strange religion years before. The temple ceremonies, the relentless reliance on men to do God's will, the belief that a woman needed a man to get into heaven. I had fallen for it all, hook, line, and sinker, and it had totally disabled me, made me unable to deal with my own misfortune and get on with my life.

While I was far from a doubting Thomas, I also knew that Mormonism no longer worked for me—if it ever had.

A strong desire to talk to Colt, who had the same roots as I did, came over me. Where did he stand on this? Where did other disaffected Mormons stand? I knew a few, but most were angry, bitter, and strident in their criticism of the church. How could I possibly fit in there, among those angry ex-Saints? I didn't think I was angry at the church. Or was I?

"Mom, I think I left a long time ago. I'm sorry to disappoint you. But do you really believe one religion will work for everyone?"

"If it's the true religion, and, Jannie, it's Jesus Christ's true and restored Gospel. I know it's true. I promise you that if you will just pray, and talk to God honestly, and . . .

Oh, I don't know. Things didn't work out the way I planned, but that doesn't make the church wrong, it just means the people in it are human, and make mistakes."

"I wish it was just the people, Mom. But I don't think that's it. I don't know where I stand right now, I really don't. I only know that it doesn't work for me."

"But you can't walk away just because it doesn't work for you, Jannie." I winced as I heard the tears begin to choke her voice. "If you know something is true, you can't just walk away."

"Then I must not know it's true, Mom. Please, can't you just let me walk away? This religion is not working for me, Mom. I don't want to be an angry. I've met some former Mormons, and they are filled with anger and hatred toward the church, and all it stands for, because no one will let them go. Then everyone asks why they won't leave the church alone. They won't leave it alone because it won't leave them alone. Please, Mom, don't turn me into that. I don't want that for myself."

"Oh, Jannie," was all she said as she sniffled and wept for a moment. I considered going to her again, but soon a soft snore emanated from the bed, and I realized she had fallen asleep.

CHAPTER FORTY

I descended the stairs and headed toward the kitchen, and felt a soft breeze wafting across my face. Puzzled, I looked to see the front door standing ajar, my purse dropped where I had left it, on the floor of the entryway.

I stopped, and prickles rose on the back of my neck. Had I not shut the door tightly when I first ran into the house, searching desperately for my mother? I remembered shutting it, but I had been in and out of this house so many times, it could have been automatic to believe I just shut the door.

I looked around and listened closely, but could hear nothing. The cold prickles continued to travel up and down my spine, and I tiptoed to the door and quietly shut it, then quickly turned the door lock and the dead bolt.

Of course, if someone had come in, I had just securely locked them inside.

I picked up my purse and fished inside it for both my cell phone and the gun I always carried, and then I returned as quietly as possible back down the hall toward the kitchen, gun pointed out. My heart racing, I disengaged the safety. Things had gotten serious. I could afford to take no chances.

I rounded the corner into the kitchen, where I saw a large man rummaging through the refrigerator.

"Get your hands up!" I screamed. "Hands up or I'll shoot."

I knew it was Mike the moment I saw him, but he looked very different. He had many days' growth of beard on his face, and his eyes were wild, the irises small, giving him a feral look. By the smell, I could tell he hadn't showered for days, and his clothes were dirty and torn.

He didn't put his hands up.

"Mike, why are you here? You need to go to the police and turn yourself in."

With my left hand, I was trying to fumble with my cell phone and unlock the keys. I'd been forced to add keylock when I found that my phone consistently called my mother whenever I stuck it in my purse. After talking to her countless more times than I cared to, I had given in and locked my keys. Now I was fumbling trying to figure out how to unlock it and somehow dial 911 without Mike noticing.

"I'm not guilty, Jannie. I already told you that. But they don't believe me. They think I did it."

He turned and reached into the fridge, as though I were not pointing a gun at him, and pulled out the milk, drinking from the jug as though he had never used a glass in his life. In a matter of days, he had become a wild animal.

"God, that tastes good."

"Where have you been hiding? Haven't you eaten?"

"Nothing but leftovers and Dumpster food. I had fast food for a while, but they froze my bank accounts, so I couldn't get money out anymore. I'm being treated like a fucking criminal, all because my wife couldn't keep her pants on."

I winced and felt my face harden as he casually dismissed, with such derision, the woman I believed he had killed.

"You should turn yourself in, Mike. If you're innocent, then you'll be exonerated, and you can get on with your life."

"I am innocent! Aren't you listening? Melissa left me that day. She left, and I left, and the next thing I knew the police were questioning me, then people starting popping up dead, and then . . . And then everyone decided I did it. I was guilty, just because I failed a few classes."

"A few classes? Mike, you've been pretending to go to school for four years when you weren't doing anything of the kind. You pretended to be applying to medical school. You've been lying for years. Of course they think you did it."

I had given up on the keys of my cell phone and resorted to prayer, instead. *Please, Mom, hear the ruckus. Please, God, don't let me die. Please, Mom, hear the ruckus and call 911. Don't teeter down here and fall down the stairs, breaking your neck and making things even worse . . .*

"I was only trying to make Melissa happy. To make her stay with me. She wanted a successful husband, and I tried, but I couldn't . . . I just couldn't . . ."

He broke down then, giant, body-wracking sobs shaking his frame. Despite all that had happened, I found myself wanting to move forward, to put my arms around him, to comfort him. It was hard for me to believe I had sometimes been slightly envious of Mike and Melissa. He'd seemed so together, so strong. Brian had always paled in comparison. So many of my childhood memories had pieces of Mike in them, I fought with myself to stay strong and focused. For an instant, I wanted to believe him.

I slowly lowered the gun, although not all the way.

"I didn't kill her, Jannie. I didn't. She was having an affair, and I found out, and then . . ."

"Mike. Turn yourself in. For your sake, and your parents' sake, turn yourself in. Brian will help you get it straightened out. He can do that."

"No, I can't. I can't." He reached one of his arms up and wiped his nose, like a kindergarten boy, and scrubbed furiously at his face. "I have to find out who did it first, so they won't blame me. I have to do that. Why did she want so much from me, Jannie? Why did she expect so much?"

"It was what we all expected, Mike. You never seemed to have a problem living up to it before."

"It's always been a lie. Always. I've always just gotten by, and nobody could figure it out. I even started believing it myself, until I flunked out. And then I couldn't tell her. I couldn't tell anyone."

"Mike, let's call Brian. He'll know what to do . . . Let me help you."

"You want to help me?"

"Of course. We've been friends for years. We grew up across the street from each other."

"You don't believe I killed Melissa?"

I hesitated, then cursed myself as I saw his face harden, and he took a step toward me. The sudden ringing of my cell phone caused me to start and drop the gun, and I cursed silently as Mike's head followed the gun as it hit the floor and skittered toward him. He made a step as though to pick it up, and I hurriedly answered my cell phone.

"Help!" I screamed into it. "Help me. Sixty-five forty-two Edgewood Drive. Call the police. Help me!"

He lunged forward and grabbed for the phone, knocking it out of my hand with a heavy swipe that left my arm aching. The phone flew through the air and hit the wall, then fell to the ground. I prayed it was unharmed.

"You bitch! You are just like her. You didn't really want to help me." He grabbed me by both wrists, so tight I thought they would snap, and I fought to keep back a scream, now afraid my mother, in her drugged state, *would* awaken just enough to toddle down here and directly into danger.

"Please, Mike, let go. You're hurting me."

From somewhere in the distance I heard the wail of a siren, and Mike heard it, too. He cursed again, then let go of my wrists, heading for the back door and out into the night. I rushed to the door and slammed it shut, locking the dead bolt and the knob lock, and then dropped to the ground, sobbing, holding my aching wrists.

The insistent pealing of the doorbell told me help had arrived. I forced myself to rise and run to the front door, carefully peering through the keyhole to see two uniformed officers standing there.

"He went out the back," I told them in a rush of words and breath, and one of them headed toward the back door while the other hesitated, asking me if I was okay.

"Go find him. I just want this to end."

Two more police cars pulled up, and neighbors began to exit their houses, most dressed in robes and nightwear, all peering over at the home of Hugh and Evelyn Fox, a house that had already been the subject of a fair amount of gossip in the past few days.

After I spoke to the two officers taking the report, I scurried over to pick up my cell phone, seeing that it had plenty of bars and appeared to be still working, and I hurried upstairs and checked on my mother, finding her safely and softly snoring away.

As I returned back downstairs, my gaze caught that of Colt Singer, who stood next to the uniformed officers, asking them questions with a hard, intent look on his face. He hurried over to me. And put his hands on my shoulders.

"It doesn't matter where you go, trouble finds you, Jannie Fox. What am I going to do? I thought you'd be safe here. I'm so sorry." His voice lowered an octave. "I'm so sorry. I misjudged this guy. I didn't really think he'd come after you. I figured he'd know that was too dangerous. But I've seen enough in this line of work that I called to check on you."

"Don't blame yourself," I said to him. "Please, don't blame yourself. He's still lying to himself, and to everyone else. He still wants everyone to believe he's innocent. Even with all the evidence, he thinks he can lie his way out of it. Poor Melissa. My poor, poor friend."

Colt pulled me to him tightly, ignoring the looks of the uniformed officers, and then asked about my mother.

"She borrowed some pills from Angela, Melissa's mother. She's out cold. My mother is not a diehard when it comes to medication."

"I'm taking you home, so we need to find someone to stay with her. I'm taking you to *my* home."

I thought about saying no, even though I wanted to say

yes. But I knew my mother would not need me again tonight. I also knew the house would be guarded safely, because I would be calling both my father and Jack. For years, they had both expounded that a man ruled the house, protected the house, protected the family. My father, who had abandoned those duties, and whom I suspected would soon be seeing the inside of a church court, having to explain his behavior, would be coming here tonight and taking care of his responsibilities.

"Dad, this is Jannie."

I'd called his cell phone, having no other way to contact him.

"Jannie, why are you calling me so late?" His voice was sleepy, and I heard the murmur of a female voice, quietly asking, "Who is it?"

"Dad, you are such a creep. You are sleeping with your girlfriend? You make me sick."

"Janica, did you call just to heap abuse on me?"

"I called to tell you that Mike Holt broke into our house and threatened me, and that you need to come home and stay with Mom to make sure she's safe."

"No, Jannie, no," I heard my mother say, and turned to see her standing in the doorway. "I do not want that man in my house. And this will be my house, mark my words. Call Jack, instead. Call anyone. But not him. Never again."

"Never mind, Dad. Never mind. Mom doesn't want you here."

"But what do you mean, Mike Holt broke in? Did he hurt you? Are you okay?"

"You lost the right to be concerned about me years ago, Dad, when you blew off Brian's behavior. I called because

I thought you would care, but I think I was wrong, and Mom doesn't want you here. Go back to sleep."

I disconnected the phone and looked my mother in the eye. She looked a lot more coherent than she had when I'd last locked gazes with her.

"Mom, I'm sorry. I was just so mad at him, I wanted him to know what had happened, and I didn't even think . . . I'm sorry. I'll call Jack."

"No, don't call Jack, either. I'll be okay. Time to stand on my own two feet, huh? If I'm going to be alone, a single woman, I guess I better get used to it."

"There will be plenty of time for that, Mom. Besides, Jack needs to know."

I got on the phone and dialed my brother's number. My sister-in-law, Karin, answered on the third ring. Jack slept like a bear in hibernation. It took a lot to rouse him.

I hurriedly explained to Karin what had happened, and she immediately volunteered to come stay with my mother.

She didn't ask Jack first, a huge step for her.

My entire family was undergoing massive sea changes.

Colt had been talking with the uniformed officers, including the one who had gone out the back door after Mike, but he walked back into the kitchen where I stood talking with my mother, then stopped, as though afraid he was interfering with something.

"Mom, Colt will assign officers to stand guard over the house. I really don't think Mike will be back. It's too dangerous. And Karin's coming over to stay with you."

"Officers standing guard sounds good," she said, staring at all the people, including the crime lab techs, traipsing through her house. "But Karin should stay home and take care of her family. I'll lock up tight. Jannie, you're staying, right?"

I hesitated, guilt overcoming me. I should stay. I should be here to make sure my mother was all right.

"No, I guess you're not," she said. "You've grown up. Of course you're not staying. Can I talk to you for a minute, Jannie? Just you and me?"

Colt nodded and left the kitchen, and my mother pulled me to the table and we both sat down.

The words she spoke next surprised me.

"I'm sorry, Jannie. I'm sorry I didn't do something more about Brian when it happened. I'm sorry I let your father and the bishop tell me it was less than what it was. It destroyed you, didn't it? I'm sorry I didn't see that."

Her words brought old emotions to the surface, and I felt as though a spear had arced through my heart.

"It's okay, Mom. Water under the bridge, right?"

"No. Someday soon we will sit down and talk about it. And everything else. When it's not so raw. When it doesn't hurt so much."

I just nodded my head. I knew my mother well. My leaving the church would not now, and probably never, be left alone. She would be after me until the end of my days to return to my roots, to my religion, to what I "knew" was right.

But just for tonight she would let it be.

And just for tonight, I would do the same.

CHAPTER FORTY-ONE

After Karin arrived, we left my mother with two police officers guarding her house, and she and my sister-in-law locked up tight inside. I knew she was probably terrified; she was alone—at least emotionally—for the first time in her entire life. She had gone straight from her family home to her married home, and had never once lived on her own. She had never understood my desire to do so, even though she didn't know—then—the secret I was hiding, the secret that was so much easier to bury when no one was around to see my odd behavior. For my mother, there had always been a man—a priesthood holder—to turn to for guidance.

Now, though, she would have to learn, as she said, to stand on her own two feet. She would have to live alone, although when I considered my father's behavior, I figured she must have been alone, in many ways other than physically, for a longer time than I had understood. Probably a longer time than she had understood, too.

Colt followed me as I drove back to his house, my stomach doing somersaults of guilt—and something else—the entire way there. I had forged something with this man I had never thought possible. Where would it go from here?

When his cell phone rang, I knew it would go nowhere, at least tonight.

"Singer."

I knew from the look on his face he would be dropping me off and going back out. When he hung up, he gave me a look of regret, as though he had known where my errant thoughts had been wandering. Perhaps his thoughts had also been wandering there, into his bedroom, where earlier we had made love.

"I'm sorry, Jannie. I want to spend more time with you, when I'm not being constantly called out. I want to really get to know you. I want to spend time with you when the world isn't filled with chaos and anger and hurt and betrayal. I hope you feel the same."

I did.

His next words stunned me so deeply it was as though I had been physically punched.

"Brandon Talon just committed suicide in the Salt Lake City jail. He hung himself."

The suicide investigation that had called Colt out in the middle of the night would take hours. I settled in on his couch, Beavis at my feet, and popped in a DVD I had found, minus the case, sitting on top of the VHS/DVD player next to the television. It turned out to be the six-hour miniseries *Lonesome Dove*. Not wanting to fall asleep until he returned—and since Westerns weren't exactly my thing—I ejected it and looked around for the case, which I couldn't find.

I set it back where I had found it and looked for other movies. I was unsuccessful, and so I turned the power off on the machine and scanned the local channels with the remote control. Nothing much was on, except for old *Seinfield* and *Friends* reruns, all of which I had seen a million times.

A breaking news announcement on KSL caught my eye, and I turned up the volume.

"Police have confirmed that Brandon Talon, an inmate at the Salt Lake City Jail, committed suicide this evening, shortly after 1:30 A.M. Talon had recently been charged with the murder of his wife, her mother, and two children. In addition, charges were expected to be filed shortly against Talon for the murder of Salt Lake City resident Ida Miller, who was murdered in an apartment located behind her home. Police believe that Talon killed Miller after she surprised him breaking into the apartment looking for the woman who rented it. The woman, whom police are not naming at this time, was a domestic violence counselor with the YWCA, and it is believed Talon was angry at her for interfering in his marriage."

I listened to the rest of the information and shook my head. Colt hadn't told me they had the evidence to charge Talon with Ida's death, and in fact, the man had hinted that he had information about it. I supposed he had been trying to pin it on someone else, most likely Mike Holt.

There was too much death, too much misery, too much betrayal surrounding me, and I wanted to escape it, wanted it all to go away.

I wandered over to Colt's bookshelf and looked through the titles, picking up one called *No Man Knows My History* by Fawn M. Brodie. I, of course, had heard of this book. It was universally reviled, at least in my small, closed

Mormon world, as lies and nonsense. The author had been excommunicated for daring to write it.

I opened it and quickly scanned the pages, my heart racing as though I had picked up a piece of vile pornography. I almost laughed at the way my mind worked, even now, at age twenty-six.

I set the Brodie book aside, telling myself I wouldn't want to read it and knowing that I would, and further scanned the titles on Colt's shelf. There was a copy of something called *Losing a Lost Tribe: Native Americans, DNA, and the Mormon Church.* A quick glance told me it was about DNA evidence that refuted LDS claims that Native Americans were descendants of the Jews. The last book I picked up was called *An Insider's View of Mormon Origins* by Grant Palmer. Did I really want to know this information? Did I want my already broken faith to be completely shattered and irreparable?

I understood why they were here on Colt's shelf. He was raised in the religion, and he was a detective. Of course he would investigate what he found puzzling and questionable. But me—should I do the same?

The pealing of my cell phone pulled my attention from the books, and I scurried over to the end table by the couch where I had set my purse earlier. I looked at the caller ID and didn't recognize the number.

"Hello?"

"Jannie, it's Brian. Mike just called me, and he wants to turn himself in. But first he wants to talk to us, to explain. I'm here at the bishop's office at our old church. His request is that he turn himself in to me, as one of his lawyers, with the bishop and you present. I've already called the police, and they are on their way. Will you come?"

"God, Brian, it's so late. And why does he want me there?" I was relieved that Mike was going to turn himself in, that soon the nightmare—at least this part of it—would be over. But I wasn't in the mood for him to continue to try to convince me he was innocent.

Brian sighed softly, and when he spoke again, his tone was gentle. "Jannie, I wanted to believe it wasn't him. He kept proclaiming his innocence, but he's finally ready to tell the truth. And he won't do it if you aren't here. He wants you—and me—to understand why it happened. He wants us to forgive him, to understand the part that Melissa had in this. That's what he said. I'm just so shocked that it came to this. But I guess after Talon killed himself, Mike just snapped. Realizing he wouldn't be charged with the other murders, because the police believe that Talon committed them, he felt secure that he wouldn't be railroaded, but he can't live with the guilt of Melissa's murder anymore. Jannie?" His voice softened.

"Yes, Brian?"

"I'm sorry I had to tell you that our old friend did kill Melissa. I'm sorry. I'm sorry for so many things." A slight sob escaped him, and a part of my heart, a tiny part that was still reserved for him, after all the years I had spent with him, pulsed.

There was a brief rustle as Brian's sobbing lessened, and then someone else spoke.

"Janica?" The voice was slightly familiar. "This is Bishop Burton." I'd recognized the voice of my old neighbor Ward Burton, an ER physician at LDS Hospital. Burton, I knew because every conversation with my mother had included something church-related, had been appointed bishop the year before.

"Mike needs your forgiveness," he continued. "Brian's pretty upset right now, too, and he could use your support as his best friend turns himself in to the police. It seems very important to Mike that you be here. Will you come?"

Burton's tones were harsh and slightly cold, but I didn't know him very well, and this was not a good situation to find oneself in.

"I'll be there in about twenty minutes."

I hung up my cell phone and went to the bathroom to tidy myself. In sweatpants and a T-shirt, I wasn't exactly dressed up, but this wasn't an occasion that required dressiness, was it? Besides, it was late and I needed to go now.

I left Colt's house and locked the door behind me, knowing that since this was his case, I would not return before he did. After I got into the SUV, I drove toward the Canyon View Stake Center, quickly hitting the automatic dial key on my phone where I had stored Colt's cell phone number. It went straight to voice mail, and I told him where I was going. I left him a message to call me, explaining about the telephone call and urging him to hurry to the scene, then hung up.

When I pulled up to the church parking lot, I could see the lights inside, but there were no police cars. I quickly locked my doors. Despite the fact both Brian and the bishop had assured me I would be safe, I wasn't setting foot inside that church until I knew the police had arrived.

When my window shattered and the gun was pressed against my forehead I screamed, and then a big hand clasped over my mouth. The rancid, unwashed smell told me it was Mike.

I stopped screaming, and he slowly removed his hand,

whispering to me to keep quiet, cocking the gun for emphasis. He undid the lock, useless now that the window was shattered, and opened the door with his left hand, the right still holding the gun pointed at my head.

"Get out, and come with me," he told me. I complied, not wanting him to kill me—as I believed he had done to Melissa, the woman he promised to love and protect for time and all eternity.

Instead of heading me toward the church, which I expected, he pulled me away from it, toward a smashed-up black truck—painfully familiar because of my accident.

"God, Mike, you ran into me with that truck. What the hell is up with that? What has happened to you? What has happened to all of us? Were you trying to kill me, too?"

"Kill you, too?" Mike's face hardened, his eyes scrunched up, and then, as if all the muscles holding him together suddenly weakened, he seemed to deflate. His face softened and tears seeped from the corners of his eyes.

"God, Jannie, how did this happen? How did you lose so much faith in me that you think I'd kill Melissa? I loved Melissa! I loved her too much. I sure as hell would never kill her."

He let go of me and swiped at his eyes. He looked up at the sky for a moment, as though to regain composure, then back at me. I should have taken the moment—his pause and loss of control—to run, but something was wrong here, and I wanted him to tell me what it was. I wanted to know. I felt like I had to know.

When he looked at me again, I saw nothing but defeat in his face. "I wasn't trying to kill you, or hurt you, Jannie. I was trying to keep you from going to the newspaper with your allegations that I killed Melissa."

"Newspaper? What are you talking about?"

"You were down there by the Tribune building, and I had to stop you. I needed time to explain, to tell you . . . but I didn't realize you had lost all faith in me. I didn't realize that it was too late."

"You need to turn yourself in, Mike. This needs to stop."

"So you can convince them I did it? Why did you do it, Jannie? Why would you lie about me like that?"

"Mike, what are you talking about? Brian said you admitted you killed her. What the hell is going on here?"

"Yeah, right, Brian said that. You think I'm that dumb? He knows I'm innocent. He still believes in me, even if no one else does. He's the one who he loaned me the truck. I needed a way to get around so people wouldn't recognize the car."

My mind reeled as I tried to make sense of all that had happened. I dug my feet in and refused to move, even though Mike was tugging at me, and the gun was still pointed at my head.

"Where are you taking me, and why, Mike? I don't understand."

"I'm going to convince you I'm innocent, or die trying. I did *not* kill Melissa! Even though she cheated on me, I loved her."

"Mike—"

A shout went up from the doors of the church, and I saw Brian and another man run out the doors toward us. Mike turned and watched them, confusion tingeing his features.

"Why is he coming over here? He said you were going to be here, so why is he . . . ?"

Mike turned to me and let go of my arm, but didn't

drop the gun, just as Brian called out, "No, Mike, no, don't do it!"

"What? What are you talking about?" Mike yelled, swinging the gun in Brian's direction.

A shot rang out. I winced but quickly realized no bullet had come close to me. Instead, I heard a thump as Mike's big solid body hit the ground. I gasped and ran to him, checking for a pulse while he looked up at me, his eyes cloudy and puzzled.

"Wh . . . why? Why did he . . . ?"

When the stillness hardened his face, all movement stopped, I knew he was dead.

"Where are the police?" I asked Brian, as he came up behind me, staring at the friend he had just shot. I was shocked to see him carrying the gun. I didn't know he even knew how to shoot one.

"They'll be here any second. I gave them the time Mike said he would be here. I didn't expect him this early. I was sure they'd be here first."

That made little sense to me, as I believed the police would have immediately come to the scene to stake it out, just to be there when Mike did arrive.

The bishop moved in behind Brian, panting as he stared at the lifeless body.

"Oh, this is terrible," Bishop Burton said, going to lean over to check for a pulse or signs of life in Mike. "I'm afraid he's dead. What a huge tragedy."

"When did you start carrying a gun?" I asked Brian, staring at him sharply.

"I've been carrying one for four years now, Jannie. I'm a lawyer. Sometimes I make enemies. I have to keep safe. You should be thankful I do carry a gun. I just had to kill my best friend to save you. Oh, God, this is awful." He put his left hand on his forehead, his right relaxed down by his side, still gripping the gun.

I wasn't thankful. Something in Mike's behavior, especially after he saw Brian running toward him, was bothering me. And where were the police?

"Mike didn't act like he was going to turn himself in, Brian. He kept telling me that he was innocent, and he was determined to convince me of that, because he believed I would turn him in to the police. You said he told you he was guilty."

"He did. He was confused, Jannie. I mean, look at him. He's been on the run for days, he rarely eats, he smells like a sewer. I'm surprised he made it this long without cracking up. I told you he confessed to me."

The bishop stared at both of us, a puzzled look on his face, and then he pulled a cell phone out of his pocket.

"I'm going to call the police, make sure they're on their way," he said.

Brian reached out and swatted the phone away and yelled, "I told you I called them. They'll be here any minute."

Bishop Burton walked backward away from Brian, shock reflected in his face as he inched away from the scene. Brian's eyes were on the bishop, and I slowly stood up from the position I had taken over Mike's body and began backing away myself. I still wasn't completely clear as to what was going on, but I knew one thing.

Mike was either innocent or had not been guilty of Melissa's death alone. Brian had set him up to come here and then brutally murdered him.

"Don't move!" Brian screamed at the bishop, and I

heard the man speak gently, both hands out, trying to placate him, although I couldn't hear his words through the ocean roaring in my ears. I continued to back up toward my car, hoping I could get inside and turn the engine on and speed away. The keys were still in the ignition, as I had not yet removed them when Mike smashed the window.

"Brian, you don't want to do this."

"This is your fault," Brian said harshly, turning to me, and I froze where I was. "Once again you didn't believe me. You believed Mike. Just like always. Good old Jannie, no respect at all for Brian. You believed Mike!"

I saw the bishop turn and run, and I hoped he'd get away before Brian saw him. That hope was dashed when Brian spun around and fired two shots at the man's fleeing back. The bishop dropped to the ground, and Brian turned back to me, pointing the gun.

"Boy, this is a mess now. This is not how it was supposed to work out at all." He sounded so defeated I almost felt sorry for him. Almost.

"How was it supposed to work, Brian? I don't understand what is going on here."

He just shook his head and gestured me to the gun Mike had been carrying, now lying on the tarry parking lot. "Pick it up."

With his gun aimed at my head, I did as I was told. What he did next shocked me. He walked to me and took the gun Mike had been carrying and trained it on me. Then he took his gun, wiped it off on his pants leg, and placed it where Mike's had been. Next he pushed close to me and poked the gun in my back, pushing me toward the wardhouse.

"Brian, why are you doing this?"

"Just shut up. I'm thinking."

When we got to the wardhouse door, I reluctantly opened it, and he pushed me in, toward the bishop's office.

"Well, you totally screwed up another one, Jannie. This would have worked if you weren't so fucking stubborn, so determined to punish me for something that happened so many years ago. It would have worked."

I stopped where I was and turned to face him. "What would have worked?"

"I save you from Mike, you see what a loser he was—what a murderer he was—and finally realize I'm the only one for you. I always have been. I saved you."

"You saved me?"

"I saved you from Mike."

"Brian, you set this whole thing up. Now you've killed the bishop, Mike, and I have a sneaking suspicion you have no intention of letting me walk away. What do you mean, you saved me? You couldn't have done any worse than if you had killed Melissa yourself."

When he winced at my harsh words, it all came to me. With the realization came a cold terror, slowly spreading from the base of my spine in both directions. Mike had been telling the truth. He hadn't murdered Melissa, Brian had.

But why?

"I told you I was going to save you. Save you from Mike. I tried to save Melissa, too, but she wouldn't listen. Mike was nobody. A complete nobody, and you all fawned over him like he was the next Jesus Christ." I gasped at the harsh words. "Melissa came to me when she found out about all Mike's lies, and she was done. It was over. She was walking, and since you'd left me behind, I figured she was the next best thing. We got a little too close, went a little too far, kind of what happened between you and me, and suddenly she was running back to Mike. She was going to tell him, the dumb bitch. I couldn't let that happen."

Melissa had slept with Brian. The thought filled me with all kinds of emotions I could barely identify, but that was secondary to my sudden need to escape, to get away from him. But how could I do that when my knees were shaking so severely, my vision blurring, my hands refusing to cooperate, my breathing rapid as the familiar panic attack set in on me?

Not now. Please, not now. It's not Brian that brings this on, it's you. Stall. Stall for time.

"But the police determined Melissa was killed in her house, on her mattress." I forced myself to speak; willed my voice to be calm. "Surely you didn't sleep with her there. Surely . . ."

Brian laughed harshly. "Oh, surely. Please, Jannie, don't be an idiot. Mike was working nights. Melissa was always alone. It was the simplest way. The only way. The police would only look at Mike as the suspect. The blood was hers. The mattress was theirs. It couldn't have been easier."

"But why dump the mattress, then? Why take it out of the house?"

There was silence for a moment, and when he spoke I heard the dark twang of mental distress in his voice. "That wasn't me. Mike's not smart. He never has been. But he was smart enough to realize that he would be the obvious suspect. When he found the bloody mattress, and put two and two together, he realized he was in deep trouble. Melissa was gone, there was blood all over the mattress, and they'd had a roaring fight the neighbors had to have heard. He panicked, and dumped the mattress and bought a new one. At first I was mad, but then I realized he'd done me a favor. It made him look even more guilty. And it's hard to hide a bloody mattress."

I felt a cloud of fog seep into my brain with each cold, calculated word he spoke. In the past few days I'd come to believe that my panic attacks were not caused by Brian. It had allowed me to let my guard down. I'd been wrong.

I could only hope I wasn't dead wrong.

CHAPTER FORTY-TWO

Instinct kicked in, and I forced myself to breathe, slowly, in and out through my mouth. When I was slightly less dizzy and nauseated, I moved a step toward Brian.

"You did save me, didn't you?" I said, determined to do whatever was necessary, to say whatever was needed, to get out of this alive. "Brian, I'm sorry. I just didn't get it. I'm sorry I didn't understand how far you were willing to go for me."

"Too late, Jannie," he said, chuckling with a forced, canned sound that set my teeth on edge and stopped me from moving even one step closer. "It's too late. Self-righteous little Jannie, couldn't even forgive me for a passionate slip, even though we were always destined to be together. No, not Jannie. Couldn't forgive me that. I had to go to *these lengths* just to bring you back around, and still you managed to *totally* fuck it up!"

Of course, none of it would be Brian's fault. Now that I realized just how far his madness had gone, I was able to quell the shaking and come up with a plan. I had to escape.

"Is that the police?" I asked, cocking my head. "I hear sirens."

"Good try, Jannie, but I didn't ever call them. I never intended to do it until it was all over and the bishop was comforting you. You should never have figured it out, except you're such a bitch you didn't trust me quite enough to make it work."

The irony of Brian's words seemed to totally elude him, I realized. I was right to never trust him. But I'd been wrong about so many other things. This had never been about Mike, or Melissa, or even me, really. It was about Brian and his twisted belief that as long as he lived his life right, everything would come to him. Everything he wanted. He was a flawed human being with a God complex. When those things he expected didn't happen, like a god, he set about rectifying the situation.

I had seriously messed with his plan when I walked away from our projected life together. Now I would probably pay with *my* life.

He stood before me now, shaking his head with disgust, and I looked around for a weapon—anything—to throw at him and distract him. We stood in the narrow hallway that led from the outside door into the chapel. On each side were closed doors—classrooms and utility closets—and the one door that was ajar and lighted I knew must be the bishop's office. I started inching toward it.

"Brian, let's just sit down and talk. Please?"

If I could get him inside the office, I could find a paperweight, or a letter opener, or something to defend myself or, at the very least, catch him off guard so I could escape.

"Too late, Jannie. You saw too much. You know now. It

would have worked if you hadn't been so damned untrusting, but I should have known better than to expect any less of you. You should never have been my eternal mate. I don't understand why God had me wasting my time with you!"

"Who the hell is that?" I yelled out suddenly, pointing to the doorway. Brian turned to look, and I took off running in the other direction, down the darkened hallway, pushing through the big wooden doors that led into the chapel. I ran up one of the aisles, heading for the side doors that were conveniently placed on each side of the chapel for ease in getting funeral caskets out, but I heard a shot before I could get that far; I dropped to the ground and crawled into the middle section of pews.

I heard soft footsteps that would slow then stop as he checked each row, looking for me. When he got close to the long wooden bench under which I hid, I carefully crawled backward several rows, making sure to stay low and not bump my head or other body part on the pews. I wasn't worried so much about hurting myself as I was about giving away my position.

"Come out, Sarah," he whispered, a loud stage whisper, even though I knew we were all alone in the wardhouse. I winced as he used the name I would never, ever answer to, even if the bowels of the world opened up, threatening to eat me alive, and it was the only way to redemption. Why had no one warned me of the power I would give up if I lived the life of a good Mormon woman? Why did so many other women not care that it happened to them?

"Jannie, this is stupid." He wasn't whispering anymore. "I'm going to find you, so you might as well come out. You've always belonged to me. You are *mine*. I know your secret name! It wouldn't matter who else you were with, I knew it first. You should have just given in to me. No one else is going to have you."

The sound of his voice told me he was getting close, so I slowly crawled backward under the pews, trying not to breathe or make any noise, my elbows scraping on the carpet, leaving rug burns that seared through me like fire. I was hoping he would continue to move forward, thinking I was heading for the side doors to try to escape.

The breathing moved away, and I released my own breath, slightly.

"Well, Jannie," Brian said, his voice a boom from the front of the chapel. "This could take all night. And I'm tired. No one knows you're here, and I can't really kill you in here, because that would be too hard to explain. And since so much time is passing, the story is getting too complicated so let's just get this over with. Come out, my sweet Sarah. You were born mine, and you're going to die mine. And no one will ever be the wiser. No one. I was enjoying this game of cat and mouse, but time's up."

Brian was wrong. He was jealous of Colt Singer, but he didn't know I had grown close enough to the detective that I had called him and told him where I was going.

I reached the back pew and inched out into the open. I knew he couldn't see me from the front of the chapel, where he had last been.

The lights, when they came on, were blinding; I blinked slightly, then tried to head back for the pews, where I would be slightly covered, but it was too late. Brian was there, panting, having run from the front of the chapel, where he must have been standing on the riser, to the spot where he saw me crouched. His gun pointed at my head, he ordered me to get up.

"You're not a very bright girl, Jannie. You never were. Did you really think you could get away from me? But despite your shortcomings, I loved you anyway. I would have taken care of you. I would have taken care of the baby. It was my job as priesthood holder. But you killed it. You killed my baby. You owed me another one."

The words were a hiss of sheer hatred, and they knocked the air out of me.

CHAPTER FORTY-THREE

The fact I'd been pregnant, that Brian's actions had resulted in a child being conceived, had been my deepest, darkest secret. I'd never told anyone. Guilt about sex had only been half the story. I'd been angry at God because Brian raped me, and God showed his anger by making me pregnant.

But no one knew. No one but Melissa, and Melissa would never tell anyone. She had held my hand that day at the Utah Women's Clinic, while the doctor had systematically and without emotion suctioned the baby from my womb while I lay sobbing on the table. She'd sworn her secrecy, her pledge of silence. How did he know?

The hand on the back of my neck that forced my face into the industrial carpet caught me by surprise. Brian, always good at playing the trump card, had held this information close to his vest, using it when he needed it most—when it would catch me off guard enough that he could get me exactly where he wanted me.

He pushed my face into the carpet until it burned, and I knew it could be the last thing I ever felt, but I wasn't giving up that easily. I screamed, a sound of primal rage and frustration, and it surprised him enough that he loosened his hold slightly. I knocked at his hand with my arm and jumped to my feet, preparing to run in whatever direction would give me shelter.

But there was nowhere to go. He stood with the gun pointed at my head, no more than two feet away, and utter despair, combined with anger, filled my body.

I stared at him with hatred emanating from my body. I only hoped he could see how much I despised him and everything he had become. He would have to kill me here, inside this chapel, where he believed he could rightfully enter and rightfully belong even though he had committed terrible crimes. I had to do something to stop him, or at least slow him down.

"Was it your baby, Brian? Was Melissa carrying your baby?"

He cocked his head slightly, looking at me with shock and surprise. "How did you know she was pregnant?"

I'd intended for this to be my trump card, the thing I would use to set him off balance, but he didn't seem surprised.

"You knew," I said, trying to pretend this information didn't hit me like a lead weight. I didn't want to think that Melissa's baby might have been fathered by Brian. "Was she going to get rid of it, too, like I did? After all, that's why you're so angry at me. Because I killed the baby you forced on me when you raped me."

Terrifying anger scored his face, his features distorted and his eyes bitter and cold. "It wasn't really rape and you know it. Even the bishop said so."

I ignored the madman in front of me and continued to

talk, words pouring out of me, words that I knew might totally unbalance him and send him—and me—flying off the edge, and yet I couldn't stop.

"It must have been yours. Once again, you are responsible for the death of your own baby. Did you know, when you killed her, that you were killing your unborn child? Too bad you didn't find the box when you broke into my apartment. How did you get in there, anyway? Without breaking in."

"Getting into your apartment was child's play. Melissa had the key, the one you gave her for emergencies. When I was there one night, I just took it. No one noticed it was missing, because you were never around anyway." His face hardened, and he jabbed the gun forcefully in my direction. "Time's up on this discussion. Head for the door now, Jannie. We're going outside, to the scene of Mike's crimes."

I didn't move. He still hadn't told me about Melissa's baby, and I knew if I gave in, if I moved, it would be the end of me.

He took four quick steps toward me and grabbed me by my long hair, pulling me him; I screamed at the pain.

"You bastard," I hissed at him. "You fucking, rotten bastard. You will burn in hell for this."

He pulled me by the hair toward the chapel door, laughing as I hissed in pain, his gun still pointed at my head.

"No, I won't burn in hell, Jannie. You know there's no hell. Just the lowest of his kingdoms, where I suppose I would be surrounded by the likes of you and Melissa, women who never deserved the glory of God or his priesthood. But I won't be there."

When his back hit the door he stopped and loosened his hold on my hair slightly, and I tilted my head and glared at him, catching the madness in his eyes as he cocked his head and reached down with one hand to open the door.

"This is the second-to-last time you will ever be inside a Mormon chapel, Sarah. You've made your bed, now you'll have to lie in it. You were never good enough to be my wife, or my eternal companion. The next time you are here, it will be in a casket, and they'll all cry over your body, never realizing how utterly worthless you really were. Oh, well. Time to move on."

"Why did you do all this, Brian? Why?"

"It's so simple. Everything I ever wanted, *everything,* Mike got. Every touchdown he ran, I handed him the ball. Every smooth word or thoughtful gesture he made toward Melissa, I coached him in. Every class he passed, I tutored him. He could barely spell his own name, for hell's sake. But he had me, good old Brian, Mike's sidekick, the product of Gentile parents."

The huge chip on Brian's shoulder had been the fact he was a convert, while the rest of us had come from a long line of Mormon pioneers—even though our families were flawed, imperfect. We had something he could never claim—a Mormon birthright, born under the covenant to parents married in the LDS Temple. It would never matter what he achieved, or what he did, he could never claim that. And it was the only thing he really wanted.

"Why did you kill Ida, Brian? Why Ida? She had nothing to do with this."

"I needed the box. I needed the proof, and she caught me. Wrong place, wrong time." He shrugged, and fiery anger roared through me as he dismissed the woman's life so casually. "She was old, anyway. Wouldn't have been around much longer."

"You needed what proof? You left everything behind, didn't you?"

"Of course not, Jannie. I meant to take the whole thing, but you surprised me and I dropped it. I still managed to grab the most important thing."

"What?"

His face was unusually serene, as though he had crossed over the top of the mountain and realized he was nearly home free. "It was a letter that Melissa wrote to Mike and you, begging for forgiveness. She also pointed a finger at me. I guess she got a little freaked out toward the end. The stupid bitch got scared of me. Of *me*!"

And that is when it clicked for me. Suddenly the scenario played out before me in startling clarity.

"Melissa never slept with you at all, did she, Brian? You pursued her when she found out about Mike, and she still rejected you. Did she come to you for advice, and you turned predator, thinking you could finally take what Mike had? And it was Mike's baby. Mike was going to be a father, something that I denied you. You didn't think he deserved it, but the truth was, you never deserved it, and you realized it right then. That's why you killed her, isn't it? You were never going to be good enough."

I watched his face change, the anger taking over his formerly calm visage, his eyes compressing and turning mean and feral. Brian had spent his entire life as second-best, and Melissa's rejection had been more than he could take. He was determined to destroy what he couldn't have.

"How did you know? How did you know I'd been pregnant and had an abortion?"

"Melissa told Mike. Big mistake. He told me everything. He had to. He couldn't even tie his shoes without me. He figured he had something I would want to know—information I needed."

Information that had resulted in three deaths—and possibly a fourth, if Brian got his way.

The door swung open and knocked Brian forward into me, and I grabbed for his gun just as Colt and three officers stormed into the chapel, weapons drawn.

Brian reacted quickly, pulling the gun out of my reach and grabbing and twisting me until he held me tight, gun pointed at my head.

"Drop the gun and let her go, Williams," Colt ordered, swallowing hard, eyes steely as he surveyed the scene in front of him. "Let go of the girl and put the gun down. Let's talk this out, but first you have to let her go."

I felt a shiver run through Brian's body, and in that instant I felt death looming closer than I had ever felt it before. I knew his intention almost before he cocked the gun.

Since he had been found out, I would be his last murder victim, and then he would take his own life. There was no way he would let me go. He simply wasn't capable. He never had been. Perhaps if we had never gone through the temple at all, even though I had bolted before we could be sealed for time and all eternity, then he would have been able to let me walk away.

But he knew my secret name, and my rejection was more than he could bear. So much rejection in Brian's life.

"Say good-bye, Jannie," he whispered as he moved the barrel slightly, pushing it deeper into my forehead, the pressure bruising, my life flashing before my eyes. I heard the shot . . .

And then I stood alone, all the pressure relieved, and there was no white light or pain—at least for me. Warm relief flooded my body. Brian lay on the ground behind me, motionless, a gunshot wound in his forehead. I turned to stare at him, and a myriad of emotions whirled through my mind. I had thought I loved this man, once. I had been betrayed by this man, too, and yet I felt a pang of regret and also pity. Brian wanted desperately to belong to our trio. Mike, Melissa, and I had all come from a long line of Mormons. The pedigree we bore, without thought, was something he obsessed about constantly. It had led him to destroy those who had what he could never obtain.

Now there was only me.

Colt moved quickly to me and pulled me into his arms.

CHAPTER FORTY-FOUR

Colt and I sat in his kitchen, both on barstools, facing each other. I needed to tell him the whole story now—the entire truth. I had to get it out, then put it behind me, so I could finally move on with my life. And I knew that I wanted Colt Singer to be a part of that life.

Irrational fear made me worry that he, too, like Brian, would not forgive my actions. But he was nothing like Brian.

"I had an abortion." The words, when they spilled from my lips, were so no-nonsense, with no warning, that I half expected him to fall off his chair, but he didn't even flinch. "I got pregnant that night, the night that Brian raped me, and I couldn't handle it. I couldn't face it. I ignored it for weeks. Even though I knew, I didn't want to believe it. And when I finally did face it, because I had no choice, because I hadn't had a period in two months, I just got rid of it. Just like that. I was all alone. All alone except for Melissa, because she went with me, and she didn't judge me, and by God, she was there for me. Just

Melissa. And I left her behind. I walked away and I didn't even know her life had come to this."

He didn't speak for a minute, then reached forward and wiped the tears from my face, and pulled me into an embrace.

"I don't care. It doesn't matter, and you didn't abandon Melissa. You couldn't have stopped this, and you couldn't have stopped Brian. You're not to blame here."

"But I am. I am the catalyst."

"Brian was an evil, sick man, who had latched on to the tenets of a controversial religion because it suited him. It met his needs, particularly the need to be more important than the woman he ruled over. It happens all the time. You're lucky you escaped. I'm sorry Melissa didn't, but we can't change that. And Jannie?"

I leaned back from his embrace and met his eyes. "Yes?"

"I'm glad you escaped. I'm glad we're here together. And if I don't get you back into bed, I'm going climb up the walls. Once was definitely not enough. I'll give you a baby if you want. I'll give you the stars. I'll give you anything you want, but you have to promise me one thing."

"What?"

"When we use the handcuffs, I get to be on top."

I laughed and he kissed me again, and then pulled me close.

No, we couldn't change what had happened to Melissa. But I knew that for all my life I'd carry a piece of guilt in my heart and soul for being involved in the destruction of Melissa.

EPILOGUE

Hurricane Brian had blown through our lives, wreaking destruction on anyone in his path. Like a real hurricane could clear deadwood and old trees, some of the effects might be considered beneficial. Brandon Talon, a man who had murdered his wife, mother-in-law, and children, had been stopped from committing further crimes by Brian.

Never again would he beat, bully, dominate, and ultimately murder someone he professed to love. It was hard to mourn his death.

Somehow, perhaps using his incredible reach and sources within the Mormon community, Brian had managed to get into the jail late at night and I had no doubt he was responsible for Talon's death. So far, no one was talking, but with Colt pressuring an investigation, I believed they would find whoever was responsible for allowing Brian Williams access to a man who was neither his client, family, or friend.

Morrison Naylor, the local attorney representing Talon, told police that he'd received a surprising call from Brian, who had met him for lunch and asked questions about the case. His client, he told the police, had seen someone lurking around my house the night Ida died.

Talon had gone to my apartment to try to pressure me— most likely with a threat—into staying away from Debbie, and in doing so, had inadvertently seen Brian. This was the card that Brandon Talon was going to play, to try to reduce his sentence.

It was shortly after he got off the phone with Naylor that Colt checked his voice mail and got my message.

"Cell phones don't ring deep in the jail," he explained later. "Too much metal."

His alarm for me had been overwhelming.

"If you ever do that to me again, I will lock you in a closet and never let you go," he whispered to me early the next morning, before the sun rose.

I didn't believe Brian would have gotten away with the crimes, even though up until the end he had seemed supremely confident that he would. At the least, some red flags would have been raised, and he would have died under a cloud of suspicion. As it was, he died a guilty man, and I would forever proclaim that guilt to the world.

I would never get my life back, those years I had lost. I would never get Melissa back, and I would find it hard to forgive myself for not being there for her when she needed me most. Perhaps if I had been, she would not have turned to Brian—an event that led to her murder. I did understand, now, why she had done what she had done. Hurt by Mike, lied to repeatedly, she had focused on someone she thought could help her. Someone she thought would want to help Mike. She just didn't know Brian well enough to realize it would turn out badly. Even knowing what she did about my experience with him. How could she, when even I didn't know just how mentally unstable he really was?

I also forgave her for giving away my secret. I chose to believe she didn't know what damage she was wreaking. Or perhaps she had only been human, and couldn't keep it in anymore.

I also felt the loss of Mike, for, fallible human though he was, he was a part of my life, and he would always be a part of my memories. He had disappointed Melissa repeatedly, but perhaps some of the blame could be placed on her. Desperate to live a different life from that of her parents, she wanted a strong man who would be a leader in the community and in our religion, a good candidate for church positions, a successful businessman. She had been unable to love Mike for what he was.

A seriously flawed human being.

Perhaps one day I could feel remorse for Brian, who had always wanted what could never be. That time would not come soon.

We tend to downplay what happens in someone else's life, interpreting it and twisting it to meet our own definition as we seek to avoid the harsh realities. What had seemed idyllic—Mike and Melissa's life—was far from it. When it imploded, the destruction was immense.

I had lost my childhood along with my friends. Almost every memory I had included one of the three—Mike, Lissa, and Brian. Memories faded with time, and there would be nothing to replace them with.

I would forever grieve that loss.

• • •

DNA testing came back on Melissa's unborn child and confirmed that the child was Mike's, not Brian's. Even though I had become convinced that Brian manufactured the entire thing, convincing himself that Melissa would come to him, because I would not, I felt a great sense of relief at this knowledge, even though the child would never take a breath. Brian did not deserve any children, spirit or otherwise, to destroy.

I was shaky in my newfound apostasy, and found myself referring back to my childhood religion whenever I could not find the answers I sought in my temporal surroundings.

It would take a lot of retraining to get away from that. I suspected it would be years, if ever.

The church authorities convened a Bishop's Court for my father several weeks after all the furor over Brian's crimes settled down. I learned from my mother that my father had not even bothered to show up, which I had to admit I understood. Being honest with myself, something I now tried to do on a regular basis, I had to admit I would also not have been present as a group of men I did not respect, or assign any authority to, decided my fate. Still, a big part of me felt my father owed them, and my mother, an explanation.

It would not be forthcoming. In typical Hugh Fox fashion, he simply ignored all that had been his past and moved forward with a new, totally different life.

"No, Jannie, that's not really right," my brother Jack corrected me when I made this observation. "Dad had to have been living on the edge like this for years. You don't just wake up one day and think, 'I'll take me a mistress, and abandon my wife and family, walk away from the religion I was raised in, and pretend the whole thing never existed.' This whole thing must have been going on, although hidden, for years."

I suppose Jack is right. My father was never as devout as my mother. His plans were really hers. His aspirations belonged to her, too. Looking back, I realized I'd been given a few glimpses into the real man, and he had been nothing like the one married to my mother. Perhaps, as with me, Mormonism had never been a good fit. I wasn't ready to talk to him right now, but perhaps, down the road, I would be able to sit down with him and finally, for the first time, get to know my father.

I am still angry at him for many reasons, but the overwhelming one is that he had pretended, for so many years, to believe that Mormonism was the one true religion. He continued this deception at my expense—and of course, the expense of my mother. Why had he never stepped up to the plate to say, "You will not do this to my daughter. She would not lie," yet he could so easily walk away from the church when the enticement was a piece of ass?

I practice swearing and using blue language a lot lately, something that gives Colt a great deal of amusement.

"It just doesn't sound right coming out of your mouth, Jannie."

"I just have to try harder," I tell him.

I swore a lot the day my mother called to tell me she had met someone else—someone special—just a month after my father left. I tried out words that had never before left my mouth. I'm sure he was a nice person. He was a widowed man, a former stake president, and his lifelong dream to serve a mission with his eternal companion had been interrupted when she'd been killed in a car accident.

"Don't tell anyone yet, Jannie, but we're planning on getting married."

"Um, Mom? You seem to have forgotten you are still married to Dad."

"Oh, I've started divorce proceedings. It's uncontested, so I suspect it won't take long."

"And your temple marriage?"

"I'm sure he will agree to have that nullified so I can marry Hank in the temple."

"And Hank's marriage?"

There was a silence there, as my mother thought about the fact that Hank had been sealed, for time and all eternity, and according to our religious beliefs she'd be sharing him with his late wife in the Celestial Kingdom.

"Jannie, I swear, you are such a wet blanket these days. It's a waste of time to even try to talk to you."

She hung up, and I smiled slightly. It would be at least a week before she called me again. I loved my mother, but if I honed my skills, it might be possible to go for weeks in relative peace and quiet.

She knew I was seeing Colt Singer. She asked about him in sly ways, and I avoided the questions in equally foxy fashion. This was mine, and for now, I was not ready to share it—with anyone except Colt.

He and I slowly forged forward, and I discovered that intimacy was a good thing. Every day we went a little further. With Colt, sex was slow, throbbing, sensual, and it made me feel more alive than I had ever been before. Of course, that wasn't hard to achieve. Perhaps we'd be using those handcuffs even sooner than I thought possible.

But I was proud of myself. I was getting pretty good at this living thing. Melissa would have been proud, too.

Reading Group Guide for
Behind Closed Doors

1. Jannie Fox is a complicated character who is relentless when it comes to fighting for other victims of abuse, and yet she refuses to see her own victimization. Colt Singer tells her she is hiding from life, and that is why she doesn't recognize it. Do you think this is true, or is there some other reason that she doesn't recognize herself as a victim?

2. While she is fighting for justice for others, Jannie lies to herself and her family on a daily basis. While these are not serious lies, they ultimately build up until her pyramid of deceit tumbles down. How is this similar to Mike Holt's pyramid of lies, and is one any less serious than the other?

3. Colt Singer is a complicated man in a complicated society. He works to bring justice to people on a daily basis, yet the biggest injustices are those from the past, and ones he can't right. How does this affect his relationship with Jannie?

4. It seems that the biggest villains in Jannie's life are her own expectations, and ultimately her own denials. What steps could she have taken years earlier to fix her problems, or were these problems unfixable?

5. Part of Jannie's problems stem from her upbringing in a repressive patriarchal society and also her complicated relationship with her father. Do you believe that things would have been different for Jannie if her father had been more aggressive and take-charge at home, instead of letting Jannie's mother run the home?

6. It seems that Jannie's father is the "reluctant" leader of their home, and in the end, he bows under that pressure. Ultimately, that was also Mike's fate, along with trying to live

up to expectations he could never hope to achieve. Does Brian also fall victim to these expectations?

7. Brian wanted to be something he never could be—Mormon royalty. The only way to achieve that was through birth, and yet he systematically set about destroying all those around him in an ill-fated attempt to build himself up. Was this an inbred mental illness, or something that beset him after being raised in the repressive Mormon society?

READ ON for an excerpt from the next
novel by Natalie R. Collins

THE WIFE'S SECRET

Coming soon from St. Martin's Paperbacks

CHAPTER ONE

"That was too much money to pay for a watermelon," Allan groused at me, as he pulled our Nissan Pathfinder into the driveway of our home. I knew we should not have gone to the supermarket together, but he'd insisted. He'd been trying for the past two days to be jovial and entertaining. To rekindle what had been lost in our relationship for the past half year. I did not know what had caused him to revert to the man he used to be, but I also knew it was too late.

"It sounded good. Refreshing."

"Too early in the season. It'll be thready and bland."

I sighed. "I told you to put it back; that I didn't need it."

"Right, and then you'll be angry at me the rest of the night. Like I really need that."

The Pathfinder came to a stop, and I angrily jerked open my door and stepped out. Walking to the rear, I opened the hatch.

The watermelon had shifted during the drive, and I saw its rapid roll toward the back of the vehicle. It hit the cement driveway with a loud thwack and burst open, black seeds, pink juice, and pulpy flesh spilling all over the concrete.

"Dammit, dammit, dammit."

"Watch your tongue, Carly," Allan said wearily, as he walked back to see the mess. "You sound like a sailor. And I told you a watermelon wasn't a good idea."

"A sailor? What the hell do you know about sailors? And just what are you trying to prove? What, Allan, what? This is what happens when I don't follow your counsel? God just shoves a watermelon out of the back of the car and smashes it to teach me a lesson? Doesn't God have more important things to worry about, like the war in Iraq, and starving children? Where the hell did you get the idea that life's lessons are taught with watermelon? Surely God's not all that concerned with your disobedient wife and her watermelon-loving ways."

Allan glowered at me and grabbed two sacks of groceries, violently swinging them as he headed to the side door of our small house. He put the groceries on the ground while he opened the screen door and, holding it ajar with his shoulder, found the right key to unlock the inside door. He stood back, puzzled, then pushed the door open wide. He shrugged his shoulders, picked up the sacks, and walked inside. The screen door shut with a soft swick.

Cursing silently, I walked to the small garage and pushed the side door open. I walked in and grabbed a long-handled push broom that was propped up against a worktable. Hanging from a hook was a dustpan, and I removed it, leaving behind the outlines in the fine dust on the wall.

Back at the car, I cleaned up the watermelon mess. I muttered and cursed as I worked, angry at Allan who had evidently left me to bring in the rest of the groceries while he went off to his study to sulk. He couldn't even put a good face on it for two full days. He'd only been making the effort since I had told him I wanted a divorce, anyway. I knew it wouldn't last long. I sighed. My reaction had been over the top, too, really. My unhappiness was making me into an ugly person I did not recognize. This would best be over soon. I had no desire to read the Scriptures with him, to attend a Sunday worship service. This was no longer my belief system. It had caused an irreparable rend in our relationship.

The late spring Las Vegas sun beat down mercilessly on the top of my head, and I was glad I'd chosen to wear a white tank top and short denim shorts. This despite the glare I had received from my husband when he saw my attire. I was the same person I'd been when we married. He, however, had changed dramatically.

After the sticky mess was cleaned up as best I could without water, I grabbed three sacks and headed into the side door, anger making my voice caustic. "Allan, despite the fact you think it's beneath your station in life, I would really appreciate it if you would come help me bring in the rest of the groceries. Allan? Allan, you can't hide . . ."

I heard a click and the cold metal of a gun pressed against my forehead.

CHAPTER TWO

The gun against my forehead moved in short, spastic bursts. My heart skipped a beat, then pulsed almost painfully. An irrational yet terrifying thought shot through my brain: What if . . . what if my husband was so angry over my lack of obedience that he'd lost control? Would he kill me because I didn't follow his directions? Was the watermelon just the proverbial straw that broke the camel's back? People killed other people, especially those they claimed to love the most, for the tiniest of reasons.

I glanced to the side, quickly. I saw a blur of black. I knew immediately that this was not my husband. I couldn't see much else. I didn't dare turn my head to look. But when we left for the store, Allan had on a lightweight dark blue shirt and jeans. A moment of ridiculous relief was swallowed by stark terror. I struggled to breathe, heavy, panting wheezes of air coming out of my open mouth.

The knocking of the gun against my skull slowed. I sensed the man—a woman would not do such a thing, would she?—who held me hostage had been anxious, but had now regained control. Why had he been so uptight? And why was he calm now?

And where was Allan?

"Down, to the ground," he ordered, his voice deep and commanding.

I dropped on my hands and knees obediently, moving away from the gun barrel, daring to sneak a quick glance. The gunman was covered from head to toe in black, including a ski mask.

There was nothing quite so horrifying as the realization you could not ever identify your attacker. But he—he could speak, breathe, and glare at you with venom-filled eyes.

"Lay down, flat. On the ground. Face down."

I complied. My muscles and sinew had turned to liquid. *Where was Allan?*

"Where are they?" he said. I felt the gun clack against the back of my head. "Where are they?"

I didn't know who "they" were. Surprisingly—or maybe not—I thought of my mother, whom I had not seen for a while. Not since I told her that her religion was not the one for me. Not since I told her she was crazy and dishonest.

"I said *where are they*?" His eerily familiar voice cut through the room, although I knew I had never met him. His broad shoulders, his authoritative stance, the way he held the gun—all were foreign to me. Yet somewhere in the back of my subconscious they triggered déjà vu flashes. The gun pushed against the back of my head.

"I don't know what you mean." My words were muffled and distorted as I spoke into the cold tile of our kitchen floor.

He turned my head manually to the left, pushing it with the gun. From that vantage point, I saw shiny, black leather shoes. The footwear of a businessman, or pastor, or funeral director. Not the shoes of a common, everyday thug.

Where was Allan?

"Where is it? Where did he put it? I know you know, and if you want to live to see tomorrow, you better tell me," he said with a menacing growl. He had gone from "they" to "it" and I still had no idea what he wanted. People or possessions, I'd give it all up, just to live through this one terrible moment.

"I don't know what you mean," I gasped.

Where was Allan?

"Don't play dumb with me. He told you, I know he did. He said you knew, too. Just before . . ." His voice trailed off.

Just before what? Was Allan already dead?

CHAPTER THREE

Allan and I had been distant and separate for months. I couldn't even remember the last time we'd touched. But the thought of him being dead reverberated through my soul.

"I don't know what you want. I don't *know*!" My voice cracked with strain. Tears scalded my eyes. If this man was telling the truth, my husband had betrayed me. Had said I knew where the "it" was. I didn't even know *what* "it" was. Did he do it to save his own life? Did it work?

"Tsk, tsk, tsk." He was measured, cool. The rank odor of perspiration emanating off him was the only indication he had ever been distraught.

Now he behaved like a professional killer. Perhaps that was what he was. My whole body trembled.

I might never walk away from this. I might die today.

"Carly," he growled. *He knew my name? Oh God, who was he? Why did he know me? What did he want?* "I am going to give you to the count of five. You are going to tell me where he put it. Or I will blow your brains out. It would not cause me a moment's remorse. There are things at stake here. Things someone like you cannot understand. I have to find those papers. I've been assigned to get them by my boss. I do not disappoint my boss. Ever. You have two choices. You can die. Or you can tell me where they are."

Papers. He wanted papers. But what papers? Allan's job as a bank manager couldn't be the source of this attack, could it? This man was not your typical criminal, with his educated tone and dress shoes. Although he held a gun to my head. Could he be looking for plans that would allow him to break into a bank and steal millions of dollars?

"I do not know what papers you are looking for. I have no idea. At this point, I wish I did, believe me, but I don't. I don't know who you are, and I don't know what damn papers you want, and I can't believe that . . ." Tears seeped out of my eyes, and I shut them tightly, cutting off the words. I wanted to be anywhere but here.

A sharp rap on the side door startled both of us. The gun pushed against my head, sharply. Pain coursed through my skull. "Carly, what the hell is going on?" my neighbor Marla Stokes called through the screen. I hadn't shut the inside door even though I knew Allan would grouse about letting hot air inside our central air-conditioned home. *Why did I have to be so stubborn? Was it really worth making Allan angry? Of course, if Allan were dead, he would never be angry again, and I would have to deal with the guilt of knowing I hadn't shut the door the rest of . . .*

"Carly?" Marla's two-packs-a-day voice was gruff, almost masculine. Its condition worsened at her job as a blackjack dealer for the smoke-filled Mirage.

The gun wavered a moment, then the pressure abated slightly. I flinched when the man pulled the gun away. I waited for the shot to ring out. Nothing. I heard the soft thump of leather soles on tile, and I turned slightly as the man in black disappeared into the den. I heard a metallic ping and a scratching noise. I knew he'd opened a window. I heard a thud, and after that, complete silence.

"Carly? Are you in there? You left all your groceries out here. You won't need an oven to bake this shit if you wait much longer. Weather forecaster said near ninety today." I heard the door push open, and the solid thwap of her footsteps as she entered. Her voice got closer, but I didn't look. My eyes were still trained on the den doorway.

"Carly, why are you on the ground? What in the hell happened here?"

She bent down and touched my hair. I jumped and screamed.

"Are you hurt? Did someone hurt you? Was it Allan?" Her voice lowered. I couldn't answer. I couldn't do anything but watch the door.

A strangled gasp coming from the den finally spurred me into movement. Instantly my body reacted, coiling up. I sobbed. *No, I could not do this. I was made of sterner stuff.* I forced myself to rise and run into the den, knowing that what I heard was not the assailant.

Allan, sprawled on the floor, gasping for air, did not seem to know I was there.

Marla followed me, then gasped, and ran back into the other room. I heard her voice as she spoke into the phone. She recited my house number and address, told them someone was shot, and no, she had no idea what had happened.

I fleetingly thought I would be suspected of shooting my husband, a complete turnaround from when I had wondered—just for a brief moment—if Allan was trying to kill me.

I moved quickly to the man who had been such a big part of my life for the past decade. I knelt down by him. I wrapped my arms around him tightly and rocked, as his blood spilled out and stained my white tank an unforgettable crimson. He gurgled softly, his eyes open but unseeing. Blood seeped from the sides of his mouth.

"Who was he, Allan? Who was he? What did he want? Why did this happen?"

I asked these questions softly as I rocked him in my arms, an almost maternal instinct.

He died seconds later.